THE COMFORT OF HIS ARMS

"Caitlin?"

This time the voice was a whisper. Cole dropped to one knee beside her, and she felt strong hands on her shoulders. The urge to lean into his embrace was overwhelming, but she resisted even though his grip was the only thing keeping her from collapsing facedown on the ground.

"Caitlin, look at me."

She did, but his image blurred. "Oh, Cole, he's just a baby."

His arms closed around her and she let her face fall against his shoulder. Cole never let go of her. She felt his hands stroking the length of her back, and his touch soothed her as nothing else had done. Slowly, her sobs subsided into mute, shuddering gasps for breath. He moved one hand to raise her face to his, and she didn't think to stop him when he lowered his mouth to hers.

The kiss was slow and gentle, like a dream they were both sharing, and she felt limp as his mouth left hers and traced the line of her jaw. The heat of his breath feathered against her throat, and she knew she should resist him while she still had the strength. The first heated touch of his lips on her skin banished such thoughts, and she dug her fingers into his shoulders and held on for dear life.

She needn't have worried. Cole wasn't letting go. His hold tightened and she hung in his arms. All thoughts of blame and betrayal were swept away in the sweet rush of forgotten passion. He held her firmly against him as he lowered the two of them to the ground and leaned over her, his face taut with desire. She raised her palm to his face, wanting to erase the bitterness, but he wanted nothing to do with comfort.

He wanted surrender.

Caitlin knew she wasn't submitting to Cole, but to herself, instead. For too long she'd denied the love and the need she felt for him, but she wouldn't squander what might be her only chance to relive the memories locked in her heart. She had tried so hard to forget, only to be frightened when she couldn't remember what it was to give herself to someone she loved. . . .

UNFORGIVEN

Lisa Higdon

Zebra Books
Kensington Publishing Corp.

http://www.zebrabooks.com

ZEBRA BOOKS are published by

Kensington Publishing Corp.
850 Third Avenue
New York, NY 10022

Zebra, the Z logo and Splendor Reg. U.S. Pat. & TM Off.

First Printing: April, 1999
10 9 8 7 6 5 4 3 2

Printed in the United States of America

For my sister, Betty Dills. There have always been too many miles between us, but you've always been close to my heart.

Also, for my brother, Thomas Costley, who taught me to love old movies.

PART ONE

One

He was going to kiss her.

The thought alone made her breathless. That and the feel of his palms braced on either side of her waist, drawing her against him. Caitlin McDonnell had had little practice at kissing, and she feared her ignorance would show. She braced herself, as if for a blow, and waited. When nothing happened, she let her eyes drift open in hesitant curiosity.

"Do I frighten you?"

"No, of course not," she managed, but her voice trembled.

"You're a pretty thing, Caitlin," Cole Thornton whispered against her lips. "Kiss me first, then I'll kiss you."

She swallowed, not certain she could go through with something so bold. Slipping away from the party had been daring enough, and she knew her father would strongly disapprove of Uncle Cam allowing her to even dance with a young man so new to town. In the shadows of the dense rose arbor twining over the end of the porch she could make out only the lines of his face and couldn't read his expression, but she heard no mockery in his coaxing voice. She inhaled the dewy fragrance of the evening mingled with the clean scent of soap and leather clinging to his skin, and she shuddered with a sudden longing to feel his arms around her. Steeling her courage, she rose on tiptoes and scarcely brushed her lips against his before pulling back as if burned.

Her retreat was only temporary, as Cole quickly saw the need to take control of the situation and claimed her mouth in a kiss that was both gentle and possessive. The heat of his lips seared her own and she sank against him, her fingers digging into the fabric of his shirt.

When he lifted his head, she gaped up at him, momentarily dazed. He traced the line of her face with his thumb and smiled down at her. "That wasn't so bad, was it?"

"No," she whispered, managing a smile of her own. His hands rested on her shoulders and she leaned forward, this time without hesitation. "Not bad at all."

His mouth covered hers, and he embraced her loosely. Caitlin knew he was wary of frightening her, so she slid her arms around his neck and drew him against her. His arms tightened around her, and she felt giddy.

"Cole! You out here, boy?"

He straightened immediately, turning away from her. "Over here, Pa. What's wrong?"

"Nothin'." A match flared in the darkness, and Caitlin caught the acrid scent of burning tobacco

as the man approached them. "What are you doing
out here?"

Cole's fingers tightened around her hand, and
Caitlin winced. She sensed his apprehension and
wondered what kind of man his father was.

"We just came outside for fresh air."

The cigarette glowed orange, illuminating a face
very much resembling Cole's, only older and hard-
ened. He chuckled. "I know damn well what you
came out here for."

Caitlin shrank from the knowing look on the
older man's face as his gaze traveled over her, and
he laughed again at her obvious embarrassment.

Cole stepped in front of her, as if shielding her
from his father's coarse manners. "Pa, don't—"

"You get around front and keep an eye on those
horses like you're supposed to be doing." He
turned back toward the doorway, tossing one last
warning over his shoulder. "Don't make me come
looking for you again."

"I'm sorry about that," Cole said, once his father
was out of sight. "I'd better get going before he
comes back."

Caitlin was trembling so that she could only
manage a nod.

Cole raised her face to his. "Can I see you again?
Tomorrow?"

"Where?" she whispered.

"To the east of your father's ranch, there's a
grove of cottonwood trees near the stream. Do you
know where I mean?"

"You know who my father is?"

"Do you know the place?"

"Yes."

"Meet me there. Tomorrow at three o'clock."

He turned without another word and disappeared into the shadows.

The afternoon sun filtered through the thick leaves of the cottonwood trees as Cole dismounted and let the horse drink from the stream. He had found this place not long after arriving in Eden and quickly made the grove a sanctuary from his father's frequent drunken rages. His dream was someday to have a spread of land of his own where such moments wouldn't have to be stolen.

He'd been full of dreams as a boy, but he was fast beginning to believe that was all they would ever be. Little by little, his father was dragging him down, and he didn't know how to get away. He had no money of his own and no place to go where the name Thornton wouldn't be met with disdain.

At the sound of hoofbeats, he glanced toward the west and saw Caitlin riding toward him. She reined her mare to a halt and smiled down at him. Her riding outfit had obviously been custom made just for her as the emerald color matched her eyes and enhanced the strands of gold in her tawny hair and, no doubt, cost more than he could earn honestly in a year's time.

He was genuinely surprised to see her. "I didn't think you would come."

"I almost didn't," she admitted, dismounting gracefully. "My father doesn't like me to go riding alone, and I had to wait until he left the house."

She didn't have to say that she couldn't stay long, and he wasted no time taking her in his arms and kissing her as he had meant to the night before. He took advantage of her startled gasp and deepened the kiss, savoring the sweetness of her mouth. Her arms found their way around his neck, and he shuddered at the feel of her fingers digging into his shoulders. She was young and innocent, but she wanted him.

He dared not push things too quickly, knowing he could frighten her so easily. He gently ended the kiss and savored the passion-dazed expression on her face.

"How did you know who my father is?" she asked after an awkward pause. "And where we live?"

"I recognized your uncle last night at the dance, and I heard him call you his niece," he explained, taking hold of her hands to stay the distance she sought to put between them. "I've been working on the Stegall spread for the last two weeks, so I've heard plenty about the McDonnells."

Her eyes narrowed slightly. "Nothing polite, I'm sure."

"I like to draw my own conclusions about people." He was tempted to add that anyone J.D. Stegall disliked had to be a decent person, but he had learned to keep his opinions to himself. "I never heard anything bad about you."

A doubtful expression clouded her eyes. "Does your father work for Mr. Stegall as well?"

"Yes, he does." The mention of his father only served to sour Cole's mood. Sean Thornton was a bastard, and he wasn't proud of being his son. He looked away, wishing she hadn't brought up the subject. "For now."

"For now?"

Cole knelt beside the stream and studied the sparkling water. A dry leaf floated into the water and was quickly swept away by the rushing current. "Hell, he never stays anywhere long."

"I overheard Papa telling Uncle Cam that Stegall had hired guns working for him." The accusation hung over him, and he could sense the distance rising between them. "Is that why you're working there?"

"For the last week I've been roping and branding calves." He stood and held out calloused palms for her inspection. He resented having to defend himself against his father's reputation, especially now that they were finally doing honest work.

Caitlin grasped his hands and held them in her smaller ones. The buttery texture of her riding gloves sent waves of desire over him as he imagined her skin even softer and smoother.

"I'm sorry," she replied in a tight whisper. "Everyone has been on edge since spring. Papa says Stegall is spoiling for a fight. That's why he doesn't want me riding alone, he's afraid Stegall's men will—"

Cole raised his fingertips to her lips, not wanting

her to finish the statement. Indeed, the men in the ranch's employ were no better than the men with whom his father usually associated. They would no doubt take delight in assaulting a lovely young girl for the sheer pleasure of doing so, let alone at the order of their boss.

"Your pa is right," he told her. "You shouldn't have come out here alone."

"I had to see you," she confessed, "I was afraid you might think—"

"That I'm not good enough for you?"

"Oh, no. That's not what I meant at all."

"Then why did you have to sneak away to see me, without telling your father?"

She rolled her eyes. "Papa would never in a million years let me ride out to meet a young man by myself."

"Have you ever tried?"

"No," she admitted, and her cheeks grew slightly pink.

"Good," he replied and gathered her close for another kiss before she would have to hurry home.

Cole trudged toward the ramshackle bunkhouse that served temporarily as his home. He inhaled deeply, breathing Caitlin's faint, lingering scent still clinging to his shirt. The sweet essence would quickly perish within the crowded quarters he shared with his father, uncle, and other men who avoided soap and water as if they were lethal.

As always, he bitterly wished he hadn't sought

escape for it only made the inevitable return that much worse.

These were the times he missed his mother the most. Their tiny Missouri farm had been humble but it was home. He fondly remembered returning from school or chores and catching the scent of supper cooking or hearing his mother sing to herself while she hung out wash or worked in her garden. Those were the happy times, when Sean was away from home, either in prison or on the run.

The hinges whined sharply in protest as Cole opened the door and ducked inside the dimness of the bunkhouse. The gaping windows allowed the dying sunlight inside, and no one had bothered to light a lantern. His uncle, Will, lay snoring on a corner bunk, and Sean had his back to Cole, guzzling whiskey from a near empty bottle.

He turned suddenly as if startled, allowing whiskey to dribble down his stubbled chin. "Where the hell have you been?"

"Out."

Sean placed the bottle on the rickety table. "God damn it, I know you been out! I want to know where."

"Just riding, Pa."

Without warning, Sean backhanded Cole across the face, and the coppery taste of blood filled his mouth. Cole didn't flinch, taking a perverted pleasure in the frustration his father felt at not being able to knock his son down anymore. They stood glaring at each other, and Cole knew the day would come when he would strike back. He tried to put if off as long as he could, because he knew one of them would end up dead.

"Just like your ma," Sean sneered, reaching for the bottle. "She'd just stand there bleeding and looking stupid."

The ruckus had roused Will Thornton from his peaceful slumber, and he swore out loud as he sat up on the edge of the bunk and reached for his boots. "Sean, I swear you make the meanest drunk I ever saw."

"Shut up, you bastard."

"Oh, I'm a bastard?" Will grinned as he pulled on his worn boots. "What does that make you, considering you got here two years before I did?"

Cole ignored the usual exchange between the two and dabbed at his lip with his bandanna. There wasn't much blood, but he could feel his mouth swelling already. Humiliation and fury simmered within him, and he cursed himself a coward for not leaving before it was too late.

He could have joined the army, worked on a cattle drive, anything, but he felt obliged to stay with his father after his mother's death. Now his name was on more than one wanted poster, and he would be a dead man the minute he set out on his own.

Sean stormed outside, and Will waited until the door closed behind him to ask, "You been sweet-talking that fancy gal from the dance, ain't ya?"

Cole glanced over at his uncle and said nothing. Will laughed. "Your pa figured as much. You gotta watch them rich women, boy. They like to lead a man on, but you ain't never good enough for them."

Cole felt a bit braver with his uncle than his father. "How would you know?"

"Had one try that stuff on me one time, but I showed her what I *was* good enough for." He crossed the room and slapped Cole on the back. "Clean up your face; we're going to town."

Caitlin's heart leapt into a fluttering dance as she caught sight of Cole waiting for her in the grove of cottonwoods surrounding the narrow stream. Their secret place.

Her stomach knotted in anticipation of his touch, and she wished their meetings weren't surrounded by such secrecy. Cole Thornton was the most decent young man she'd ever known, but her father would only consider him the son of a hired gun and forbid her to see him. And Duncan McDonnell always saw that his orders were obeyed.

She hated lying to her father, but she wouldn't give Cole up for anyone.

The old mare nickered softly in recognition of Cole's gelding. The two had become quite chummy, and Caitlin smiled to herself as Sophie quickened her pace as they entered the shadowed glade. Cole caught her reins and offered the sugar lump he never forgot.

He chuckled at the way she greedily consumed the treat and sniffed his pocket for more. "Hey there, old girl."

"I think she's sweet on you." Caitlin remarked as Cole secured Sophie's reins around a low-hanging limb.

He reached to help her down from the sidesaddle. "What about you?"

She lingered against him, savoring the feel of his hands about her waist. Without waiting for an answer, he lowered his mouth to hers, and she shuddered at the feel of his arms enveloping her. He ended the kiss in a lingering touch, nuzzling his lips at the base of her throat. His breath was hot when he asked again, "Are you getting sweet on me?"

Caitlin hesitated, not certain exactly how honest she should be with a man like Cole. With anyone else, she would bat her eyes and pretend to be astonished at his brazen question, but she couldn't look into the blue depths of his eyes and offer anything but the truth. "You know I'm very fond of you."

"Fond of me?" he mused, taking her hand and leading her toward a faded blanket he had spread out near the stream. "People are fond of saltwater taffy and berry pies. I want you to think more of me than that."

Settling herself on the blanket, Caitlin waited until he had stretched his long form beside her. She smoothed her skirt around her ankles and found her voice long enough to say, "I could ask you the same question. I mean . . . ask if you're sweet on me."

He took her hand and pulled her toward him,

lacing their fingers together. "You're the best person I've ever known. For the first time in my life, I have someone who understands me, someone I can count on."

His declaration went right to her heart, and Caitlin didn't wait for him to kiss her. She leaned forward without hesitation and covered his mouth with hers. He took her in his embrace and rolled her beneath him, kissing her with unrestrained ardor.

She could feel a tension in him she had not sensed before, and she tried not to flinch when he cupped his palm over her breast. His touch was gentle, kneading the soft mound, and she knew he could feel the nipple harden beneath her blouse. Indeed, her whole body was aching for his touch, and she barely comprehended his intent when he tugged at the lacings of her bodice.

Only when his lips left hers to claim the taut peak of her nipple did she manage a strangled protest. Heat washed over her, and she was lost to the waves of pleasure sweeping over her. She combed her fingers through his dark hair, shivering at the feel of his tongue on her skin.

"Caitlin!" a voice called. "Caitlin McDonnell!"

They froze at the sound. Cole recovered first and rushed to his feet, pulling her up along with him. Frantically, she tugged her bodice together.

"Is that your father?" he whispered.

She shook her head. "Over here, Uncle Cam!"

A man topped the hillside, looking down on the guilty pair. "Caitlin, your father is looking for you."

"What's wrong?"

"Stegall." He made his way down the hill, sparing a glance at Cole. "Several of his drovers were caught poisoning one of our wells. Thankfully, they were stopped before any poor animals were able to drink. Things are going to get ugly, and the thought of a young girl out alone is rather unnerving."

"I wouldn't let anything happen to Caitlin." Cole's glance never wavered. "And she's in no danger from me."

"My boy, I'm not the man you'll have to convince of that."

"Uncle Cam, you won't say anything to Papa, will you?"

Cameron McDonnell studied his niece before reminding her, "You know I don't like choosing sides between you and your father."

"Oh, please, Uncle Cam," she pleaded. Caitlin wasn't afraid of her father, but she didn't want his disapproval directed at Cole. "He won't listen and he gets so angry—"

Cam held up a hand to silence her pleas. "All right, but just this once. You two need to wait until this unpleasantness blows over and then do your courting in the proper manner."

"I doubt Duncan McDonnell would approve of me any more than he would now."

"Indeed, you had best be glad I'm the one who found Caitlin. I am somewhat more . . . understanding than my brother." Cameron held out his hand to his niece. "His approval is something you should have considered earlier."

An awkward silence fell over the trio, and Caitlin cast a pleading glance toward her uncle. Covering his chagrin with an exaggerated clearing of his throat, Cam turned to round up Caitlin's mare.

Tears threatened as Caitlin turned to say her goodbyes, so filled with uncertainty. "I'm sure Papa will make me stay close to home now."

"You need to stay close to home." Cole squeezed her hands in his. "I don't want anything to happen to you."

"But when will I see you?" she managed, her throat nearly closed as she fought back tears. "What if we never have—"

He wouldn't let her finish the question, kissing her quickly. "Don't worry. I won't let you get away that easy."

"Come along, Caitlin," her uncle urged. "You'd better be safely at home when your father returns."

Cole approached the bunkhouse with more than the usual apprehension. The ranch was all but deserted, and he feared that Stegall had indeed sent his men out against the McDonnell ranch. He simply would not go, he swore to himself. Raiding another ranch for money was no better than robbing stages, and he'd had enough of that.

As he drew his mount to a halt, his uncle called out, "Don't bother unsaddling, boy. Your pa is waiting on us in town."

"Town?" he repeated. "In the middle of the week?"

"He decided now is the time to clear out."

Cole's whole body froze at the words. "You mean leave town all together?"

"Hell, yes. We don't need any part of Stegall's feud with McDonnell, and I'll be damned if I'll get shot to save another man's property."

Cole could only stare as Will ducked back inside the bunkhouse long enough to collect Cole's saddlebags, his meager possessions hastily crammed inside. Once again, he found himself face to face with an opportunity to escape the outlaw band. Adrenaline rushed through his veins, and his heart began to pound loud enough to drown out everything Will was telling him about his father's plans for the immediate future.

Not only did he have an opportunity to escape; he had a reason to stay.

Caitlin.

A hasty plan began to form in his brain. He could get a job on Duncan McDonnell's ranch and prove himself worthy of Caitlin. Once he earned enough money, they could get married and start their own place and—

"What's the matter, boy? You deaf?"

Cole turned to see his uncle already mounted and ready to ride. "Your pa don't like to be kept waiting."

Cole remembered Eden as a busy town, and there were always dozens of people hurrying in and out of various businesses. He would wait until they reached town and inform his father of his decision to remain. Sean wouldn't dare start trouble in town and risk the sheriff noticing them and realizing who they were. It occurred to him once again how unusual a trip to town in the middle of the week was. "What's he doing in town?"

Will only shrugged. "Unfinished business."

The First National Bank of Eden, Texas, sat square on the corner of Main and Cairn Streets, facing the general store and a seamstress shop. The livery was at the opposite end of Cairn, far enough away so that the odor of horses and manure would not offend the sensitive noses of those patronizing local merchants. Sean Thornton was waiting for them behind the livery, and the sight of him set off alarm bells in Cole's head.

He was sober.

Sober and clean shaven. He wore a dark hat pulled low over his brow, and the anticipation in his narrowed eyes was all the confirmation Cole needed. The only thing more important to Sean than whiskey was money. Stealing other people's money, that is, and Cole knew Sean was already planning a heist.

"What took so long?" he demanded of his brother.

Will shrugged toward Cole. "Had to wait for your boy. You said don't come without him."

"I hope you've had enough of that prissy little gal to last you." His voice was thick with contempt, and it occurred to Cole that Sean would despise Caitlin simply because he loved her. "Just be glad your screwing didn't cost us this job."

"What job?" Cole demanded in a voice little more than a whisper.

"The bank." Will's eyes were veritably shining with anticipation as he secured the three horses to a makeshift hitching post. "The safe's full as a tick, and there ain't no armed guard."

Of Sean, he asked, "Is everyone in place?"

"Everyone?" Cole repeated as Sean nodded in assurance. "Who's here?"

"Men I can *count* on."

His father's slur was of no offense to Cole, and he decided he didn't owe Sean an explanation or even a goodbye. Once the robbery had begun, he could simply slip away in the confusion and hope he never saw his outlaw family again. He could only look on with numb fear as Will and Sean secured bandannas over their faces and drew their guns.

"You stay here with the horses," Sean ordered. "And don't let me down."

They disappeared around the corner of the livery, and Cole held his breath, dreading the sound of gunfire and screams of panic. He had never gotten used to the practice of terrorizing innocent people and taking their money. Sean had never forgiven him for refusing to search a woman clutching a baby. Cole had seen her slip her wedding ring in the folds of the child's blanket, but he wouldn't stoop to frisking a frightened woman and a crying baby.

Since that incident, Sean always punished him by giving him the lowly task of waiting with the horses.

The loud crack of gunfire startled him, and he peered toward the street, refusing to believe that his father would be stupid enough to burst into the bank with guns blazing. Quiet but malevolent was always Sean's style, and he never fired his weapon unless challenged. Getting in and out as quick as lightning was the secret to eluding capture. Edging a little farther toward the street, Cole heard shouts of panic and confusion and the shattering of glass.

He recognized his father's voice, cursing and ordering someone to "run like hell." Will appeared at the entrance of the alley, his pants leg dark with blood, but he managed to hobble quickly toward Cole, clutching a bulging cloth bag in his arms.

"Get the horses, boy!" he shouted, his voice strained. "Hurry!"

Two men, vaguely familiar to Cole, were not far behind Will, and they hurried to claim another pair of waiting horses. Sean finally made his way into the alley, one hand clutching his gun and the other was pressed tightly against his bleeding side. Father and son caught sight of one another at the same time, and genuine fear for Sean's life flooded Cole's mind and overshadowed his thoughts of escape. He mounted his horse and reined the remaining mare behind him as his father stumbled toward rescue. Cole used his spurs to urge the frightened horse toward the sound of gunfire and the smell of blood, and he prayed that Sean would be able to ride.

Men from the town were already blocking the alley and speed would be imperative to their escape. Cole was not ten feet from his father when the blast from a shotgun cut through the mingled shouts and curses. Silence fell over the crowd, and Sean Thornton was thrown against Cole's horse, his eyes wide and vacant.

"Pa!" Cole cried out loud, grappling at his reins as his mount shied from the scent of human blood. Sean sank to the ground, and his blood soaked the hard-packed dirt beneath him. Again, Cole shouted, "Pa!"

Will cursed. "Come on, damn you, can't you see he's dead?"

The harsh words startled Cole back to the horrible reality, and he turned his mount and followed after Will and the other men. The townspeople could be heard shouting threats and more gunfire followed them. Cole knew that a fast horse was the only hope he had of staying alive, and he leaned forward, urging the animal on even faster. He hoped to God that Will knew where he was going.

If the good people of Eden had horses saddled and waiting, the end of the Thornton gang would no doubt have come that day. Instead, all but Sean managed to escape with their lives. The men his father claimed he could count on had disappeared, and Cole feared his horse would drop trying to keep pace with his uncle. Will finally brought his lathered horse to a halt, and Cole did so as well.

"We agreed to split up if anything went wrong." Will could barely speak between ragged gasps for air. "Ed and Tom will catch up with us later."

"Pa is dead," Cole said, as if saying the words aloud would change things. He couldn't believe Will wasn't the least bit concerned. "We can't just leave him back there."

"It's the risk you take, and us getting killed won't do him no good." Will turned his horse in the direction of a narrow sloping path. "There's a cave down here by a stream. I already stashed some supplies inside, just in case."

"You and Pa have been planning this ever since we came to Eden. Haven't you?"

Will glanced over his shoulder, a humorless chuckle escaped his lips. "The bank *was* the reason we came to Eden. Sean didn't want you to know anything about it."

Cole followed Will in stunned silence. It had all been a farce. The story about working for Stegall, Sean's pretense of wanting to go straight, and Cole realized that everything he'd told Caitlin was a lie.

They reached the bottom of the hill and allowed the fatigued horses to go directly to the stream. Will slowly slid from his mount, cursing his own preference for tall horses. "You'll have to dig this ball out of my leg."

Cole didn't flinch at the grisly announcement. He had learned how to remove bullets years ago, and he'd had plenty of practice since. Leaving his horse to drink, Cole slid from his saddle, startled to find his denim-clad thigh plastered to the leather. He placed his palm against the sticky fabric of his pants and it came away a mottled shade of red.

Cole was sickened to realize that he was covered in blood. His father's blood.

Caitlin sat at her dressing table, nervously combing the tangles from her wet hair, and she winced at every snarl. Uncle Cam had ordered her upstairs the moment they arrived home, advising her to have her dress changed and her eyes dry before her father returned. She pressed a damp cloth against her cheeks, but they remained flushed. Her eyes were puffy and red, and the moment she let her guard down the tears began anew.

Any chance she had of sweet-talking her father into accepting Cole as a suitor was now ruined by circumstances beyond their control. Papa had forbidden her to even dance with their own ranch hands at his last birthday party. Lord knows, he would send her to a convent if he learned that Cole was one of Stegall's ranch hands.

She was much too nervous to struggle with arranging her hair, so she simply pulled it back from her face with a pair of combs. She drew a deep breath and shuddered against another batch of tears. Crying wouldn't help.

She decided to slip downstairs and see if Papa was home yet. She was anxious to learn what had happened between the cowhands, hoping against hope that the situation had been greatly exaggerated. Halfway down the stairs, she heard her father's voice coming from the library.

"These things usually turn out much worse," he was saying. "A lot of innocent bystanders could have been killed."

"Indeed, I read an account just last week of a much more violent episode in Kansas." Uncle Cam's voice rose slightly to be heard over the clinking of glass as he poured whiskey for himself and Papa. "It's a miracle only one man was killed, on either side."

Caitlin gripped the stair rail. A man had been killed. Forgetting her timidity, she ventured into the library. "Who was killed?"

Duncan McDonnell started at the sound of her voice. "Caitlin! I thought you were upstairs. Cam said you weren't feeling well."

"Who was killed? What happened?"

"Those cutthroats Stegall hired as ranch hands robbed the bank," he informed her bluntly. "Poisoning the wells was merely a tactic to divert everyone's attention away from town."

"Especially the marshal," Cam concluded as he crossed the room, handing the glass of whiskey to his brother. "Evidently, they had been planning the holdup since coming here. However they failed to anticipate the bank's unique policy of arming all the clerks."

"Who was killed?" Caitlin demanded.

"An outlaw named Sean Thornton," her father said, somewhat startled by her tone. "How does any of this concern you?"

Caitlin could feel the color draining from her face. She couldn't believe it. Cole didn't like to talk about his father, but she never dreamed it was because he was an outlaw who robbed banks. Now the man was dead, and she panicked, afraid something had happened to Cole.

Cam hurried to her side and gripped her elbow, steadying her. "You'd better go back upstairs and lie down," he advised, giving her a warning look. "I'll have Maggie bring a tray up to you later."

Caitlin turned toward the doorway, and her legs threatened to give way. She stumbled to the stairs and held tight to the rail as she forced herself to climb all the way to the top. Her mind was a blur of panic and fear, but one thing was clear. She had to find a way to reach Cole.

Caitlin had never ridden by herself at night, and she couldn't stifle her apprehension. The sliver of moon offered no light, and she feared she might become lost. She was taking a tremendous gamble by slipping out so late, but she knew Cole wouldn't leave without giving her some clue as to how to find him. Uncle Cam had warned her to forget she ever knew Cole, saying that he had obviously misled her and used her, all the while knowing about the bank robbery.

She wouldn't consider the possibility, but she made no protest to her uncle and waited for Cole to contact her. After two days, she convinced herself that Cole must have left some message for her at their secret place. A note or a sign of some kind that she alone would find and know how to find him.

As she neared the dense grove of cottonwoods, a coyote howled nearby and Caitlin's horse shied. She struggled to bring the mare back under control and decided to walk the rest of the way, leading the frightened animal. Feeling her skirt pocket for the derringer she had never carried before, she tried to reassure herself.

Once ensconced by the thick shadows and the towering trees, she felt a little safer. She could hear the stream not far away, but she held tight to the reins.

A twig snapped behind her, and she froze. She held her breath and listened as the footsteps grew near. She retrieved the tiny pistol and whirled to face a man approaching her from the shadows.

"Cole!" She recognized him even before he removed his hat and ran gratefully into his waiting arms. "Oh, Cole, I was so afraid something had happened to you."

"I'm all right," he assured her, burying his lips in her hair. "Don't worry about me."

"Is it true that your father was killed?" His only answer was a thinning of his lips into a dark frown. "I'm so sorry. I lost my mother only three years ago, and I know how you must feel."

He shook his head. "I doubt your mother was anything like my pa."

Caitlin hadn't forgotten the menacing look on his father's face or the way Cole tensed at the sound of his voice. "I'm just glad you weren't involved in this."

"What makes you think I wasn't involved?"

She hesitated. The possibility had not even occurred to her. "You weren't, were you?" He didn't answer, and she pointed out the obvious. "You're still here. Papa said the gang rode out of town as fast as they could, and a posse of ten men couldn't find them."

"I had to see you one last time." He cupped her face between his palms. "I've been here since sundown, hoping you'd come."

His lips claimed hers before she could respond, and she sank against him, numb with the knowledge that he was now an outlaw.

"You shouldn't be here," she whispered. "If they catch you—"

"Don't think about that," he said, forcing a smile for her sake. "I wish things were different, Caitlin. I'll miss you."

Her arms tightened around his waist, and she felt the sting of budding tears. "You just can't leave me. Oh, Cole, isn't there some other way?"

He thought for a moment. "You could come with me."

As if on cue, the wind picked up, stirring the dry leaves that lay at their feet. A shiver ran up Caitlin's spine, and she shook her head. "I couldn't."

"Why not?" he challenged. "You love me. You want to be with me, and you know I'll take care of you."

"Papa would kill me."

"Not if he doesn't know where you are."

She couldn't imagine living on her own, doing as she pleased, and not having to seek Duncan McDonnell's approval, but it sounded wonderful. To be free and independent, and best of all, she would be with Cole.

"All right," she breathed. "I'll go with you."

Two

Caitlin tried to hide her disappointment as best she could, but Cole immediately sensed her reluctance.

"It's just for tonight," he assured her as he took her hand and led her into the abandoned shack. "We'll catch up with the others tomorrow."

"The others?"

"My uncle and his men."

Caitlin hadn't even considered with whom or where they would be staying. Her only thought had been that she and Cole would at least be free of their domineering fathers and live happily ever after. Reality was quickly catching up with her.

"Cole, we can't stay here," she whispered, swatting at a spider's web. "This place is filthy."

"Because no one lives here," he reminded her. "We have to stay out of sight for a while—besides I've slept in places much worse than this."

It was on the tip of her tongue to tell him that she had not, but she thought better of it. The last thing she wanted to be was a nag, but as she glanced around the dirty little room she couldn't imagine actually spending the night here. Especially her first night alone with Cole.

Her apprehension grew just thinking about the night ahead. She knew he would expect to sleep with her as if they were married, and she suddenly felt timid. As if he read her mind, Cole untied his bedroll and spread it out near the far wall where the floor was somewhat clean. Her face grew warm, and she could feel her eyes grow wide as she watched him.

He rose to his feet and crossed the room, taking her hands in his. "Your fingers are like ice, Caitlin."

"This is the first time I've ever been away from home by myself. I mean without my father or uncle," she replied, her breath catching in her throat as he brushed his lips against her cheek. "I suppose I'm a little nervous."

"You're scared to death," he countered and drew her close, his arms encircling her. "I understand, and I think we'll both be better off with some sleep."

She pulled back to study his face, trying to read his meaning. He smiled the soft solemn smile that made her fall in love with him, and whispered, "We have the rest of our lives together. We can wait for a better place than this."

Relieved, she sank against his chest. "I do love you."

"I know," he whispered against the part in her hair. "I hope you never regret it."

He led her to the bedroll and they settled down for the night. Caitlin lay with her back against his chest, and the steady rhythm of his breathing lulled her to sleep.

The little town they rode into was nothing more than a wide spot in the rode. Cole could see the disappointment on Caitlin's face, and he didn't blame her. For two days, she had ridden her horse into the ground only to find their final destination a desolate mining town. Will had arranged the sanctuary long before the robbery was carried out, and Cole knew there was no better place to go.

"We'll hole up at Sally's place," he had told Cole when they separated. "She'll hide us out as long as we need."

Sally Jessup had been Will's part-time mistress as long as Cole could remember. Whenever he was broke, running from the law, or not in prison he would show up at her door, and she always believed he would stay for good this time. Inevitably, something would lure him away, or sometimes Sally would just plain throw him out when he drank too much or hit her once too often, but they always ended up back together. For a while.

"That's Sally's place," he said, pointing to a two-story house that stood at the end of the street. "We'll go around back."

Sure enough, Will's horse was tied behind the shabby building, and Cole helped Caitlin down from her saddle and hitched their mounts beside his uncle's. He took her hand and tried to reassure her, but his own misgivings got in the way.

He knocked lightly on the door and received no answer. He knocked again, a little louder.

"Can't we just go in?" Caitlin asked, her weariness showing on her face. "They are expecting us, aren't they?"

Before he could answer or knock again, the door flew open and a woman's shrill voice reverberated through the empty alley. "Cole Thornton! This can't be you! You was just a kid last time I seen you!"

Sally lunged through the doorway and threw her arms around him in a hug that knocked the breath out of him. She thumped him soundly on the back, and he felt smothered by the cloying scent that always seemed to cling to her. He set her away from himself and tried to appear glad to see her. "How are you, Sally?"

"Oh, you know me, always full of piss and vinegar." Her eyes darted to where Caitlin stood behind him. "Who's she?"

"This is Caitlin." That was all Sally needed to know about her for now. He put his arm around Caitlin and drew her near. "Honey, this Sally Jessup."

"H-how do you do?" she managed, but her eyes were wide with shock at the sight of the woman standing before them clad in nothing but a chemise, drawers, and a gaudy silk wrapper that gaped open in the front.

"Ain't you a fancy thing?" Sally smiled knowingly at Cole. "I guess you'll both be staying here with me and Will."

"That's what we had planned."

"Well, come on in," she said, and Cole hoped that Sally's friendly nature would make Caitlin feel at ease. "You can stay in the back room upstairs."

They entered the house through the kitchen, and Cole felt his stomach tighten at the enticing aroma of food cooking on the stove. Something with beef and plenty of onions, and he hoped there was a lot of it, whatever it was.

"Well, well, look who finally showed up."

Cole turned to find Will lounging in the doorway, wearing only his britches and a knowing smile. "I had a feeling you wouldn't be showing up alone. I told Sally to have plenty of clean sheets stashed upstairs."

"Will!" Sally scolded, even as she laughed at his coarse humor. She crossed the room and yanked a hair from his chest. "What a thing to say!"

"Damn, woman, don't ever do that again!" Will shoved her hands away from his bare chest. "I ought to blister your ass."

"My ass is covered, your chest ain't," she goaded him. "If you want something left alone, cover it up."

He caught her by the arm and drew her against him, planting both his hands across her generous backside. She shrieked with laughter, and he swatted her hard.

Cole glanced over at Caitlin, wincing at the horror on her face. She had never been around people like Will or Sally, and he hated that she would always associate him with these two and know that Will was his blood kin. He took her hand, startling her from her disbelieving trance, and tried to sound casual. "Why don't we go upstairs and get settled in?"

She nodded and followed him toward the hallway. As they passed through the doorway, Will caught Cole by the arm, all traces of humor gone from his face. "We got business to discuss, boy."

Cole glared at his uncle, having no intention of discussing the bank robbery in front of Caitlin. Right away, Will let go of his arm, but Cole didn't back away. "It can wait."

Will glanced at Caitlin. "I don't want no woman interfering, you hear me?"

Cole didn't miss the new tone of authority in Will's voice or the subtle threat. His father had always had complete say-so, and now Will expected to step in as boss. Cole knew Will didn't have enough patience and would get them all killed.

"I hear you, Will." Cole hated being obligated in any way to Will, but he'd been seen in Eden and had to have a place hide from the law. The first chance he had, Cole intended to take Caitlin and leave, but for now he wasn't about to start taking orders from Will. "I said I'd be back. Didn't you hear me?"

Without waiting for his uncle's reaction, he turned and led Caitlin down the hall toward the stairs. She held on tight to his hand, but he waited until they were behind the closed door of their room to speak.

"I know you think they're trash." He wouldn't let her deny it. "Maybe they are, but right now this is the safest place for us."

He put his arms around her and hated the way she trembled. He wanted her to feel safe with him, and he committed himself to convincing her of that as soon as possible.

"Your uncle doesn't want me here," she whispered, her breath feathering against his throat. "What if he won't let me stay?"

"That's not for him to decide," Cole assured her. "He was never boss, and he won't be now just because Pa died."

Caitlin waited until she was certain Cole had gone downstairs before sinking to the bed. Every inch of her body ached, and she was afraid to even look in a mirror. A sob rose unexpectedly in her throat, and she buried her face in her hands. She felt like a frightened child wanting to run home where she would be safe and warm.

A knock at the door startled her, and her voice was a raw whisper: "Come in."

"Brought you a few things, honey." Sally bustled into the room, her ample bosom bouncing with each step. "Cole told me you didn't have time to pack."

The statement hung between them, and Caitlin knew that Sally was fishing for information about her. She only nodded and said, "That was very kind of you."

"Don't think nothing of it." She shoved a bundle of folded clothes into Caitlin's arms and crossed the room to the bureau by the bed. "There's soap and towels in this top drawer. Just make yourself at home."

When Sally was out of the room, Caitlin all but ran to the washstand, pouring a generous amount of water into the bowl. She took a towel and a block of plain soap from the drawer and began washing her hands and face. She had never felt so gritty in her life.

Upon inspection of the things Sally had brought her, she was pleased to find a modest nightgown and a pair of drawers, each made of fine white cotton material. She was certain they were store bought and had never been worn. She certainly couldn't picture Sally wearing anything so prim.

She checked the door to make sure it was locked and hurriedly began to undress. Her skirt was all but stiff with splattered mud that had dried only to be splattered again. Her shirtwaist had fared no better, and she was horrified to find her chemise streaked with sweat and grime.

Once undressed, she made good use of the soap and water, though she would have given anything for a decent bath. At last she felt human again and slipped the nightgown over her head. Sally had said nothing about dinner, but Caitlin would rather starve to death than set foot downstairs wearing only a nightgown. The solution came with a knock on the door.

"You decent, honey?" Sally called. "Cole asked me to bring you a bite to eat."

"Thank you so much." Caitlin hurried to unlock and open the door. "Please come in."

Sally placed the tray on a narrow table near the window. The aroma of food made Caitlin's stomach clench in anticipation, and she wondered if she should invite her hostess to join her while she ate. Instead, she tried to smile and said, "You've been so nice to me. I appreciate everything very much."

Sally seated herself and motioned for Caitlin to take a seat. "Honey, you're going to need a friend if you're fixing to get mixed up with this bunch."

Caitlin sank into the remaining chair and faced Sally. "What do mean?"

"I mean, do you even know what you've gotten yourself into?"

Caitlin ate without tasting the food, all of her attention was focused on Sally and her stories of the Thornton gang. Sally, herself, had met Will Thornton in a small town in Kansas, and they had been together ever since, for the most part. Someday, she hoped, they would settle down, but for now Will had to stay on the run if he wanted to stay alive.

Caitlin knew that. "He's wanted for robbing the bank in Eden."

"Oh, that job has just barely made the papers." She shrugged as if the bank robbery was of no consequence. "The Thorntons are wanted in at least six states, not counting the Indian Territory. Except for Sean, now."

"Even Cole?"

"He's a Thornton, isn't he?" Sally leaned forward. "He looks just like his pa, and he was a real son-of-a-bitch. Treated Cole's ma like dirt, and I know he's what drove her to her grave."

When Caitlin had finished eating, Sally left her alone with her thoughts, and she had a great deal to consider. What had she fallen into?

To hear Sally tell things, Cole and his whole family were nothing but a ruthless gang of outlaws. She had assumed that the bank robbery was a one-time occurrence and wouldn't happen again after the disastrous outcome.

Just then, the door opened, and Cole stepped inside. His dark hair was damp and combed away from his face, and she felt a blush creep over her whole body when she saw the look in his eyes. He crossed the room and held out his hands to her, taking her in his arms.

"Is everything all right with your uncle?" she asked in a small voice.

"Let's not talk about that now," he whispered, running his hands over her bare arms. Lowering his head, he let his mouth lightly graze the sensitive skin just above her collarbone. "You smell so sweet."

She sank against him and felt the heat of his body through his shirt. There was no turning back. Cole was all she wanted, now he was all she had.

He led her to the bed and turned back the faded bedspread. The sheets did look clean, and Caitlin understood what Will Thornton had meant earlier. He urged her to sit on the side of the bed and knelt before her, pressing his lips against the inside of her palm.

"Caitlin, I want you so much," he said in a low voice. "I don't want you to be afraid of me."

"I can't help being nervous," she managed despite the lump in her throat. Her voice sounded calm but her insides were tangled like a nest of water moccasins, and she couldn't believe that he didn't hear her heart slamming against her breastbone. "Things are happening awfully fast."

"If something is right, there's no need to wait." He leaned forward and kissed her, gently at first, and then his mouth grew demanding. Her lips yielded, and she couldn't repress the moan that rose from her throat as his tongue stroked the inside of her mouth, filling her with the taste of him.

When she placed her arms around his shoulders, he pressed her down on the bed and smoothed her hair back from her face. "I've never seen your hair like this. All loose around your shoulders. It's beautiful."

He kissed her again, deeper than before, and this time she kissed him back. He pulled away from her for a moment and stripped off his shirt, tossing it to the floor. The sight of his naked chest increased the apprehension coiling in her stomach, and his skin was hot to her touch when he returned to the bed. She savored the clean, masculine scent of his flesh, and he encouraged her to explore his body.

She slid her palms over his shoulders, just barely letting her fingers brush against the hard wall of muscle of his chest. His hand slid to the tiny buttons of the nightgown and deftly unfastened every one, revealing her bare breasts. He said something, but the words were muffled as he lowered his mouth to the soft mound. Caitlin could barely suppress the cry of pleasure that rose unexpectedly in her throat as he drew the nipple into his mouth and gently grazed the tip between his teeth. He transferred his attention to the other breast, and Caitlin cradled his head in her arms.

Abruptly, he pulled away from her and stood beside the bed. Caitlin felt somewhat dazed as she looked up at him, and she could only nod when he said, "Caitlin, I'm going to put out the light."

Darkness filled the room, and she heard the thump of his boots hitting the floor. Her heart began to pound with the realization that he was removing all of his clothes, and she would soon be shed of the borrowed nightgown. Before she could consider the wisdom of taking this huge step, she felt his weight settle on the bed.

Her eyes grew accustomed to the darkness, and she could make out the lines of his face as he gazed down at her. He kissed her again, but this time his hand traveled the length of her torso and settled on her thigh. His fingers gathered the thin material of her nightgown and raised the garment almost to her waist.

"Cole," she gasped, feeling genuine panic. "I can't—"

He silenced her protest with a gentle kiss, but the feel of his fingers between her legs was still a shock. He touched her softly at first, tracing the hidden recesses of her body, and then his caresses grew bolder. He opened her body to his tender exploration, and Caitlin thought she would die as he discovered secret places that sent spirals of pleasure washing over her.

Her reluctance seemed to dissolve, and she thought nothing of being naked beneath him when he removed her nightgown. All that mattered was the feel of his skin against hers and the intense pleasure that hovered just beyond her reach. Her breathing was nearly as labored as his, and she was dimly aware of his weight settling between her thighs.

She closed her eyes and anxiously awaited what he would teach her next, only to be startled by the feel of something large and hot straining at the entrance of her body.

She gasped at an unexpected stab of pain and the instinctive knowledge that more pain would come. "Cole, please, don't—"

"Shh, honey, don't be afraid," he whispered against her throat. "The first time is never easy for a woman."

His hands slid to her bottom, holding her still beneath him, and he pressed his body more firmly against hers. She bit the inside of her jaw to keep from crying out, and her entire lower body tightened in protest of the sudden intrusion.

He lay still as death, and she clung to his shoulders as the pain slowly subsided. He kissed her gently on the forehead and then the mouth. His hips began to move and he balanced his weight on his elbows, thrusting in and out of her in a steady rhythm.

She lay stunned at the feel of his manhood surg-

ing into her body again and again and at the sheer
beauty of his desire for her. He was consumed with
it, and she wished she could see the expression on
his face. The muscles in his arms bunched beneath
her fingers, and she could feel sweat beading across
his shoulders. He groaned low in his throat and collapsed on top of her, his breath hot against her
breast.

"Oh, God, Caitlin, I love you."

Those were the magic words that made the experience beautiful, and she combed her fingers
through his hair. "I love you, too, darling."

He rolled onto his back, drawing the covers over
their naked bodies, and gathered her close to him.
He brushed a kiss against her forehead. "You're
not sorry, are you?"

She shook her head and prayed she wouldn't be
in the morning.

Caitlin awoke with a start, realizing that she was
in bed alone. Cole's clothes wore gone, and she
guessed the hour to be midmorning by the angle
of the sun shining through the faded curtains. She
stretched beneath the covers and every muscle in
her body protested sharply, and she winced at the
unexpected soreness between her legs.

She knew she needed to get up and see about
her clothes, but she wasn't ready to face Cole in
the light of day. What did men and women say to
one another after something so intimate transpires
between them?

Rolling out of bed, she snatched the nightgown from the floor and slipped it over her head. As she fastened the tiny row of buttons, Caitlin's hands froze at the sight of blood smeared on the sheets. It wasn't nearly time for her monthly cycle, and she felt her face flame as the cause for the blood dawned on her.

She stripped the sheet from the bed and wadded it into a ball. She searched the bureau and found the clean bed linens that Cole's uncle had so crudely referred to the night before. Once the bed was made and the soiled linen hidden under the bed, she washed her face and combed her hair as best she could before venturing out of the room.

From the top of the stairs, she couldn't see past the front hall, and she strained her ears for any sound of someone in the house. She couldn't believe she was fortunate enough to find the house empty long enough for her to see to her clothes and get back upstairs.

She padded into the kitchen on bare feet and found the room to be eerily quiet. She spied a washtub in one corner and knelt beside it to find her clothes soaking in cold water. Sally had said she should wash them in the morning, but Caitlin had never washed clothes before and didn't know where to begin.

"Well, good morning, your highness."

Caitlin nearly jumped out of her skin at the sound of Will Thornton's voice, and she whirled around to find him crossing the room toward her. She rose to her feet, realizing too late that she was pinned in the corner, and did her best to sound nonchalant. "Good morning, Mr. Thornton."

He laughed out loud. *"Mister* Thornton? Hell, girl, we're practically family. You just call me Uncle Will."

She managed a nervous smile. "All right."

He let his eyes travel the length of her nightgown. "How'd you sleep last night?"

"Fine, thank you."

He smiled, and her insides shrank as he took another step toward her. Standing not three feet away from her, Will reached out and stroked her cheek with his calloused fingers. "You sure are a pretty thing."

"I have to go upstairs now." She bolted past him, not caring if he knew she was frightened, but his instincts were honed and quicker than hers. He caught her upper arm and hauled her back to face him. "Please, Mr. Thornton, I need to go."

"Uncle Will, remember, honey. Why don't you let me see what you got on under that nightgown?"

"Get your hands off her, Will."

Cole. Caitlin's knees buckled with relief, and she ran toward him the instant Will released her. His arm snaked around her waist, and she pressed her face against his shoulder.

"Now, Cole, we was just getting to know one another," Will told him. "No cause for you to get all worked up."

"Go upstairs, Caitlin."

The last thing she wanted was to be the cause

of trouble between him and his uncle. "Cole, I'm all right, really it's—"

"I said, go upstairs."

The anger in his voice was mild compared to the fury in his eyes. She backed away from him and hurried toward the stairs.

Cole glared at his uncle. "Don't ever touch her again. Do you hear me?"

"Is that a threat?" Will mocked, reaching for a bottle of whiskey Sally had hidden behind the china cabinet. "What are you gonna do about it?"

"She's mine, Will. That means off limits to everyone, not just you."

"Is that what she told you last night? That she was yours and no one else's?" He uncorked the whiskey and took a long, deep drink. "Just wait 'til things get tough. I can't wait to see how fast she'll run back to her rich daddy and forget you ever existed."

Cole didn't flinch, but Will had voiced his deepest fear. He knew Caitlin loved him, but how could he expect her to stay with Will pawing her every chance he got? By God, if he lost Caitlin, he wouldn't let Will be the cause of it. "Leave her alone, Will. I won't tell you again."

He turned without another word and hurried up the stairs to the room he shared with Caitlin. He turned the knob slowly and peered inside before opening the door all the way. Sure enough, Caitlin was curled up on the bed, crying miserably, and he silently cursed Will Thornton. He stepped inside the room and closed the door, causing her head to snap up at the sound.

"It's just me, honey." The wide-eyed fear on her tear-streaked face tore at his gut, and he sat down on the bed and gathered her in his arms. "No one's going to hurt you. I swear it."

Her crying had stopped, but her whole body was trembling. "Cole, I don't want to stay here."

His heart sank. "It won't be for long."

"Please, let's go somewhere by ourselves," she begged, wiping at the tears on her face. "Anywhere."

He drew a deep breath and tried to decide the best way to explain to her what it meant to be a wanted man. "Honey, the law is looking for me, and they will be for a while. If someone recognizes me, I could be sent to prison or even killed."

She paled at the statement. "How long before it will be safe?"

"A week or so, and then we can go somewhere nice."

"A week," she repeated in a whisper. "But I don't even have any clothes to wear."

"I've taken care of that," he said, pleased by the change in subject. He got up from the bed and opened the door, retrieving the bundle he'd left in the hall. He presented her with what he hoped would prove his ability to provide for her. "See what you think."

She peered inside the bag and gasped with delight at the assortment of feminine garments. "Oh, Cole, this is wonderful. How did you do it?"

"I went over to the mercantile and talked with the storekeeper's . . . wife. She put together everything you might need, and she even had a ready-made dress that should fit you. She said for you to come over anytime you like so she can measure you, and she'll make you some more."

She stood up and rushed toward him, throwing her arms around him. "Oh, thank you so much."

He kissed her then, deep and slow, savoring the feel of her soft curves pressing against him. His body responded instantly, and he forced himself to end the kiss. She would be too sore and tender for him to take her right now, and he desperately wanted to make sure she enjoyed the next time he made love to her.

"Cole!" she breathed. "What if that woman recognized you? She might send for the law."

"I doubt it." He chuckled, kissing her forehead. "There's no sheriff here, and besides, she's wanted herself for worse things than I am."

"A woman?" she gasped. "Goodness gracious."

The following week dragged by, and Caitlin began to fear that they would never leave. She kept her distance from Will, but he never failed to catch her alone in the hallway or some other corner when she least expected him.

"I'm not a patient man," he had whispered against her ear when she tried to pull away from him. His fingers dug painfully into her arm. "I'll have my time with you, missy. Don't think I won't."

Besides her fear of Will, Caitlin was consumed with guilt over the worry and grief she knew she was causing her family. Poor Papa. She understood now that he had meant only to protect her, and she knew Uncle Cam would blame himself for keeping her relationship with Cole a secret. It made her sick to think that she might be the cause of animosity between two brothers who had worked side by side every day of their lives.

Cole had made her promise not to contact her family, fearing their location would be divulged, and she knew that Papa would indeed send an army to bring her home. She was also afraid of what her father would do to Cole, and Cole had made a few gory predictions, all involving his genitals.

Finally, Will declared that it was time for him and Cole to venture out long enough to contact the other members of the gang and settle up from the robbery. "As far as Sean's share of the money goes, Cole and I will divide that between ourselves. Sort of like our inheritance."

"I don't want his money." Cole's voice was gruff, and he never looked up from his supper. "You keep it."

Caitlin didn't care about the money, but she sensed Cole was refusing the money out of shame for the way his father died. That night in bed, she pillowed her head on his chest and tried to reassure him. "There was nothing you could have done to keep your father from being killed."

She felt his muscles tense. "I don't want to talk about it."

"Cole, try to understand—"

"I said I didn't want to talk about," he all but growled and turned away from her. "Go to sleep, Caitlin."

When he kissed her goodbye the next morning, he apologized for snapping at her. "I'll bring you back something pretty."

That had been three days ago, and she was beginning to worry more with each passing hour. Being cooped up in the house was bad enough, but Sally was beginning to grate on her nerves. The woman slept half the day and never offered to prepare the meals or help clean up. It wasn't that she expected Caitlin to wait on her, she simply didn't care whether the work was done or not. When she was downstairs, all she did was sit at the kitchen table, smoke thin black cigars, and talk about herself.

It was nearly noon, and Caitlin hadn't heard a peep from upstairs the whole morning. She ate breakfast by herself when it suited her and began ironing a stack of shirts that had lain in a basket for Lord only knew how long. She hated to think that she was honing her domestic skills out of boredom.

A sudden noise came from the front room, and she was positive she heard the front door open. Cole was back! She rushed into the parlor only to find a scantily clad Sally bidding goodbye to a pudgy gray-haired man.

"I'll let you know when it will be all right to come

back," she assured him, boldly rubbing against him. "Be patient, sugar, you know I'll make it worth your while."

"You always do," he all but panted, handing her a wadded bunch of paper money. "Just let me know."

Sally closed the door behind him and began counting the money. She glanced up and found Caitlin gaping at her in disbelief. "Now, honey, you got to promise me you won't say nothing about this to Will *or* Cole, you hear?"

"That man paid you?" Caitlin couldn't believe her eyes or the nasty conclusion forming in her mind. "He paid you for . . . for . . ."

"He paid me for five minutes on my knees and ten minutes on my back," Sally stated matter-of-factly. "And, believe me, he got his money's worth."

Caitlin moved aside as Sally flounced past her into the kitchen. She plopped down at the table and lit a cigar. "Is there any coffee made?"

"I'll make a pot."

"Thanks, hon, you're a doll."

Caitlin moved automatically to the stove and began filling the coffeepot with water. Her hands were trembling so that she nearly spilled ground coffee all over the floor, and bile rose from her stomach. She gripped the counter, afraid she might actually be sick. How could the woman do something like that?

While the coffee perked, Caitlin returned to the ironing, her face burning with the humiliation Sally should have felt. When the coffee was done, she filled two cups and sat down at the table. She could feel Sally staring at her, and to her surprise the woman began to laugh.

"What's so funny?"

"You." Sally drew deeply on her cigar, her eyes sparkling with humor. "You look like you've seen a ghost."

"I just don't understand."

"What's to understand? I got to eat and pay rent like everyone else." She spooned sugar into her coffee and stirred the steaming brew idly. "I'm not exactly cut out to be a blacksmith."

Caitlin shook her head. "There are other jobs."

"Like what? Being someone's maid? No, thank you."

"But what about you and Will?"

"I care about Will, don't get me wrong." A wistful look came into Sally's eyes as she gazed over her coffee cup, but it vanished as quickly as it appeared. "He's not the kind of man anyone can count on. I have to make my own way and not depend on him."

Caitlin sipped her coffee and grimaced at the bitterness. She had forgotten to add cream or sugar. She reached for the sugar bowl, but Sally's next words stopped her cold.

"You'd better start thinking how you're going to take care of yourself."

She pushed the coffee away, not wanting it anymore. "Cole and I are getting married. I don't plan on being on my own."

"When did he propose to you?"

Caitlin hesitated too long before answering, and Sally concluded the truth. "He hasn't."

"Not in so many words." She rose from the table, not wanting to continue the discussion. "Why else would he have asked me to come with him?"

"Maybe he needed somebody to iron his shirts."

Infuriated by the remark, Caitlin whirled around to face Sally. Before she could retaliate likewise, the back door burst open, and Will stumbled inside with Cole slumped against him.

"Help me get him upstairs, damn it! If I don't get this bullet out of him, he'll bleed to death."

Three

The last time Cameron McDonnell had seen his brother cry was when he was five years old and Duncan was eight. They had been waiting for their father to come up from the coal mine, as was their habit on Fridays. On Friday, wages were paid and Quintan McDonnell would give each of his boys a ha'penny to spend anyway they pleased. The hour was late when the men finally emerged from the mines, bearing only bad news for the boys along with their father's battered body.

They had followed the macabre parade all the way to the tiny cottage where their mother would have supper waiting. Sometimes, in his dreams, Cam could still hear her agonized sobs, but it was the sight of his older brother with tears streaming down his face that let him know it was a black day for all of them.

Now he had to sit and watch Duncan's eyes glisten as he tried to blink away tears shed for the loss of his only child. A loss that Cameron could have prevented, and now his lack of foresight had cost his brother the most precious thing in his life.

"She wouldn't just *leave* like that," Duncan said

more to himself. "I know I've been strict with her, but I always loved her and saw that she had everything she wanted. Someone has abducted my daughter, and all that idiot marshal wants to do is pose for a bunch of newspaper reporters."

"Duncan, there is a possibility that Caitlin did leave on her own."

"What makes you say that?" he demanded. "Do you know something I don't?"

He forced himself to look his brother in the eye. "Caitlin confided to me that she had a sweetheart."

A stormy look came into Duncan's eyes, and Cameron decided against telling him about the day he had found the two of them alone together in the woods. He'd never suspected that the well-mannered young man was the whelp of a monster like Sean Thornton.

"Who is he?"

"Now, Duncan, don't rush to conclusions—"

"Tell me who he is, and I'll have him brought here in chains if need be!"

Cameron took a deep breath and said, "His name is Cole Thornton. His father was the man killed during the bank robbery."

Braced for a violent reaction, Cameron watched morosely as Duncan merely sank back against his leather chair, his face ashen. "Sweet Mother of God."

"I can't believe that he would harm Caitlin, but—"

"Taking her away from her family *is* harming

her!" Rage slowly filled Duncan's face, and he gripped the arms of his chair until his knuckles turned white. "I'll hire every man Pinkerton has, and when I find them. . . . If he's even *touched* her, by God, I'll have his balls mounted on a plaque and hang them right there on that wall."

Cameron could only hope that his would not hang beside them.

Caitlin had never wished for her father more in her life. She sat huddled in a dark corner of the hallway, her head propped against her knees. She covered her ears when she could no longer take the groans of agony coming from inside their bedroom, and feared she would go mad not knowing whether Cole would live or die.

Sally had set her out in the hall shortly after Cole had been placed on the bed and his blood-soaked shirt removed. Will had threatened to "slap the shit out of her" if she didn't stop crying, and Sally intervened, warning Caitlin that her hysterics would only upset Cole and make things worse.

"Stop it! Damn it, you're killing me!" she heard him rasp, his voice raw with misery.

"Be still, God damn it, or I'll never get this out and you will die!"

Cole's reply was lost in another groan of pain, and Caitlin could hear Sally telling him to lie still and it would all be over soon. Sobs racked Caitlin's body once again, but no tears came from her raw and swollen eyes. She buried her face in the folds of her skirt, the one Cole had bought her, and tried to muffle the sound of her crying.

If Papa was here, he would know what to do, and he would take charge of the situation. He would send for a doctor, the finest doctor available, and he would see that Cole had medicine to ease the pain. She rocked back and forth, bargaining with God for Cole's life.

After what seemed an eternity, Sally opened the door and smiled at her. "Come on in, hon. He's going to be fine."

Caitlin was so weak from crying that Sally had to help her to her feet and all but lead her inside the room. Her gaze locked on Cole's form sprawled on the bed. He was pale, and she swore he wasn't breathing. His upper chest and shoulder were swathed in long strips of linen, hastily torn from a bedsheet, and he gave no reaction when she spoke his name.

"He needs to sleep," Sally explained. "You'll need to watch him during the night in case he has a fever."

"If you can't handle it, say so now," Will called as he stood washing his bloody hands in the basin. "You won't be no good to him if you go to pieces like some kid."

"She'll be fine, Will," Sally insisted, leading him out of the room. "You need some rest yourself."

Caitlin sank to the chair by the bed and stared at Cole's ashen face. He was so still that she actually placed her hand on his chest to assure herself that he was breathing. His skin felt clammy, and she wondered if she should cover him with the blanket. She had never taken care of a sick person, but she knew someone with a fever could easily become chilled.

Once the blanket was tucked around him, she didn't know what else to do but sit and wait. And pray.

She dozed some, but every stirring of his breath made her jump to her feet, terrified that she would fail to respond to his needs because she was sleeping. By the time the first hint of daylight peered in the window, her body felt as though she had been beaten. With only a straight ladder-back chair to sit in, her joints were stiff and her muscles ached with the effort to stand.

Sally peered inside and whispered, "How is he?"

"Still sleeping," Caitlin replied. "I haven't seen any signs of fever yet."

"It's still early." She moved to stand over him and shook her head, glancing sideways at Caitlin. "You look like death warmed over. Go lie down and get some rest while I change these bandages. I'll come get you if he wakes up."

She hobbled downstairs, desperate for a drink of water. Her throat was raw and her tongue felt like sandpaper. Her stomach ached from being empty for so long, and she wondered if she could even keep food down. Upon reaching the kitchen, she drained the dipper three times before her thirst was eased, and she glanced around, wondering what she might find to eat.

Too tired to cook anything, Caitlin saw the pan of biscuits she had made the day before. Even fresh from the oven, the biscuits had been barely edible, but she was hungry enough not to care. She managed to get one biscuit down with a few more dippers of water, and she decided that was enough for now. She would sleep just a little while and then return to Cole.

"I think those biscuits would taste a lot better with some gravy, don't you?"

She froze, realizing that she was alone downstairs with Will. In her exhaustion, she had let her guard down, and he sensed the opportunity like a wolf stalking a lame calf. Steadying herself against the counter, she turned to face him.

"Did you look in on Cole?"

Will smiled at her obvious attempt to remind him of Cole's presence in the house and the warning he had given Will about her.

"I sure did." He crossed the kitchen floor with a lazy stride and stood before her. "He don't know he's in this world and might not wake up until tomorrow."

His meaning was clear, and Caitlin swallowed hard before speaking. "You had better leave me alone or I will tell him."

"No, you won't," he countered, tracing the outline of her breast with one finger. "You won't say anything, because you want him to think of you as some kind of angel. Not a dirty little whore who screwed his uncle on the kitchen floor."

He moved to kiss her, and Caitlin knew she had to act fast. She turned away from him, but he caught her by the hair and brought her face within inches of his. His fingers twisted painfully in her hair, and he ground his lips against hers. She reached blindly behind her, hoping to knock enough dishes onto the floor to create a momentary distraction.

Her fingers found the handle of the butcher knife.

She bit down hard on his tongue as he tried to force her mouth open, and she gagged on the taste of his blood. He jerked back and raised a hand to slap her.

"Don't you dare," she warned him, brandishing the knife inches from his face. "I'll cut your throat."

"You don't have the nerve." He laughed at her and reached for her wrist.

She drew her arm back, just out of his reach, and knew she would have only one chance to save herself. She lowered her arm and thrust the razor-sharp blade against his crotch. "Maybe I don't have the nerve to kill you, but I'll make sure you never try to screw anyone on a kitchen floor again."

His face paled white as a sheet, and genuine fear flashed in his eyes.

"I think she means it, Will."

His head whipped around at the sound of Sally's voice, but Caitlin never took her eyes off of him. He backed away from her as if he'd been scalded, and the fear in his eyes turned to hatred. "Bitch," he growled before storming out the back door.

The knife clattered to the floor, and Caitlin turned to brace her arms on the counter, fearing her stomach wouldn't hold her meager breakfast. The stench of tobacco smoke reached her nostrils, and she gagged but managed not to vomit.

"I've never seen Will Thornton tuck tail and run like that." Sally began dipping water into the coffeepot, the thin cigar dangling between her lips. "He won't be sniffing around you for a while, that's for sure."

Caitlin couldn't believe Sally could act so casual when she had just seen the man she claimed to love trying to rape her. "I hate him. And I won't spend another night in this house as long as he's here."

"You're just going to run away and leave Cole when he needs you?" Sally set the heavy coffeepot on the iron stove and turned to face her. "What were you expecting, Caitlin? That Cole was some knight in shining armor taking you to his castle? You'd better wise up and start acting like a grown woman."

"By that do you mean I should be subjected to assault and rape on a daily basis?" Caitlin was furious that Sally would dare lecture her after what had just transpired. "Perhaps he should offer me money the next time."

She turned and ran upstairs, not caring whether or not she had hurt Sally's feelings. She slipped inside the bedroom and found Cole staring up at the ceiling, his eyes half open. Hope flooded her heart, and she knelt beside the bed. "Cole, can you hear me? It's Caitlin."

Slowly, his head turned toward the sound of her

voice, and he managed a weak smile. She covered his hand with hers and smiled back at him. "You're going to be just fine," she assured him, squeezing her fingers around his. "I'm sure of it."

He nodded and tried to speak but he could barely get the words out. She leaned forward and he repeated, "I was afraid I'd die before I got to see you again."

Tears slipped down her face and her heart ached with love for him. He drifted back to sleep, and she pressed her forehead against his arm. She prayed she could endure Will's presence just long enough for Cole to recover and take her away. Remembering the fear in Will's eyes made her feel a little safer, but she knew he hated her now, enough to want revenge. She rose to her feet and searched the bureau drawers for the pistol Cole had taught her how to use.

Cole watched Caitlin move about the room when she thought he was asleep. Her eyes were troubled, and she stared out the window for long periods of time.

She wants to go home.

He knew how close he had come to dying, and that the experience had completely unnerved her. He had succeeded in his campaign to win her trust and prove that he could protect her from harm, only to turn out to be nothing but flesh and blood like anyone else.

Her father, on the other hand, remained a stalwart of strength and security, tempting her with escape from the ugly world Cole had brought her into. Loving her wouldn't be enough. Cole had to make her see that he could give her everything her father could, and then she would stay. Unfortunately, there was only one way for a man like him to have that kind of money, and Cole felt his plans of abandoning his outlaw days crumble.

"Caitlin." She turned at the sound of his voice, momentarily startled. "Can you come here for a while?"

"Of course." She smiled and neared the bed. "Do you need anything?"

"Sit here beside me." He held his hand out to her and pulled her down on the bed they had not shared since he had been wounded. "I've missed you."

She shivered at the touch of lips against her throat. "I've been right here every minute."

"But your mind is a million miles away." Cole turned her face to his and kissed her mouth. Her lips yielded beneath his, and he slid one hand to her breast. He grew hard just from the feel of her, and he traced her mouth with his tongue. "Lie down with me, Caitlin. I need you."

"Cole, if that shoulder were to start bleeding again, you would be in serious trouble." She all but jumped off the bed and began folding a stack of clean bandages.

It was the first time she had ever refused him, and he knew it had nothing to do with his health. She had yet to question the circumstances under which he had been shot, and he wondered if she even wanted to know. He had risked his life for his share of the holdup money, and he intended to use it to win back her confidence. Now he wondered if he would ever have enough.

"As soon as I can ride, we'll be leaving for Santa Fe," he stated, and the relieved smile on her face confirmed his suspicions. "I know you're as sick of this place as I am."

"What will we do in Santa Fe?"

He leaned back against the pillow and watched her approach the bed with caution. "Will has a few old friends there, and the law looks the other way, most of the time."

The relief in her eyes disappeared. "Why can't we go somewhere by ourselves?"

"Santa Fe is the safest place." He sensed her resentment, but he knew she would offer no explanation if he asked. "Will knows people who can help us, and I can't turn my back on him."

"Why not?"

"He's my blood kin," he reminded her. Bright spots of color rose in her cheeks, and she turned back to the stack of bandages.

"Caitlin, it would have been a lot easier for him to leave me to die." Cold sweat broke out on his forehead every time he recalled the feel of the bullet slamming into his shoulder and seeing his own blood soaking into the dust. "He risked his life to save mine, and I won't forget that."

Without a word, she collected his empty supper dishes and left the room.

Santa Fe was everything Cole had promised it would be. Twice the size of Eden and constantly growing, the city boasted saloons, theaters, and at least five restaurants that used linen tablecloths and real silver. What delighted Caitlin the most was the hotel where she and Cole had registered as Mr. and Mrs. Townsend. Compared to Sally's house, it was absolutely luxurious. A maid came twice a day to tidy the room, and they slept on clean sheets every night.

It would have been glorious if Will and Sally weren't right across the hall. He had not spoken a word to Caitlin since their encounter in the kitchen, but she didn't believe for a minute that Will was avoiding her out of fear. She never left the room without Cole, and she locked the door every time he went out.

Cole's reluctance to part ways with his uncle troubled her more every day. Eventually, their money would run out, and he would be faced with the prospect of robbery again. Will would not hesitate, and she feared Cole would feel an obligation to go along. Caitlin knew what would happen to her if Cole didn't survive the next shooting. She would be out in the cold on her own, and she knew she had more to fear from Will than merely rape.

A hundred times, she had started to tell Cole

about Will's assault on her and the threats he'd made since, but every time she lost her nerve. Sally's blunt warning that Cole had yet to mention marriage had made her wary of her circumstances for the first time. She believed Cole loved her, for now. If she became a complication to his loyalty to his uncle he could easily send her away, and she would have no claim on him.

Will's threat that Cole would think she was "a dirty little whore" still rang in her ears. Cole might not see things the way she did, but Caitlin was beginning to wonder if she was any better than Sally. Cole was supporting her, and she was sleeping with him in return. The only difference was Sally did not limit herself to one man.

She watched him as he moved about their room, admiring his masculine beauty but remembering that Sally had said he looked just like his father. She wondered if Cole realized how dangerously close he was to following in his father's deadly footsteps. He glanced over and caught her staring at him, and he crossed the room in her direction, smiling.

"Happy?" Cole murmured against her neck as she reclined in the copper bathtub, surrounded by perfumed bubbles.

"Delirious," she replied, craning her neck to see his face. He knelt beside the tub, and she thought for a moment he would undress and join her. "You're not going out tonight, are you?"

"Just for a little while." His teeth nipped at her

collarbone, and she dabbed the end of his nose with bubbles. "You could come with me."

She hesitated. "To the saloon?"

"No one will bother you as long as you're with me," he assured her. "You can watch me win at poker, and Sally won't have to be the only woman."

"I doubt she minds that." Caitlin rose from the tub and reached for a snowy white towel, wrapping it around herself as she stepped onto the floor. Water puddled around her feet, but that would be the maid's problem. "I would feel out of place."

"Your place is with me," he reminded her as she began toweling herself dry. He reached for the towel and ran it slowly across her breasts. "I like showing you off. I see men looking at you and hating me for being such a lucky bastard."

Her breath caught as he lowered his head to her breast and drew the nipple into his mouth with enough force to cause her to flinch. She grasped his head, but he wouldn't relent until she was limp with desire and unable to stand without holding on to him. With little effort, he carried her to the bed and placed her in the center of the huge mattress, never taking his eyes off of her as he shed his clothes.

He captured her hands and held them over her head while he kissed her, long and deep, and then his mouth left hers and sought out the sensitive flesh of her belly. His traced the outline of her navel and pushed her hands away when she tangled her fingers in his hair.

Caitlin shuddered at his intent, and was too

shocked to prevent him from lowering his mouth to her most intimate place. His tongue made a gentle foray, at first, and soon grew more demanding, entering her with heated strokes. She struggled against the waves of desire that coursed over her body and threatened to sweep her away.

Cole showed no mercy, ignoring her pleas to stop before he drove her mad. She dug her heels into the thick comforter beneath them and writhed in sweet agony as he brought her to a shattering climax, more intense than any she had yet to experience. She was weak with release as he spread her thighs and drove into her with such force that she feared the bed would collapse out from under them.

"Tell me what you want," he demanded, gripping her buttocks as he thrust into her again and again. "Tell me."

She searched his eyes, trying to discern his meaning, and then she knew. "I want you, Cole. Just you."

He let his head fall against her breast, and she wrapped her arms around him as he shuddered with release. She was tempted to ask him what it was that he wanted, but her nerve failed as it had every time before.

"Caitlin," he whispered against her ear. "Caitlin, are you awake?"

"Mmm," was her only reply. "What time is it?"

"Almost eight."

She rolled over onto her back, surprised to find

that he had already shaved and dressed. Stifling a yawn, she asked, "What are you doing up so early?"

"There's a horse trader in town from Mexico," he explained, brushing away any lint that might cling to the brim of his hat. "I want to see for myself if his stock is as fine as his reputation."

She nodded. "Be careful."

He had been gone less than ten minutes when a knock came at the door. Caitlin ignored the summons, surmising that Cole would use his key, and she wasn't about to let anyone else inside the room. A second knock came followed by a muffled voice. "Housekeeping, miss. I need to tidy the room."

She groaned against the pillow and called back, "Could you come back later, please?"

There was no response, and she breathed a sigh of relief and turned back to catch a little more sleep. She heard the key turn in the lock and the door open.

"Cole?"

There was no reply.

"Cole, is that you?"

"Are you Caitlin McDonnell?"

She pulled the tangled sheet around her stark naked body as best she could and sat straight up in bed. A short, wiry man stood in the doorway, peering at her as if he were trying to pick her out of a crowd. "Get out of this room!"

"Are you Caitlin McDonnell?" he repeated, politely doffing his hat.

Her eyes narrowed, and the prickle of a different kind of fear settled over her. "Who are you?"

"If you're Caitlin McDonnell, I'm the man who's taking you in."

"Taking me in?"

His smile was friendly, but she didn't miss the flicker of triumph in his eyes. "Yes, ma'am. I'm taking you back to Texas."

"I'm not going anywhere with you."

"Now we can do this two ways." He made no attempt to enter the room but stood just inside the doorway as if he were patiently waiting for the two of them to leave on a holiday. "Either you gather your things and come along peaceably, or I'll take you by force, and I'll march you through the hotel lobby naked as a jaybird if I have to."

She moved to reach for the pistol Cole kept in the nightstand, but her instincts came too late.

"Ah, ah, ah, young lady," he scolded playfully, pointing a revolver directly at her. He reached inside his pocket and produced a pair of handcuffs, dangling them from his index finger, but the gun barrel never wavered. "I had hoped these wouldn't be necessary."

He advanced no more than two steps before a figure loomed behind him, and the butt of a pistol connected soundly with his skull. The man crumpled to the floor, and Will Thornton stepped over his prone body.

"Son of a bitch," he muttered, kicking the man's pistol across the floor. "Who the hell is he?"

Caitlin could only shake her head. "I have no idea."

He leaned over and searched the man's pockets, producing a pocket watch, wallet, assorted change and bills, and a folded notice which he scanned quickly before tossing it onto the bed. With shaking fingers, Caitlin reached for the paper, startled to find her own name printed boldly across the top.

"Information leading to the safe return of . . ." Her voice trailed off, and she gasped. "Ten thousand dollar reward."

"Hell, I might carry you home to Daddy for that much."

Caitlin had not considered the lengths to which her father would go to find her. Her family had no way of knowing that she had left of her own free will, and the natural assumption would have been that she had been abducted.

"What am I going to do?" she said more to herself.

Will took the notice from her shaking fingers and studied it before stating, "You had better get your ass home before you get Cole hung."

She blanched at the thought. Duncan McDonnell had earned the reputation of a ruthless man who never turned the other cheek and who protected what was his. Would he even care that she had wanted to run away with Cole?

"I'll make my father listen. I'll explain everything."

Will folded the notice and shook his head. "Cole's

not stupid. If he finds out about this, he won't stick around long enough for you to tell your daddy anything."

Without stopping to think, she pleaded, "You won't tell him, will you?"

His eyes narrowed and, too late, she realized her mistake.

His gaze dropped to the sheet she had clutched over her breasts. "Why should I do you any favors?"

Without warning, he reached out and snatched the sheet away from her naked body and gripped her shoulders, forcing her to meet his gaze. "Are you going to make it worth my while?"

His fingers dug painfully into her flesh, and she squeezed her eyes shut against the gloating triumph in his eyes. She knew, as well as he, that she didn't dare scream, and she cursed herself a thousand times over for not retrieving the pistol after all. She felt the mattress dip with his weight, and he laughed when a sob escaped her throat.

"Come on now, honey," he taunted, pushing her down on the bed. "You ought to be an old pro at this by now."

Caitlin's first instinct was to beg him to leave her alone, but her pleas would only add to the delight he took in humiliating her. Still, she couldn't bear the thought of submitting meekly to his abuse. She struggled to escape his grip, praying she could get to the nightstand before he realized her intent.

"Don't push your luck, girl," he warned, yanking her head back by a great handful of her unbound hair. "You won't look so pretty with your front teeth knocked out."

She froze, glaring up at him, when a faint groan drew her attention, and they both turned toward the forgotten intruder sprawled on the floor. Raising his head a fraction of an inch, the man groaned again and lapsed again into oblivion. Will released her none too gently and swore aloud.

With one last malevolent glance at Caitlin, he warned her, "You owe me now, and you had better remember that."

Without another word, he turned around and collected the hapless intruder and dragged him out into the hall. When the door closed behind him, Caitlin collapsed onto the bed, shaking so hard her teeth rattled.

"So, now you want to be a horse trader?"

Cole glanced over his shoulder just as Will neared the livery, but he returned his attention to the mares being shown in the corral. On the opposite side of the lot, several potential buyers could barely stifle their admiration of the animals, and the trader noted each and every reaction.

"You picked one out yet?" Will prodded, leaning against the fence.

Cole shook his head. "Just looking."

"Too rich for your blood?" When Cole gave no response, he only shook his head. "Mine, too. Hell, it won't be long, we'll both be busted."

Glancing sideways at his uncle, Cole knew where the conversation was leading, and he wanted no part of whatever scheme Will was concocting. With more nerve than foresight, Will was quickly proving how desperately he lacked the keen, ruthless instincts of his late brother. Few men were willing to throw in with them now that Will was calling the shots, and Cole couldn't help feeling a grudging respect for his father's capabilities.

"There's money to be made in horses," he ventured, gesturing toward the group of men clambering to give Juarez any price he named for one of the prize mares. "Even cattle."

"Rustling?"

"No, not rustling," Cole snapped, wondering if Will had ever had a decent thought in his life. "Raising cattle . . . ranching. We could buy land in California or even here in New Mexico—"

"I had all the cowpunching I want back in Texas!" Will straightened and faced Cole, his face taut with revulsion. "And I've shoveled behind enough horses to last me a lifetime."

Cole couldn't recall ever seeing Will do any such work but didn't bother to point out the fact. Instead, he decided to confront the inevitable. "In that case, what did you come out here for?"

"Opportunity." He leaned forward, his eyes all but glittering. "You can buy a whole herd of horses . . . better than those."

"How?"

Will glanced around. "Not here. Let's get a drink at the saloon."

Knowing Will wouldn't rest until he'd been heard, Cole followed him toward the row of saloons and dance halls open for business twenty-four hours a day. Despite the early hour, each establishment was already enjoying a brisk trade, and they were lucky to find an empty table out of earshot of the other patrons.

Cole listened patiently as Will spelled out his plan to waylay a stage leaving Santa Fe bound for California, rumored to be carrying a large amount of gold. "All we have to do is ride out the day before and wait for it to come right to us."

"And then what? Come back here like nothing happened?"

"Hell, no," he sneered. "We make tracks for Mexico."

"Mexico?" Cole was caught completely off guard by that. Never had the suggestion been made that they should leave the country altogether. "What about the women?"

Will laughed. "Who gives a damn? I'm talking about more money than the two of us would see in a lifetime."

"If we can't come back for them, how will they find us?"

"They won't, if we're lucky." When Cole didn't respond, Will's temper flared. "Hell, boy, what's wrong with you? They got women in Mexico."

"You're not going to tell Sally about this, are you?"

"No, and, by God, you better not, either!"

"You really expect me to leave Caitlin stranded here?"

"Send her home if it will make you feel better, but you're not dragging her along."

He glared at Will, who appeared to be amused by the predicament. "I told you before, I'm not sending her home. That's final."

The older man's grin slowly disappeared, and he leaned across the saloon table and lowered his voice. "You have wasted enough on that girl, and now you're wasting my time and risking both our necks. I already said we'd meet up with Tate and Richmond day after tomorrow."

Cole knew Will needed him more than he would ever admit. Will had always depended on Sean to judge the risks of every situation and didn't trust his own judgment to go on a job without reliable backing.

"You don't speak for me, Will." Cole leaned forward and met Will's challenging glare. "I'll do what I want, whether you like it or not."

"Just what is it you plan on doing?" Will's eyes narrowed with apprehension and anger. "Besides sit here whining about a piece of ass."

Cole started to warn him never to speak that away about Caitlin again, but he knew Will would never understand what it meant to be in love. "You've wallowed with whores so long you can't begin to understand how I feel about her."

"What I can't understand is what makes you think she'll stick around when the money's gone." Will drained the whiskey in his glass. "Once we're busted, Miss High and Mighty will run home to Daddy. Then how will you feel about her?"

"You're wrong; Caitlin would never walk out on me."

"She's never done without, Cole, and she won't have to as long as her family is waiting for her." When Cole didn't reply, he added, "Blood is thicker than water. You remember that."

Cole flinched at Will's caustic words, knowing only too well the truth they held. He'd gone through most of his money providing the luxuries she considered everyday necessities, and he really had no choice but to take part in the heist Will was planning and hope it would be his last. He was already making plans for his share of the money. Plans for himself and Caitlin to make a fresh start and put the outlaw gang behind them.

He glanced at his uncle, wondering if Will had ever even considered anything besides a life of crime. "The time will come when her family will accept that she belongs with me. They'll have to understand—"

"This is all they understand."

Will slapped a folded newspaper onto the table, and Cole could only stare at the grainy photograph of his father's corpse propped inside a crude wooden coffin, surrounded by stone-faced men bearing badges and rifles. He tried to read the marshal's version of the events of that day but found no truth in the words. Sean Thornton was a drunken thief, but he deserved better than being shot in the back by men too cowardly to ride after him.

At last, he looked up to find Will gauging his reaction and waiting for his response. Cole folded the newspaper and slid it back to his uncle. "I think it's time we quit before we end up the same way."

"The hell you say," Will snarled. "I wouldn't give those bastards the satisfaction of scaring me."

"I'm not scared of them," Cole insisted. "We can't outrun the law forever. As long as we're wanted, we'll never have a moment's peace."

"You didn't used to talk like this. That fancy little gal has put all these ideas in your head." Will snatched the bottle of whiskey and poured himself another drink, downing the liquor in one swallow. "I've saved your ass too many times for you to back out on me now."

"I don't owe you anything, so do what you want and I'll worry about Caitlin." Cole rose to his feet and threw one of his precious few remaining coins on the table. "Drinks are on me."

He was halfway to the swinging doors when Will's voice rose above the din of saloon conversation. "I guess you didn't owe your pa nothing, either."

Cole's steps faltered, but he never looked back and stepped out into the bright sunshine, hurrying toward the hotel. He bounded up the stairs and knocked on the door before using his key.

"It's me, honey."

She was in his arms before he was all the way inside the room, trembling like a frightened child. He held her close, asking, "Caitlin, what's wrong?"

She pressed her face against his shoulder and shook her head. Drawing a ragged breath, she looked up and said, "I'm so homesick, Cole. Can't I go home just for a visit?"

The question stunned him, and he stepped back just enough to get a good look at her face. He was bewildered by the misery in her eyes, and he was positive she had been crying. "If you go home, I'll never see you again."

"Of course, you would," she insisted. "I just want my father to know—"

"Do you really think your father would let you come back to me?"

She didn't answer right away, and the look she gave him was almost apologetic. "He must be so worried about me; he might even think that I'm dead. If I could just go home long enough to explain—"

"Just wait until we get settled somewhere," he bargained. She began pulling away from him, and he let his arms fall to his sides. "Then you can write to him and tell him you're all right."

She hung her head and whispered, "We're never going to be settled. Not as long as you stick with Will."

It was nothing he hadn't told himself a thousand

times, but hearing those words from Caitlin's lips cut Cole to the quick. If he wanted any kind of life with her, it would have to be away from Will and the lure of easy money. He nodded silently, steeling himself for the upheaval the next few days would bring

Four

"Cole, you promised." Caitlin's voice quivered and her eyes shone bright with unshed tears. "You promised no more robberies."

"Please, honey, try to understand." He crossed the room and reached to turn her toward him. She flinched away from his touch, and he didn't miss the sob she tried to hide with a cough. "We're broke. All we need is enough money to get us—"

"That's what you said last time," she reminded him.

"I'll be careful," he insisted,

"Careful?" At that, she did turn to face him, her chin tilted slightly. "Were you being careful when you were shot? You almost died, Cole, and you might not be so lucky this time."

He drew a deep breath, knowing she was right, but he had no other options. They couldn't leave or stay without money, and a stage holdup was always a sure thing. Unlike a bank robbery, you didn't have a town full of unlikely heroes willing to risk interference. On an isolated stretch of road, a stage could be stopped and picked clean in minutes, and passengers were rarely foolish enough to risk harm to themselves.

"I didn't get shot during a holdup."

Surprise instantly registered in her eyes, but she said nothing. They had yet to discuss the events leading to the shooting, and he had thought she was afraid to ask. Now he knew that she simply assumed he'd been in the middle of another robbery, and the realization stung. Of all people, she should know this wasn't what he wanted, but she saw him in the same light as she did Will. And his father.

"The men who helped my father rob the bank in Eden came for their money." That much she knew, but not once had she asked what had happened. "Will insisted on keeping Pa's share of the take, and he told them that I was to have a fair and equal share. They didn't like the idea one bit."

"And they shot you," she concluded as if it were that simple. "How do you know who to trust?"

"Can I trust you?" he asked, gaining her attention. "If I tell you something, will you swear not to repeat it to another soul?"

Her eyes narrowed slightly. "Tell me what?"

"Will won't be coming back with me." He let her digest that bit of information before explaining. "Once the money is divided, we'll be going our separate ways. For good."

It was the truth, only Will didn't know about it yet.

"Will it be safe for you to return?"

"That's the tricky part," he admitted and

cringed at the reluctance in her eyes. "You'll have to meet up with me after a few days."

Her eyes grew wide. "Meet up with you? How can I possibly—"

"It's all worked out," he assured her. "Three days from tomorrow, you take the stage to Nutan and check in at the hotel."

"What if . . ." she hesitated. "I mean, how will I know you're on your way?"

"If I don't show up within four days, you wire your father and go home."

"If I do that—"

"If I don't show up, you'll know I'm either in jail or dead, and either way the safest place for you is with your family."

She let her head fall forward to rest on his shoulder. "My God, Cole, we can't go on like this."

"We're not," he reminded her. "This is it, and we'll be out."

Cole scanned the horizon once more and an uneasy feeling began to settle in his gut. There was no sign of life along the desolate stretch of road, and he found it impossible to believe that a stage burdened with gold would be taking this route to Santa Fe. He glanced over his shoulder to find Will still asleep by the smouldering campfire, and frustration began to build.

Once again, Cole had followed Will on a wild-goose chase for reasons that now paled in the face of disappointment and failure. He would never reach Santa Fe before Caitlin left for Nutan, and he felt sick at the prospect of facing her with the fact that the last of their money had gone to buy a stage ticket that had taken her nowhere. He tried to find consolation in the fact that one of his promises would be kept, and that was that Will would not be returning with him.

Kin or not, loyalty could go only so far, and Will would have to make it on his own just as Cole would do. The sun was barely up and if he hurried, he just might catch Caitlin before she left on the stage. Resigned, he began saddling his horse.

"Where do you think you're going?"

His anger flared at the tone of authority in Will's voice, but Cole resisted the urge to lash out at him. He was through with Will and refused to be goaded into pointless arguments. "It's no concern of yours."

"What the hell does that mean?" Will reached for his boots and hurried to get them on his feet. "No concern of mine?"

"I'm through with your big plans that never pan out." Cole began gathering his remaining gear, barely sparing a glance in Will's direction. "Where's your stage, Will? The one with all the gold?"

"It'll be along." Will was on his feet by now, his hurried movements belied the forced nonchalance in his tone. "Just wait and see."

"That's what you said yesterday."

"So you're just gonna leave?" he snapped. "Strike out on your own?"

"No, I'm going back for Caitlin first. We'll go from there."

"She ain't waiting for you in Santa Fe, if that's what you're thinking." A cold smile inched across Will's face. "I figure she's halfway back to Texas by now."

Cole's hands stilled over the bedroll he was securing to his saddle. "What do you mean?"

"I mean I got tired of waiting for you to get rid of her." He knelt beside their dying fire and tried to stir a little life into the ashes with no luck. "So I did what had to be done."

"Get rid of her?" Cole crossed the narrow space between them and jerked Will up by the collar. "What did you do to her?"

Stunned, Will struggled against Cole's grip, but the younger man hung on. "I didn't do anything to her, by God. Her daddy put a price on her head, and Santa Fe was crawling with men looking for her. All I did was let them know where they could find her."

Cole felt his insides turn cold as ice at the thought. Caitlin's father had enough money to send half of Texas after her. He shoved Will hard, causing him to stumble and fall. His mind began to reel with hundreds of possible scenarios. A woman alone would be no match for bounty hunters, and Caitlin frightened easily. What if she resisted?

Will swore a blue streak, insisting, "They would have caught up with her sooner or later. It's best you weren't around to get yourself killed."

"I can take care of myself, and Caitlin."

"Really?" Will sneered. "Then why do you suppose she told me about the reward and not you?"

Cole froze in his tracks, knowing Will would say anything to justify his actions. "I don't believe you."

Will shrugged and reached inside his shirt pocket. "You don't have to believe me. Believe this."

Cole hesitated but caught the crumpled paper when Will let it fall from his fingertips. The bold print leapt off the page, punching a hole in Cole's heart, and he scanned the text detailing Caitlin's disappearance, the fear that she had been abducted, and her family's desperation to have her safely returned home.

"If you were my daughter, I wouldn't want you back let alone offer a reward."

Caitlin tried to ignore her captor's insulting remarks, refusing to even look at him when he spoke.

"I can't wait to hear what your pa has to say about you playing the whore for a bank-robbing horse thief. I'll bet he never figured you were so far down in the gutter."

"He must have known." Caitlin couldn't have held her tongue if she tried. She was sick of being sermonized by a bounty hunter who reeked of cheap whiskey and cheaper women. "He sent someone who wouldn't have to look very far to find me."

"Why, you mean-mouthed—"

"Sit down, Charlie," his partner growled from beneath the dusty Stetson perched low on his forehead. Caitlin was certain he'd been asleep, but he sat up and shoved the hat back in place atop the unruly mop of dark hair. "Touch her, and you won't see a dime of that reward money."

Caitlin breathed a silent prayer of thanks, her bravado vanished. She wasn't fool enough to believe for a minute her other escort was interested in her welfare. Jack Simon had been the one waiting for her at the stage office in Santa Fe and the one who secured the biting handcuffs about her wrists, boasting that he'd had them specially made to fit a woman.

His only interest was delivering her to her father and collecting the reward, and he was ever-mindful of the stipulation regarding her *safe* return. Otherwise, she would have fared much worse, and she understood now why *dead* was always listed first in the phrase *dead or alive*. It was, Simon had told her, the only way to be certain you would collect.

Glancing out the stage window, she wondered how close they were to Eden and how much farther she was from Nutan. There would be no way of getting word of her capture to Cole without alerting the law of his whereabouts, and the law was waiting for him in Santa Fe, certain he would come looking for her. Guilt settled around her shoulders like a heavy woolen shawl, and she couldn't escape the fact that her presence would lead to Cole's demise just as Will had predicted.

Her throat began to burn, and she swallowed hard against the threat of tears.

The stage eased to a stop near a ramshackle building that might have been taken as deserted if not for the lights burning inside the windows. Sundown was fast approaching, and the driver refused to risk being on the road after dark. Simon grumbled something to himself about reaching Texas before Christmas, but Charlie was more than anxious to partake of the food and drink offered at the rest station.

Neither man offered to help her down from the stage, and the driver was already unhitching the tired horses. As best she could, Caitlin managed to step down from the stage despite her shackled hands, but her legs threatened to give way beneath her. Catching hold of the stage door, she righted herself and followed her captors inside the shack.

A woman was stooped over a black iron pot that dangled above the fireplace, and from the smell Caitlin prayed it wasn't their dinner she was stirring so vigorously. She straightened up to have a look at her patrons, and her eyes went right to Caitlin's bound hands.

"Got a troublemaker there, have you?"

"She ain't had a chance to cause no trouble," Simon bragged as he shed his coat. "And she ain't going to."

"You see to it she don't," their hostess warned, pointing her long-handled spoon at Caitlin. "I'll put you out in the barn for the night, little lady, don't think I won't."

"Forget about her, Maude," Charlie piped up, settling himself at the crude wooden table. "A man could starve to death waiting on you to quit yammering."

"Not you, Charlie Tuggle," she snapped. "You could eat a buzzard out of house and home."

Caitlin ignored the rest of their rhetoric, thankful to have the woman's attention diverted from her. Jack crossed the room to a narrow wooden cupboard and retrieved a bottle of whiskey. He wasted no time in pulling the cork and turning the bottle up for a long drink. He grimaced but took another drink before passing the bottle to his partner. Charlie's taste was less discriminating, and he nearly drained the bottle in only three gulps.

"Give me that," Jack growled, snatching the bottle away from Charlie. He crossed the room and held the bottle out to Caitlin. "How 'bout a drink, little lady?"

A shiver ran up her spine at the sound of the soft, coaxing tone he used. Until now the prospect of spending the night in their company had only been distasteful, not frightening, and she feared she had badly misjudged Jack's wariness of her father. Any show of fear now would be as good as surrender.

"No, thank you," she managed sweetly. "I'm not accustomed to drinking liquor."

"That's right." He jammed the cork back in place and set the bottle on the windowsill. "You're a lady."

She tried not to shudder as he fingered a fallen lock of her hair and tucked it behind her ear. "It's hard to believe you were running with that bunch of cutthroats. You look so young and sweet."

"Everyone makes mistakes." Her feigned sincerity was convincing enough to actually draw a little understanding into his dark eyes. Her hopes of winning his sympathy were quickly dashed as he let his hand fall to her shoulder and began pulling her toward him.

"If you intend to eat, you'd better get to the table." Maude's sharp order drew his attention, and Caitlin breathed a desperate prayer. "And I don't intend to wait on your prisoner, woman or not."

Jack frowned as the surly woman slammed a bowl of stew on the table and waited impatiently for him to be seated. "I ain't got all night, and I'd just as soon feed it to the pigs if you don't want it."

He breathed a curse and made his way to the table. When Caitlin didn't follow, he turned and said, "Sit down and eat something."

"I'm not hungry."

"Humph," Maude snorted as she turned away, obviously disappointed at not being able to refuse Caitlin.

"Then sit down over there." Jack pointed to a rickety-looking rocking chair by the window. "I won't be long."

She sat down, wincing as a split in the wooden seat bit into her thigh, and she knew he'd seen her apprehension. Her heart sank even lower at the prospect of fending off Jack's attentions without angering him. She glanced toward Charlie, who was already devouring a bowl of stew with feral enthusiasm. He bothered with neither napkin nor spoon, using chunks of bread to scoop large mouthfuls of food into his mouth.

Twice already Jack had warned him not to touch Caitlin, and she felt sickened at the thought of what might happen if Jack withdrew his protection. Maude certainly wouldn't lift a finger to help her, and the men knew it as well as she.

A clicking noise drew her attention to the window, but she could see nothing in the gathering shadows. Before she could turn away, the sound came again, this time slightly louder and more insistent. A moment passed before she realized that tiny pebbles were striking against the glass, and someone was deliberately trying to gain her attention.

She hesitated, refusing to let naive hope build in her mind. For all she knew another bounty hunter lay in wait for her outside, waiting to steal her away from Jack and Charlie. She felt Jack's eyes on her and turned to find him watching her intently as he licked grease from his fingers. She decided then that even Apaches would be a viable alternative.

"I need to go outside."

They all gaped at her, and Charlie was the only one dense enough to ask, "What for?"

"What do you think, what for?" Jack demanded before turning to Maude. "Walk out with her, will you?"

As if his request didn't merit a response, she went

about her business as if he hadn't said a word. Charlie rose from his seat, but Jack ordered him to sit down. "You're so drunk you couldn't find the sun in broad open daylight, let alone a privy in the dark."

Rising from the table, Jack motioned to Caitlin to follow him, ignoring Charlie's bitter complaints about being treated like a hired hand. Once they were outside, Jack slipped his arm around her waist and began leading her away from the building. She tried to twist away from him, but he held tight.

"Easy there, darlin'. You don't want to fall."

"I can manage on my own."

He laughed and released her none too gently, causing her to stumble. "Go right ahead."

By sheer determination, she managed to right herself and regain her balance. When they reached the broken-down outhouse, Caitlin held out her bound wrists. "I can't do this with these things on."

At his skeptical look, she exclaimed, "How far could I get with you standing right outside the door?"

He hesitated then reached for the keys in his pocket. As he removed the irons he warned one last time, "Don't make me hurt you."

With trembling fingers she reached for the door but froze at the unmistakable sound of a revolver being cocked.

"Don't make me kill you, you son-of-a-bitch."

Relief and apprehension spiraled through her at the sound of Cole's voice, and she spun around just in time to see the butt of his pistol connect with

Jack's skull, rendering the man unconscious. Cole clamped a hand over her mouth before she could cry out his name, and he searched her eyes. She understood he meant for her to be quiet and nodded her compliance in earnest. He released her, stooping to deal with her hapless guard.

Cole collected the man's gunbelt and snapped the handcuffs on Jack's wrists. Satisfied, he rose to his feet and led Caitlin down a narrow path away from the main road. She hurried to keep up with him, stumbling twice but never turning loose of his hand.

Briars tore at her long skirt as they ran through the dense brush, and her lungs were burning by the time they reached the spot where Cole had left his horse. She collapsed in his arms and tried to slow her gasping breath enough to speak.

"How . . . how did—" She swallowed. "How did you find me?"

"Are you sorry I did?" he demanded, pinning her with intense scrutiny.

"What do you mean?"

"If you want to go home, tell me now." His expression was deadly serious, and the tone of his voice made her shiver. "I'll march you right back up that hill and put you on the stage myself."

She was incredulous, stunned by his anger. He wanted to believe her, she could see the war of emotions in his eyes, and she had no doubt who had planted suspicion in his mind. "I'd just as soon you did if you're taking me back to Will Thornton. I won't put up with him anymore, Cole, not even for you."

His eyes widened slightly in surprise, but realization and anger caused him to scowl down at her, his fingers tightening around her arms. "What did he do to you?"

"Nothing," she replied. "Not yet, at least, but my luck won't hold out forever. Eventually, he'll catch me off guard, and—"

Cole pressed gentle fingers against her lips. "No, no, he won't. I promised you I wouldn't be coming back with him. You should have told me about this, Caitlin. So help me, I would've killed him."

She wanted to believe him, but she couldn't help reminding him, "He's your blood kin."

"But you're my soul." His lips found hers and she reveled in the ardent kiss and the feel of his arms about her. Reluctantly, he ended the kiss and squeezed her hand. "We'd better get going."

He reached to untie the horse's lead from a low-hanging tree limb. "They'll be after us as soon as he comes to."

"Where are we going?" she asked, realizing she had nothing, not even a change of clothes, with her. "If they follow us—"

"Caitlin," he said, taking her hand in a tight grip. "I'm going to take care of you. You've got to start trusting me."

Five

"The best men you have," Duncan McDonnell sneered at the claim. "You assured me they had found her! What the hell went wrong?"

Cameron flinched at his brother's anger, though it was not directed at him, and he feared the strain of searching for Caitlin was taking its toll on a man accustomed to having his way. "Duncan, hear the man out. I'm certain—"

"All I've done is listen, now I want answers, not promises."

Oliver Parker had the unfortunate responsibility of answering to Duncan regarding his company's efforts to locate Caitlin, and Cameron feared the worst judging by the panic on the man's face. Whatever he was about to say wasn't going to be what Duncan wanted to hear.

"Well, sir, it seems the young lady escaped."

"Escaped?" Duncan shook his head as if to make sense of it all. "What do you mean, she escaped? She was being rescued, not arrested."

Parker dabbed at his upper lip with a white handkerchief. "Evidently, she did not wish to be returned and managed to get away from the men

who found her. It is almost certain she had an accomplice. Her lover, no doubt."

"Get out of my house." Duncan's voice was
barely more than a whisper, but the ominous tone
was unmistakable. Parker was on his feet and nearly
stumbled over a table in his dash to escape further
reprisals.

"At least, we know that she's alive." Cameron
desperately tried to sift a few grains of hope from
the disappointing news. "Perhaps you should consider the possibility that she wishes to remain with
this young man."

"Then why doesn't she contact me? A letter or
a telegram, anything."

"What would you do if she did?"

Duncan drew a deep breath and admitted, "I'd
go wherever she was and drag her home by the
hairs of her head. She's my daughter, for God's
sake, I can't turn her loose to the wolves just because it's what she thinks she wants."

Caitlin didn't mind the cold so much, but the unexpected rain made things miserable. For two days,
they had ridden in a constant drizzle that soaked
their clothes, their bedrolls, even their food. Guilt
ate away at her every time she glimpsed Cole's stoic
expression. It was for her sake that he had separated
from Will, and she wondered if he regretted the decision already.

"Cole will get tired of you slowing him down,"
Will had warned her more than once, and she was

terrified to think that he might be right. She should have wired her father as soon as she learned of the bounty and his desperation to find her. No doubt, he would have come for her, but her father was not an evil man. Once he realized how much she loved Cole, Papa wouldn't have hurt him.

But he would have insisted on taking her home, and she was too selfish to risk losing the man she loved on the off chance she could make her father listen to reason. She loved Cole, and, even for his sake, she hadn't the strength to walk away from him.

Just thinking how close she had come to never seeing him again made her shudder and tighten her arms around his waist. The horse trudged up a steep hill, and they had to duck their heads to dodge tree branches heavy with damp leaves. Thunder rumbled in the distance, and Cole swore under his breath.

They topped the hill, and Cole scanned the endless rain-soaked grassland. His eyes narrowed and he turned to her. "Looks like a cabin just behind those trees. You stay here while I see if anyone is living there."

She watched him hurry down the hill and disappear into the dense growth of trees and prayed they would have somewhere warm and dry to spend the night. The horse tossed his head and spattered Caitlin's already soggy clothes with moisture from his own soggy coat.

"Thanks," she hissed, her irritation short-lived as

she caught sight of Cole returning up the hill, a look of relief on his face.

She took hold of the horse's lead and met Cole halfway down the slope. He took the reins and led the way down a narrow path toward a small cabin.

One look inside the shabby little structure assured her that it had indeed been abandoned for quite some time. Broken dishes littered a bench shoved against the wall, and the layer of grime on the floor was unmarred by footprints. Compared to another night in the open, it looked like heaven.

"Can we have a fire?" she asked, wincing at how childish such a request sounded. A smoking chimney would signal their presence to anyone within five miles of the cabin, but she had endured bone-numbing dampness for two days. "Just a small one, perhaps?"

He crossed the room and took her in his arms. "A small one will be enough to make some coffee and dry our gear."

Hunger can be more frightening than armed attack. Caitlin tried not to let it show, but she was near panic the second day Cole was unable to hunt for game. Blurred tracks near the cabin indicated that riders had passed by and that not enough time had passed for the rain to wash them away altogether. A rifle shot could easily be heard a mile away, and Cole refused to risk drawing attention from anyone passing by.

The fire was risk enough, and she tried to be

grateful for that. What bread they had had long since grown stale, and the bacon had been enough for only one meager dinner. Cole had saved the bacon drippings and shown her how to make gravy out of water and their precious supply of flour.

She stirred the murky concoction, but there wasn't enough flour to make it thicken nor enough bacon drippings to give it flavor. She glanced toward the spot where Cole stood staring out the window. He looked worried, but she also sensed he was angry over something.

She hated knowing that he could do better without her. He could travel faster, need fewer supplies, and would not have the worry of someone else's safety and comfort.

Suddenly, he turned around, and she started, dropping the wooden spoon to the floor.

"Caitlin, I have to do something." He crossed the room and stood over her. "I can't take you into any town as long as there is a price on your head."

She could only look up at him, nodding slightly.

"We can't stay here and go hungry."

Again, she only nodded.

"I have to find a way to hunt or find a farm where I can trade for supplies."

She opened her mouth to protest, but he stopped her. "I doubt anyone would recognize me."

"You can't leave me here alone."

"It'll be for only one day," he assured her. "If

I leave before daybreak, I should be back by sundown."

The town was closer than he had suspected, and
he could have reached the outskirts on foot in less
than an hour. As a precaution, he'd left his horse
in a dense grove of trees. The sound of a horse
riding into a sleeping town might as well be a
trumpet, and he'd been betrayed once before by
the squeal of a stallion catching the scent of a
mare in season.

The sun wouldn't be up for at least another
hour, and he crept along the lots strewn with gar-
bage and broken bottles. This wasn't the first time
he'd stolen food to keep someone he loved from
going hungry, but it hadn't seemed as cowardly
when he was eleven years old.

Chickens were too noisy, storekeepers knew to
lock up anything that could be carried away, and
restaurants never yielded anything but the leavings
from their customers' plates. Cole knew better than
to waste time on any of them and hurried for the
saloon—his best hope of scrounging something decent to take back. Whores never go hungry, Sally
had bragged many a time, and he hoped the case
would be the same here.

He made his way along the back of the building,
confident no one would take notice of a few missing
items. He slipped inside a storage shed behind the
saloon and collected as much as he could carry: apples, cheese, and potatoes. He forsook the canned

peaches, knowing they would be too cumbersome to carry.

He emerged from the shed, glancing about. He was halfway across the lot when a flash of white caught his eye a split second before a woman's scream knifed through the darkness.

"We got a prowler!" she cried. "Somebody get out here!"

The back door was flung open and a man ran down the steps, hastily tugging up his suspenders and trying to tuck in his shirt at the same time. "Stop right there! Take another step, and I'll blow you to bits."

Cole knew there was no way in hell to explain his way out of this, and he wouldn't risk a gunfight that might leave Caitlin waiting for a dead man. Dropping his burden, he dashed toward the edge of the clearing. Once within the dense growth of trees, no one would find him in the dark, and all he had to do was get to his horse.

His relief was short-lived. The pounding of footsteps just behind him registered too late to avoid whatever it was that caught him between the shoulder blades and knocked the breath out of him. He fell forward, dimly aware of the ground rising up to meet him, but everything went black before he hit the dirt.

"Wake up, boy. You hear me?"

Cole squinted up at the man looming over him and groaned when daylight reached his eyes. How could he have been so stupid? Leaving the horse at the bottom of the hill had been the worst mistake he could have made.

Glancing around, he realized he was in a jail cell.

"Where were you going in such a hurry with all that food?"

Not certain what the best answer was, Cole tried to sound earnest when he said, "My family has been without supplies for two days. I had no choice."

"What family is that?" Another voice came from the other side of the bars. "Your pa is dead, and Will Thornton was on the other side of Santa Fe day before yesterday . . . robbing a stage."

He froze at the recitation, and for a moment even the pounding at his temples ceased. The cell door rattled and whined in protest of being opened, gratefully slamming closed. Heedless of his aching head, Cole swung his legs over the edge of the narrow cot and would have been on his feet if not for the hand landing on his shoulder.

"Not so fast. Are you sure about this, Luke?"

"He's a Thornton all right."

Cole raised his eyes to the hulking figure looming before him. The daylight pouring through the barred window gleamed off the badge pinned to his sheepskin coat, illuminating the phrase U.S. MARSHAL.

"Sean Thornton's boy," the marshal clarified. "Anybody ever tell you how much you look like that son-of-a-bitch?"

"My mother did," Cole answered without hesitation.

The marshal only nodded. "A decent woman, your ma. Never did understand how she got tangled up with the likes of him."

Cole had often wondered the same thing. "You knew my ma?"

"She used to visit your pa whenever he was in jail, back when I was a county sheriff." He shrugged, as if the situation still perplexed him. "I tried to tell her he was no good, and now you're turning out just like him."

"No, I'm not," Cole countered. "I cut all ties with my uncle, and I'm going it alone. Who are you?"

"Luke Yeager, United States Marshal. Looks like you've run into a little trouble." He turned to the town deputy. "What's the penalty for armed robbery in this town, Clive?"

"Armed robbery?" Cole's first thought was of Caitlin alone and waiting for him, and he began to panic. "How can you—"

"You were armed and you were stealing," he pointed out when the deputy only gaped at him in astonishment. "I can make those charges stick, and you'll rot in Yuma for ten years."

Cole swallowed hard, not certain what to say or do.

"Unless . . ." The word dangled from Yeager's lips, and Cole looked up, unable to squelch the hopeful reaction. "Unless you're willing to help me out, then I might be able to see that the matter is overlooked. First offense and all."

"Help you out?"

"Your uncle and two other men robbed a stage just outside of Santa Fe three days ago. The driver and one passenger were killed." He paused long enough to let Cole digest the information. "You help me bring them in, and I'll see to it you walk away from this."

"How can I help you? I don't even know where Will is now."

"Well, he's not in Santa Fe, and his lady friend swears she doesn't know where he is, either."

"He said he wasn't going back to Santa Fe."

"You mean he told you he was planning to rob that stage?"

"I thought he was trying to trick me into leaving town." Cole prayed Yeager didn't think he was in on the stage holdup. "I didn't think there was any stage."

"Why would he trick you into leaving town?"

Cole faltered, realizing how close he'd come to revealing his relationship with Caitlin. No doubt, Yeager would know about the reward and take her back to Texas personally. Groping for an answer, he said, "He wanted to get rid of Sally . . . the lady friend, and he figured I'd warn her."

The marshal laughed at that. "Well, he sure as hell got rid of her. She's already working at the saloon . . . upstairs."

Cole blanched at the idea of Yeager talking with Sally, who would be only too happy to tell everything she knew about Caitlin. He knew Will wouldn't have told her about the reward, but he braced himself as the humor drained from the marshal's face.

"Where did he plan on going after he left town?"

"Mexico."

The marshal swore out loud. "Mexico, hell, he knows the law can't touch him there. You'll have to get him to come back across the border."

"How?"

"He's your uncle, you should know. What matters the most to him?"

"Money," Cole answered without hesitation.

"Then that's our bait." Yeager nodded, pleased at the prospect. "We'll lead him to believe there's another stage, and you're going to take him to the money."

Cole shook his head. "He won't go for it. Not if he's safe in Mexico."

"Oh, he's safe all right," Yeager scoffed. "Safe and poor as Job's turkey! The stupid bastard robbed a stage on its way to pick up a payroll. The most he got was ten dollars, if that much."

Cole knew Will's greed would outrank his common sense any day, but what assurance would he have? Finally, he asked, "What if it doesn't work out?"

"The only way it won't work out is if you double-cross me and warn him ahead of time. If anything goes wrong, I'll hang you myself."

"And if I don't help you?"

"I'll have you in Yuma by nightfall, unless I have to shoot you trying to escape."

Cole didn't bother weighing his options. There were none. Right now, all that mattered was getting back to Caitlin. "How do I get in touch with him?"

Yeager smiled and turned to the deputy. "Get a pencil. We got a telegram to write."

Will—

I have to admit you were right, and I sure wish I'd listened to you. I'm flat busted and by myself, but I know of a job you might be interested in. If you're willing to catch a stage, send word.

Caitlin froze at the sound of an approaching horse. Her first instinct was to throw open the door in hopes of finding Cole just outside, but fear and caution rendered her motionless. He had been gone longer than he said he would be, and far too long for her not to believe something had happened to him.

She strained her ears for the sound of voices and shivered in the chill of the cabin. Earlier, she had doused the fire, fearful of alerting anyone to her presence, and her fingers and toes were numb from the cold. Her breath caught at the sound of a saddle creaking as someone dismounted, and she would have given anything if that door had a bolt.

The door groaned and opened slowly. "Caitlin?"

"Cole!" she cried, letting the pistol fall to the bed. She was in his arms before he was all the way inside the cabin. "Where have you been? I've been so worried—"

He silenced her questions with a hungry kiss, his embrace desperately tightening around her. Her heart sank, and she knew that something was indeed wrong.

"What happened?" she whispered when his lips left hers to seek the sensitive flesh of her throat.

"Nothing," he murmured. "Nothing at all."

"Why were you gone so long?"

"I didn't want to come back empty-handed."

She glanced down to find a cloth sack in his hand, and she gasped at the weight of it when he thrust it into her arms. "My goodness, what is it?"

"Enough to last you at least a week."

A tingle ran up her spine. "Last *me?*"

He removed his hat and ran his fingers through his hair in the nervous gesture she'd come to recognize. "Yeah, we need to talk about that."

"About what?"

"Caitlin, if I could get enough money together, how would you like to go to California?"

"California?" she whispered. "Why so far away?"

"So we can start all over. Do things right." He tossed his hat onto the scarred table and reached for her hands, drawing her near. "We can get married, have a real home, and not have the law breathing down our necks."

Hope and dread clashed within her. He'd just spelled out her every dream, but at what price, she wondered. "What about the money?"

His arms tightened around her. "I found work

not far from here. On a ranch. I'll be gone about a week, but I'll have enough for us to get away from here."

"A week?" She returned his embrace, clinging to his shoulders. "You're going to leave me here alone for a week?"

"You'll be safe, just keep the rifle handy." He pulled back to study her face. "This is our only chance."

She was unprepared for the anguish in his eyes, the desperation. Obviously, their situation was far more dire than he was telling her, and she prayed she would never need to know the truth. Instead, she raised her hand to his face as if to erase the worry she saw there. "If you think it's for the best, then that's what we need to do."

Relief flooded those blue eyes, and he buried his face in the length of unbound hair that hung over her shoulders. His lips found the sensitive flesh at the base of her throat, and she arched against his touch as his tongue traced the spot where her pulse throbbed madly just beneath the skin.

The need to feel his touch was rivaled only by the need to assure herself that his feelings for her had not lessened because of the turmoil she had caused. She tried to speak, to express once again how sorry she was for being so much trouble, but he silenced her faint whisper with a deep, drugging kiss that banished all doubt of his desire for her. She was limp in his arms by the time he placed her on the bed and shed first her clothes and then his own.

His touch was gentle, almost reverent, compared

to the urgent passion they normally shared. She smoothed her hands over his broad shoulders, trying to ignore the uneasy feeling she had that this might be more than an expression of passion between two lovers. Cole traced every line, every curve of her body with his fingers and then again with his lips, as if memorizing every detail. As if this might be the last time.

She shuddered at the thought, but managed to disguise her apprehension as desire with a kiss that shattered his control. Pressing her down against the coarse blanket, Cole's gaze never wavered from her face as he drove his body into hers. She closed her eyes against his intense scrutiny for fear her anguish would be revealed by threatening tears.

If this was going to be their last time together, she didn't want tears to be part of the memory.

He left just before sunrise the next morning, taking little with him. Caitlin's heart was in her throat as he fervently assured her he would return within the week and expected to find her ready to leave for California. She could only nod, resigning herself to plan for his return rather than preparing for the worst.

Cole, himself, had confirmed her fears by instructing her to return home right away if he was not back in ten days. She didn't ask why, and he looked relieved. Now she watched him ride away until there wasn't so much as a glimpse of him in the distance. She ducked back inside the cabin as if she could bolt the door against the eerie silence.

The drafty shelter now felt damp and chilling, and she was painfully aware of the consequences building a fire could bring. Cold seeped into her bones, and already she doubted whether or not she could remain here for a week. The least she could have would be a fire to keep from freezing to death. After all, not one soul had even approached the place in the time she and Cole had been hiding here.

Not that you know of.

The thought made her turn away from the fireplace in search of something, anything, to distract her from being so cold. The stark interior was just about as clean as it could ever hope to be, and she failed to see the point in sweeping a dirt floor. She stared down at the hard-packed earth, realizing that until three months ago she had never swept any type of floor. Indeed, she had learned a lot since leaving home.

Home. The word seemed to buzz in her brain, and she marked each passing hour as one less before the week would be up. As much as she missed her family, going home would be accepting that something had happened to Cole, and she would never know what. She tried to reassure herself that if she did go home, Papa would somehow find out what happened to Cole.

The possibilities ran through her mind, each more dismal than the one before. Working around cattle was dangerous, and men had died working for her father. There were plenty of reasons Cole might not be able to return when he said he would, but again and again she considered the sinister possibility that his fears were of the law and gunfire.

She was ashamed for even thinking it, after he'd risked so much to save her. Determined to put such doubts from her mind, she took to the task of being ready to leave for California the moment he returned. Once they arrived and were legally married, she would write to Papa and not worry about reprisal. Even Duncan McDonnell couldn't challenge a union sanctioned by the church.

Caitlin needed to somehow wash her clothes and wished she had others to change into. If she washed her things now, they would be dry by sundown. She could even iron them with the flatiron the cabin's last resident had left behind. She spied one of Cole's shirts under the bed and bent to retrieve it. As she straightened up, a crumpled piece of paper tumbled from the pocket and she frowned. It looked like a telegram. She unfolded the slip and read in disbelief the message from Will Thornton.

Glad you finally had enough. Am busted, too, and only too happy to meet up with you so we can take the stage. Remember, blood is thicker than water.

The paper fell from her fingers and floated to the dirt floor, and for a moment Caitlin feared she, too, would drop. She couldn't blame Will this time since it was obvious Cole had sought him out, nor could she blame Cole. It was her own fault for being stupid enough to believe she could change him. And that he loved her enough to want to change.

Six

"A young lady like yourself ain't got no business out walking all alone."

Caitlin nodded in agreement. "I didn't have any choice. I have to get to the nearest town."

She hadn't known what else to do but leave. Cole wouldn't abandon her; she was sure of that. He wouldn't have rescued her from Jack Simon if he wanted to be rid of her. Or did he realize too late that she would stand between him and rejoining his family?

He had tried. At least, she kept telling herself he'd tried to be what she wanted. She couldn't bear the thought of listening to any more excuses about Will being his kin, and how they needed the money so desperately, and this was going to be the last time. If anything, he would probably be relieved to find her gone.

"Do you even know where the next town is?"

Caitlin shook her head, whispering, "No, sir."

She didn't have any idea. She'd just started walking and walked until her feet were numb, but she didn't dare stop for fear she might not have the strength to start again. She didn't stop when the peddler's wagon came into view, even when he slowed the team to match her pace, and the mules were gaping at her as if she'd caused them a great deal of inconvenience.

"Victory is at least ten miles farther down the road." The old peddler eyed her with open speculation. "You never would have made it."

"I can't thank you enough for letting me ride with you."

"Bah, I don't need any thanks. How'd you come to be lost?"

"I'm not lost," she admitted. "I was waiting for someone to come for me, but I . . . couldn't wait any longer."

Understanding flickered in his eyes. "So you just took off hoping to find your way to town?" She nodded, and he went on. "Well, just be glad you weren't turned in the opposite direction. There's a little town back yonder a whole lot closer, but the train don't run there."

Caitlin sank back against the wagon seat and tried to reassure herself with the knowledge that a train could have her home in a day or two. The peddler went on to advise her about the many dangers of traveling alone.

At last, they reached the small town of Victory, and Caitlin thanked the kind old man again for his help. He smiled and helped her down from the wagon, pointing toward the far end of the main street. "Right down yonder is the freight office."

A crowd was already forming around the wagon,

and the peddler wasted no time in proclaiming the quality and rarity of the merchandise he had brought to town. Caitlin waved goodbye and turned toward the freight office.

The little man behind the glass glanced up from his work, his brow knitted with annoyance. "Yes?"

"I'd like to . . ." Caitlin's voice faltered, and she fingered the few coins in her pocket. "I need to send a telegram. How much does it cost?"

His annoyance grew. "Twenty-five cents for the first twenty-five words. Two cents apiece for each one after that."

When she nodded, he hastily shoved a piece of paper and the stub of a pencil toward her. "Write it out."

As it was, she didn't need even twenty-five words to plead for help and safe passage home.

"Who to?"

She hesitated, imagining her father's fury and disappointment. "Cameron McDonnell, attorney-at-law, Eden, Texas."

Caitlin peered out the window as the train neared Eden. Because of the early hour, she hoped there would be few people gathered at the depot. Uncle Cam would be waiting, and she hadn't the strength to face anyone else. She had slept little the night before, dreading having to face the disappointment in her father's eyes.

"Eden, miss." The porter smiled down at her as

he made his way to the front of the car. "Your stop, you said."

She nodded, wishing she could think of something to say to let him know how much his kindness had meant to her.

Caitlin had forgone the dining car at dinnertime the day before and then again at supper. Uncle Cam had wired enough for the ticket right away, but she hadn't thought to ask him for pocket money. After paying for the telegram and buying cheese and crackers for breakfast, she feared the few remaining coins would hardly afford a meal in the luxurious dining car.

After the other passengers were sleeping, the porter lingered in the aisle near her seat. "Anything I can get for you, miss?"

She shook her head. "Thank you, though."

He studied her thoughtfully, rocking back and forth on his heels. "Pardon me for saying so, but you don't look like a girl who needs to miss any meals."

Her face flamed, and her gaze fell to her folded hands.

"After the war, I decided to make my way north. I thought being free was all I needed. Wasn't long 'til I was hungry and scared."

Caitlin peered up at him, wondering if his story was true or if he was testing his assumptions about her predicament.

"Just outside of Joplin, Missouri, a white lady caught me stealing eggs out of her chicken coop, and I knew I was hung. Instead, she took those eggs from me and cooked them for my breakfast along with enough bacon to feed two men. I never forgot that kindness."

He turned away and Caitlin caught sight of a linen napkin lying on the seat beside her. Wrapped inside, she found two chicken legs and a corn muffin. It was such a simple gesture, but the compassion it represented brought tears to her eyes.

The brakes began to screech as the train pulled into the station, and the sudden blast of the whistle made her jump in her seat. She was home. Suddenly, she couldn't move, and her heart was beating ninety to nothing. Torn between elation and terror, she forced herself out of the seat and down the aisle toward the exit. She made her way down the steps and onto the deserted depot platform, wondering if the train was early.

"Caitlin?"

At the sound of her father's voice, she turned to find him standing at the end of the platform. He looked older, and her heart broke to see the deep lines creasing his handsome face, knowing she had caused each and every one. Papa had never been anything but good to her, and she'd paid him back by disgracing his name.

He moved to step toward her but hesitated, and the lines around his mouth deepened when he repeated, "Caitlin?"

Perhaps it was the quiver in his voice or the flash of fear in his eyes, but suddenly she was running toward him, into his open arms. She collapsed against him sobbing like a child waking from a nightmare. "Papa, I'm sorry. I'm s-s-o sorry."

"Shh, child, don't cry." He held her close and stroked her hair. "You're home. That's all that matters."

"I'm so ashamed," she whispered. "Please don't hate me."

"Hate you?" Duncan framed her face with his palms and forced her to look at him. "Oh, Caitlin, I could never hate you."

The porter appeared on the platform, carrying someone's luggage. He stopped and smiled approvingly. "Seems coming home was the right thing to do."

She managed a smile, but had to sniffle before she could speak. Caitlin suspected he'd found an excuse to see that she wasn't stranded with no one to meet her. "You've been so kind to me. Thank you."

Duncan slipped a hand inside his coat pocket and withdrew several bills, placing them in the porter's hand. "I thank you, too."

Keeping one arm around her shoulders, he led her toward the end of the platform. Their carriage was waiting, and she caught sight of Uncle Cam talking with the driver. He glanced in their direction, and his expression sobered.

Caitlin forced herself to meet his gaze, realizing she had betrayed him more than anyone. He had kept her secrets, and she'd made him an accomplice to her deceit. Without a word, Cam drew her into his embrace, and she felt the tears starting all over again.

"I'm sorry," she whispered. "I never thought things would turn out like they did."

"I hope you've learned a valuable lesson," he admonished gently. "I certainly have, and I'll never keep anything from your father again. You should have sent that telegram to him . . . not me."

Caitlin blinked back her tears and admitted, "I was afraid he wouldn't let me come home."

"How could you think that?"

The wounded look on her father's face only added to her guilt, but she knew there were things that needed to be said. "I know I've disgraced you, and you have every right to be ashamed of me."

"There's no shame in being young and foolish, and all that's happened is behind you." Duncan slipped his arm around her shoulders and drew her close as he opened the carriage door. With an indulgent smile, he said, "Let's get you home."

Cole slowed his horse as he neared the clearing where Will had promised to be waiting. No one was around, but he hadn't expected a welcoming party. He slid from the saddle and let the horse nose around the clump of brush nearby while he skirted the clearing, looking for any sign that someone had been there.

"Looking for somebody?"

He turned to see Will trudging up the steep hill that led to a washed-out ravine below. Cole didn't miss the man's gloating expression and knew he would have to listen to Will crow about being right.

"So she ran, did she?"

"I sent her home." Surprise immediately registered on Will's face, and Cole offered a hasty explanation. "She pitched a fit when I sent you that telegram, and I told her she wasn't coming between me and my kin."

Will nodded in approval. "I tried to tell you that would happen. You're better off to be rid of her."

Cole couldn't resist wondering out loud, "I never will understand what she had against you."

Without even the decency to look contrite, Will only shrugged and grinned slightly. "She knew I saw her for what she was. A spoiled, rich bitch who needed to be put in her place."

Cole had to look away, afraid the sudden rush of anger would show in his face and betray him. He had to get through the next few hours, and then he would be through with Will for good.

"Well, let's get going. The others are waiting on us."

Cole stopped in his tracks. "The others?"

Will made no apologies. "After Santa Fe, I threw in with Jess Martin. When I got your telegram, he was only too happy to come along and help us out."

Cole swallowed back a thousand questions along with a good deal of panic. Yeager was expecting only Will and a saddletramp or two. Not a cold-blooded killer like Martin. Even Sean had considered the man dangerous, and Cole couldn't believe Will would join the ranks of such a monster.

When Cole made no reply, Will added, "Martin won't put up with any bullshit, and you'd better be right about this stage."

Without another word, he turned and made his way along a narrow path leading down the ravine. Cole followed him, stopping short when he caught sight of three men seated around a small fire. Each man eyed him with blatant distrust and suspicion, and he tried not to think what would happen if Yeager's plan backfired. A fourth man emerged from a nearby alcove of trees and studied Cole with bemusement.

"So this is the whelp you've been whining about." He grinned slightly. "He's no boy, Will. I can't see him letting you kick his ass, let alone screw his gal."

Will's face paled considerably, and Cole turned toward him to demand an explanation. Martin laughed at both their reactions. "So it was all talk? I figured as much."

"You know I like to go on." Will tried to sound amused but knew he was being made a fool. "Besides, that's all in the past. I say it's time for me and Cole to get away from all those penny-ante heists and start seeing some real money."

"He's the one who set up this job," Martin reminded him. "All you've done is drink up my whiskey and talk. I don't need talk."

"You won't be disappointed," Cole interjected. He didn't like the direction the conversation was taking, and he scrambled to divert attention from

Will's long list of shortcomings. "This stage is carrying an army payroll . . . three months' worth."

"You'd better be certain of that."

"I'd stake my life on it."

"You just did." Martin turned to the men near the fire. "Get the gear and get ready to ride out of here. We got a stage to catch."

Cole led the way, and Martin insisted on riding beside him, watching his every move. Twice, Will tried to rein his horse in line with theirs only to have Martin order him to the back. Cole knew his every move was being scrutinized, and he tried to sound casual when he said, "The road is just below that hill, and the stage is due here anytime."

For a moment, Martin made no reply and kept his gaze pinned on Cole's face. Cole didn't flinch or look away. He only shrugged and grinned slightly. "I'm not afraid to lead the way if you'd rather not."

A muscle twitched in the man's jaw. "Step aside."

Cole was glad to, and he and Will brought up the rear as the band of thieves made their way toward the road. The minutes dragged by, and Cole could feel all eyes upon him.

At last, the stage lumbered into view, and the team of four horses strained to maintain speed against the incline of the road. The driver fought to hang on as the vehicle bounced over the deep ruts crisscrossing the path. Cole swallowed hard as Martin raised a dark bandanna over his face and motioned for the others to do the same. Will gave him a sidelong glance and nodded slightly.

A shot rang out and one of Martin's men rose from behind a copse of trees and aimed his rifle for the driver. The horses reared and strained against their bits, startled by the sudden attack. The driver fought to control the team and duck bullets at the same time. The stage came to a halt, and the driver tossed down his weapon and held his hands high above his head.

"Don't shoot, mister," he pleaded. "Don't shoot."

Martin came forward and ordered, "Hand over that strongbox."

Cole lagged behind the bandits that swarmed around the stage, feigning wariness.

The driver motioned toward his coach. "Inside. There."

At his signal, one of Martin's men stepped forward and jerked the passenger door open and shouted, "Everybody out!"

Glancing back toward his boss, the man never saw the rifle butt coming toward his skull, and the sickening thud rendered him senseless before he hit the ground. With no reaction to the unexpected turn of events, Jess Martin merely stepped over the prone body of his lackey and repeated the order.

Cole had no idea what would happen next, but nothing had prepared him for the eruption of gunfire as lawmen poured from the stage, their guns drawn and blazing. Martin was the first casualty, his chest carved out by a shotgun blast, and his band of thieves scattered like frightened little girls. Will swore and ran toward the horses, shoving Cole aside, but the startled beasts were intent on their own escape.

Will managed to catch hold of the mane of a paint mare and struggled to launch himself into the saddle. She rebelled against the unwarranted brutality and reared in protest, throwing her assailant to the ground. Will cursed and scrambled to his feet, but the mare had already put a good amount of distance between them.

"Don't move a muscle, or I'll blow you to kingdom come."

Yeager advanced on Will, the shotgun poised and ready, and Cole felt cold fingers grip his insides. His apprehension, however, was wasted, for Will was completely lacking in heroism and complied in earnest.

"Don't shoot," he pleaded. "Don't shoot."

"Throw down your weapons," Yeager instructed. "Nice and easy."

Cole looked on, remembering Will's flight from the bank in Eden. He'd run like a scalded cat with no concern for his brother's fate.

"Pick up those guns."

Cole realized Yeager was speaking to him, and so did Will about the same time.

"You bastard," Will ground out, struggling against the handcuffs Yeager was trying to fasten around his wrists. "You set me up, you son-of-a-bitch."

"Shut up," Yeager panted, kicking dust in Will's face.

Another lawman was shackling the remaining two survivors, while his comrades inspected their own wounded. Cole tugged the bandanna away from his face and watched as Will was handcuffed. He tried, he really tried, but he couldn't dredge up any guilt or sympathy, only relief that at last he would be free and Caitlin was waiting for him.

Cole urged his weary horse toward the tiny cabin, anxious to feel Caitlin's arms about him, and he couldn't wait to tell her that they no longer had to hide or fear being captured. When he rode into the clearing, he halfway expected her to rush out to meet him, and he wasted little time dismounting and securing the horse.

There was no sign of her and he frowned. She had to have heard the horse, and he tried to ignore the prickle of dread crawling up his spine. He scaled the rotting steps and knocked once. The door swung open on wobbly hinges. It was not even shut. Making his way inside, he found nothing amiss that would indicate forced entry or a struggle of any kind, but neither did he find any signs that the cabin was occupied.

The fireplace stood cold and empty, and a fine layer of dust had settled over the plank table. He knew a moment of relief when he caught sight of his rifle propped against the wall alongside the few personal belongings he had brought with them.

At the end of the table sat the bundle of food he'd left with Caitlin four days ago. It had hardly been touched, and he peered inside to see for himself. He crossed the tiny room and rummaged through the satchel, finding his clothes packed neatly away, and he grew even more puzzled.

He stood and glanced around the room, not certain what to do. The narrow bed had been neatly made, and he caught sight of something lying atop the faded blanket. It was a neatly folded slip of paper, and sickening dread settled like a stone in his stomach. It was the telegram Will had sent in reply to his own.

Vaguely, he remembered cramming it into one of his pockets, but he'd forgotten about it in the midst of all the confusion. He cringed at the thought of Caitlin reading Will's harsh reply and the conclusions she must have drawn.

On the back, he recognized Caitlin's polished handwriting.

Blood is thicker than water, and I won't waste my life on a man determined to throw his away.

The little man behind the glass glanced up from his work, his brow knitted with annoyance. "Yes?"

"I'm looking for someone." Cole ignored the man's deep frown of irritation, and continued. "A girl, about nineteen. Blonde and pretty."

"Have you tried the saloon?"

"Don't push me, mister, unless this town's got a real good doctor."

The shiny bald head popped up at that and he

glared at Cole. "I see a lot of people. Can't remember them all."

Cole braced his hands on the ticket counter. "You'd better start thinking. Most likely, she would have been going to Texas."

A flicker of recollection flashed in the man's beady eyes, and he licked his lips. "Would she have had to wire for the money?"

"Most likely."

He flipped through a ledger and nodded. "A wire came from Eden, Texas, to purchase a one-way ticket. First class."

The cabin was small and rickety and burned like a pile of dry leaves. Cole stood close enough to feel the heat from the flames as the remaining beams crumbled into a charred heap of smouldering embers. The iron bed frame had melted into a twisted knot of blackened metal, and Cole felt his heart do the same.

He had betrayed everything for her. Not just his family, but his sense of honor. Always he had taken pride in the fact that, despite his outlaw heritage, he had never compromised the values his mother had tried to teach him. He'd convinced himself that he'd had no choice, but there was always a choice. He could have been man enough to tell Yeager that he was no traitor and what he could do with his threats and deals.

But all he'd been thinking about was Caitlin. Keeping her safe, getting back to her, and not los-

ing her to her family's claim on her. He'd sold his
soul to keep her by his side, and she was already
long gone.

Caitlin closed her eyes and tried her best to will
away the nausea, but every time she raised her
head off of the pillow the room began to spin and
her stomach roiled. Sweat popped out on her forehead, and she braced herself for another dash to
the basin. The sickening waves passed, and she
dared to feel relieved.

It had been this way for a week. At first, she
assumed it was grief that made her sick, but as the
day wore on she would feel better only to awaken
the next morning feeling worse than the day before.

She wished now that Uncle Cam had not pressed
Papa to tell her about the Thornton gang being
slaughtered in an ambush by federal marshals. There
was no Thornton gang, only Cole and Will, who were
both now dead. She buried her face in the down
pillow and fought back the tears that constantly
threatened.

Oh, God, she'd been so angry when she read
that telegram, but now it seemed such a little thing
and her reaction so childish. Every time she recalled the spiteful words she'd written on that telegram, she cringed in shame, perversely relieved
Cole had never read them.

Sunlight seeped around the edges of the draped

window, and she knew she should dress and go downstairs, but she felt weak as a kitten.

A knock came at the door, and Maggie bustled inside without waiting for an answer. The room was suddenly permeated with the unbearable odor of food, and Caitlin gagged.

"Brought you some breakfast, dearie."

"Please," she managed, brandishing a hand to halt Maggie's approach. One look at a plate of quivering scrambled eggs would do her in. "Take it away."

Maggie placed the tray on a bureau near the door and crossed the room to stand over the bed. She pressed her palm against Caitlin's forehead and frowned. "You don't have a fever. What's wrong?"

"Something I ate, I suppose."

"You haven't eaten enough this week to keep a bird alive, let alone make anyone sick."

Caitlin could only shake her head. "I don't know what it is."

She felt the bed dip under Maggie's weight and turned to find the older woman seated on the edge of the bed peering down at her with a thoughtful, worried expression. "Caitlin, how long has it been since you had your monthly?"

Gaping up at her, she tried to remember. So much had happened, and she'd scarcely given thought to her physical condition.

"You've been home for nigh onto six weeks, and you haven't had any . . . soiled linen." Maggie chewed on her lower lip. "Do you know what it means when a woman's cycle doesn't come?"

Realization caved in on her, and Caitlin shook her head. "No. It can't be."

"Can't be?" Maggie repeated, her expression doubtful.

"I mean . . . not now." Caitlin felt panic well up inside her. "Not now, please, God, not now."

PART TWO

Seven

"Three bears! Three bears!"

"Not until you have your jammies on." Caitlin tickled Jamie's belly and resumed buttoning his pajama top. She finished the last button and said, "Go get your storybook."

Caitlin never went a day without thanking the Good Lord for blessing her with such a beautiful child—a little boy with dark hair and blue eyes, so much like the father he would never know. In her heart, she grieved that Cole had been cheated out of knowing his son, but she didn't deny being grateful that little Jamie's life would never be tinged by the ugliness that had spoiled everything for her and his father.

The day he was born, she vowed not to let the mistakes of her youth cast shame on an innocent babe, and the priest christened him James Duncan McDonnell without question—James after Caitlin's baby brother who'd lived only three days and Duncan after his grandfather. It was, after all, Duncan's name and the power it represented that silenced even the sharpest tongue, and any questions about the child's parentage were never breathed aloud.

The day would come, she knew, when the child would have questions of his own that she would have to answer, but for now he needed only her unconditional love and devotion. She couldn't honestly say who adored the baby more, her father or Uncle Cam, and they doted on him.

Jamie was the center of her universe, and each day brought laughter and adventure as she watched him grow. It seemed only yesterday he'd been a chubby baby who could barely crawl, and now he was learning to tie his shoes. Eagerness usually outweighed skill, and the laces would end up in a knot Caitlin could barely untie.

The best time was in the early evening hours when Jamie, fresh from his bath and sleepy from a busy day, would climb onto her lap and fight to stay awake while she read a bedtime story. He almost never made it to "The End," but she wouldn't put him right to bed.

Sitting in her grandmother's rocking chair, she would hold him close and savor the feel of his warm, sleeping body against her breast. He had grown so much and changed so fast that she feared another three years would yield a boy too old for fairy tales and lullabies. For now he was still her baby, and she refused to squander one precious moment.

Tonight was no different than any other, but she lingered a little longer than usual. From the nursery window, she watched the twilight fade to night and the stars fill the sky. She pressed her lips against Jamie's forehead and rocked slowly back and forth, loving his sweet baby scent.

"I think the coast is clear."

She started at the sound of her uncle's voice and glanced over her shoulder to see Cameron lounging in the open doorway of the nursery. "What do you mean?"

He chuckled. "Our guest asked me to bid you good night. He finally decided you were going to be all night tucking Jamie in."

"It's really none of his business."

Caitlin stood and crossed the room, placing Jamie in his tiny bed and drawing the covers over his shoulders. For the past month, Dr. Nelson Carroll had come calling every Saturday evening, and he was not the least bit discouraged by Caitlin's blatant lack of interest.

"He's a nice enough fellow," Cam pointed out as Caitlin closed the nursery door. "Nice looking, well educated, and very successful. I hear that every woman in town is out to lure him to the altar."

"I hear the same thing about you." For the first time, she recognized genuine concern in his eyes. "Uncle Cam, please don't worry about me. I'm just not ready to even think about getting married."

His expression only grew more troubled. "Caitlin, are you sure you're not . . . waiting for someone who's never going to return?"

She was stunned by the question and even more by her reluctance to answer. She drew a deep breath and said, "I gave up on that years ago."

"I didn't mean to upset you." He hugged her, and she closed her eyes against unexpected tears. "I worry about you, that's all."

"I wish you wouldn't." She tried to smile. "Nothing can hurt me as long as I have Jamie."

"I wish I knew what made you such a cold-hearted son-of-a-bitch, Cole Thornton."

Cole almost smiled at the observation, but he chose to ignore the petty insult and sank back in the steaming tub of water. He reached for the whiskey waiting alongside a stack of clean towels. No doubt he had as much trail dust inside as out, and he wanted to be rid of it.

"I'm talking to you, damn it!"

A hairbrush suddenly plopped into the bathtub, no doubt aimed at his head, and splashed a good deal of soapy water onto the floor. Slowly, he uncorked the bottle and regarded the sullen woman across the room. "I didn't pay for talk."

Bright spots of color were visible even beneath the garish rouge she wore, clashing with the kohl smeared around her eyes. She couldn't dispute that he'd paid for her just as he had the bath and the whiskey, and he'd chosen to savor the latter and was through with her. He wasn't flattered by the disappointment in her eyes. No doubt she had hoped to have one customer for the evening instead of eight or ten.

Once he left, she would have to go back downstairs where a barroom full of cowhands and wranglers were anxious to spend their wages for the month. Cole hated to see hard-earned money wasted, but it wasn't any of his concern what they did with the money he paid them. As long as he got a day's work for a day's wages, he was satisfied.

"Want little ol' Rita to scrub your back?"

He glanced up to see her sidling toward the tub, deliberately letting the front of her wrapper fall open. Breathing a curse, Cole rose from the now tepid water and began toweling himself dry. "I think I'm clean enough."

"Come on, darlin'. We're just getting started."

He flinched at the feel of her hands on his bare ass, and he managed not to be rough when he pushed past her to retrieve his britches hanging over a chair. He had nothing against whores, but tonight he would have preferred to be alone. Drovers needed little reason to celebrate, and the men had all chipped in and sent her to express their appreciation for their unexpected bonuses.

"Sorry, sugar." He hitched the denims on as quickly as he could and buckled his belt. "No time."

"You know something, Thornton?" She was pouring herself a generous portion of whiskey. "You got no feelings at all."

He finished tucking in his shirttails and reached for his dusty Stetson. "I got no use for feelings."

She said something snide, but he was halfway down the hall and wasn't listening anyway. Downstairs, his men were well into the throes of debauchery, and he declined several drink offers, a card game, and a return trip upstairs with a woman so drunk she could hardly stand up.

He stepped outside the saloon, surprised by the chill in the air. Pausing to light a cigarette, he glanced around the growing town. Two years ago, there had been barely half a dozen rickety buildings, and the livery had been the nicest one in town. Now the main street was a row of sound structures with glass in all the windows and wooden sidewalks.

Before long, wagons would arrive with men bringing families to the area. The town would become a city, and the saloon and livery would be hidden behind rows of respectable establishments: merchants, restaurants, even a church, perhaps. Cole didn't look forward to the area being tamed, or the prospect of moving on when it did.

He had no desire to live in some quaint little town with all the trappings of so-called decent society, and he'd be damned if he'd let a bunch of gelded family men set themselves up as a town council and start taxing land he'd paid for with sweat and blood. For once in his life, he had something he could call his own, something no one could take away.

He tossed the match into the dusty street and watched the wind pick it up and toss it to and fro. There was some consolation in the knowledge that he could sell the land for far more than it was worth, and settlers would fight for the privilege of buying it. He'd given little thought to what would happen then.

He would move on, of course. Maybe north toward Montana or farther west toward California as he'd always hoped. He drew deeply on the cigarette, but the biting sting only sparked the bitterness he felt at the thought of those dreams he'd constructed about California.

He exhaled a curse and tossed the cigarette away before heading toward the livery to claim his horse. No amount of time or distance could banish Caitlin from his mind completely. The slightest recollection of the past or merely saying her name tore at his gut as if it were yesterday she'd run out on him.

In retrospect, it all made sense to him now. The minute he'd mentioned marriage, she realized how bleak their lives would be and bolted for home to escape being tied to him for the rest of her life. Going straight meant working for every speck of food or stitch of clothes, and she would have been miserable.

He would have been miserable, too. Going hungry and working like a dog had been hard enough, but he couldn't have watched Caitlin suffer what he'd been through the last few years. She would have ended up hating him, and he wondered if that could possibly be any worse than her having no feelings for him at all.

Behind him, he could hear the raucous laughter of men reveling in all the heathen pleasures their wages could afford and he grudgingly envied them. When Caitlin left him, he rode until his horse gave out and found himself in a town boasting only a saloon and a livery. He drank better than half a bottle of whiskey and sought the company of a sporting woman, determined to prove one woman was the same as any other.

He was never sure if it was the whiskey or the stale odor of cheap perfume, but neither sat well on an empty stomach, and he ended up alone in back of the livery, sick as a dog, without having even touched the woman who kept his money. It was a long time before he took another drink, and even longer before he spent his money for a woman. A good deal wiser, he knew to expect only release, not pleasure.

The livery was dark, and he called out to the man on night watch that he was saddling his horse and going home. The gelding was just as anxious as he to get out of town and soon the cluster of buildings was a good distance behind him. At night, the expanse of prairie was endless with no horizon to denote where the earth ended and the sky began. Only the stars separated the heavens from the earth, but Cole paid them no attention. He never admired what wasn't within his grasp.

State Penitentiary

"Good afternoon, Warden."

"Good afternoon, William. Come in."

Will Thornton nodded meekly and made his way inside the warden's office. The old fool was positively glowing at the humble showing his prize inmate was making, and he added a little hesitation to his step, just to make it good.

"Now, don't be nervous," Warden Stone reassured him. "This is Mr. Kessler and Mr. Carrington. They represent the parole board, and I've been telling them what remarkable progress you've made in the last three years."

Will managed to keep his head lowered when he risked a glance in their direction. These men were no fools, and they scrutinized every move he made. He would have to make this good.

"You may be seated right here." Stone gestured to a chair beside his desk. "These gentlemen have reviewed your case, and they wish to ask you a few questions."

Carrington wasted no time. "You've been in and out of jail most of your life."

"Yes, sir." His voice was barely a whisper.

"What for?"

He shrugged. "Stealing, mostly."

Kessler was quick to correct him. "Armed robbery."

"Your older brother was a great influence on you, wasn't he?" Stone prompted.

Again, Will shrugged. "He was the oldest. I couldn't go against him."

Carrington quickly pointed out, "But when he died, you continued criminal activity."

"Not at first. My brother's boy got hurt, and I couldn't leave him behind. The other fellas came around thinking we had money." He turned toward Warden Stone and raised a harried, imploring expression. "I had to do something."

"So loyalty to your kin created your predicament," the warden concluded. He glanced toward Kessler and Carrington and added, "And the boy he risked so much to help was the very one who betrayed him in the end."

Will bit the inside of his jaw, afraid talking about Cole would betray the anger still seething beneath his pretense of reformation. He swallowed hard and decided on an answer he knew Warden Stone would appreciate. "I suppose he really done me a favor by that."

Carrington removed his glasses and leaned forward. "How do you mean?"

Will raised his head just enough to let the son-of-a-bitch see the sincere expression he'd perfected. "I'd be dead by now if I'd kept on like I was. Prison has given me time to think and see how much of my life I wasted."

The warden smiled, so proud Will thought the man was going to bust. "What are your plans for the future, should you be released?"

Will almost faltered on that one. For three years, he'd been planning, dreaming, living for the day he got out of this hellhole. He was going to find Cole and skin him alive, and then there was the score to settle with his little woman. Miss High and Mighty.

He was looking forward to that. She would wish like hell she'd been more obliging to him when she had a chance. He'd had three years to think of hurting her in ways she didn't know existed. The thought of having her beneath him, pleading for mercy, made his heart race, and he fought to gain control of his thoughts. Even Warden Stone's liberal notions wouldn't excuse him from getting a hard-on in front of the parole board.

"I just want to live my life in peace," he stammered, fearing his face was flushed with anticipation. "I've done ranch work and shouldn't have much of a problem hiring on to a cattle drive."

"Not many folks are anxious to hire ex-convicts," Kessler reminded him. "Especially one with the name Thornton."

"I reckon they'll be willing to trust your judgment." The man's eyes narrowed and Will didn't back away from the challenge. "If you're willing to give me a second chance, other folks will, too."

Warden Stone cleared his throat. "I think you've answered enough questions for today, William. The board will meet next week to consider your petition, and I'll advise you of their decision right away."

Will rose and shook each man's hand, politely thanking them for their time. The approving smile returned to the warden's face, and Will shook his hand, as well. He strolled back to his cell at a leisurely pace and flopped down on the bottom bunk.

"How'd it go?" his cell mate asked from overhead. "They swallow that bullshit?"

"Hook, line, and sinker." Will folded his hands behind his head and smiled to himself. He had no idea where Cole might be by now, but he was willing to bet he knew someone who did.

"All gone, Mommy! All gone!"

Caitlin pretended to be astonished by the sight of her son's empty plate. "My goodness, Jamie, you've eaten *all* of your breakfast?"

He smiled proudly, clapping his sticky hands. "Ev'y bite."

"That's wonderful." She discreetly removed the bib he detested so and began wiping his mouth with her napkin. "You'll grow up to be a big boy."

Duncan McDonnell peered over his morning newspaper and smiled proudly at the child. "Big and strong like his grandpa."

"Better suave and handsome," Cameron McDonnell declared as he entered the dining room, taking his seat across from Caitlin. "Like his uncle."

Duncan frowned. "Yes, the world's oldest eligible bachelor."

"I'm sure he will be favored with all those qualities." Caitlin brushed Jamie's dark hair away from his face with her fingers, his blue eyes smiling up at her.

Always, when she least expected it, the resemblance to Cole would catch her off guard, and an unexpected pang of sorrow would touch her heart. Not enough to bring her to tears or cause anyone to notice, but just enough to let her know that she could never put the past behind her completely.

Her fingers lingered against Jamie's downy cheek

until he pulled away, his attention turned toward the tiny wooden horse he'd insisted upon bringing to the table.

"What time do you need to leave for town?"

Her father's words forced her attention back to the present, and she tried to remember what they had been talking about before Jamie's exuberant outburst. She faltered but remembered the ladies' luncheon she would be hosting at the church. "I need to be there early, to make sure everything is set up properly."

"I have business to attend in town, and I would rather you not drive by yourself." He laid the newspaper aside and reached for his coffee. "I'll be meeting with the mayor most of the morning, and you can ride home with me."

"Papa, I'll be home long before nightfall."

He or Uncle Cam always found an excuse to accompany her wherever she went, and she failed to understand her father's vigilance after so much time had passed. Even when they learned the fate of the Thornton gang, he remained wary, and it hurt to think that she would never regain his trust.

Caitlin knew the argument was pointless, but she persisted. "There's no need for you to go to so much trouble."

"It's no trouble." He dismissed her objections and the subject, turning his attention to his brother. "What about the orphanage? Is everything ready?"

Jamie clamored to get down from the table, and Caitlin lifted him out of his highchair as she listened to the details regarding the opening of the new orphans' home.

At first, Caitlin had only agreed to serve on a benevolent committee endeavoring to better the plight of children in existing orphanages, but one visit to such an institution convinced her something greater had to be done. Her enthusiasm had been contagious, and her father had generously agreed to fund her campaign for children's welfare.

The combination of Caitlin's sincerity and her family's prestige guaranteed success, and Uncle Cam had taken care of the legal matters. The first of several privately funded homes would be opening its doors in less than a month, and every newspaper in the state carried editorials for and against the campaign.

Criticism only made Caitlin more determined, and she invited every newspaper editor to attend the opening ceremony. Uncle Cam had already assigned himself to be her chaperone for the trip, but she didn't mind. He had been such a great help to her and she was pleased he would be there.

Eden, Texas, was still nothing but a pissant little town full of cowhands and do-gooders. Will Thornton barely dodged two women trying to sell him a raffle ticket for some cockamamie church picnic, and he had to duck inside a general store to miss a second pair working the other side of the street. He could imagine the look on Caitlin McDonnell's face if he walked right up to her at a church picnic and asked her to dance. That would well be worth the cost of a ticket, but not worth denying himself the pleasure of catching her alone somewhere.

He figured the quickest way to find Cole would be to find out when Duncan McDonnell's daughter got married and where she lived. He wouldn't be surprised if they were living in Eden, living off her daddy's money. That would sure as hell be convenient, and he wondered how much McDonnell would be willing to pay to keep his little girl alive.

The storekeeper was busy with a customer, and Will slipped to the back of the store unnoticed. Money wasn't what he wanted now. He wanted Cole to suffer and Caitlin to regret ever looking down her nose at him. They would be only too happy to pay him off and be rid of him. The last thing he wanted was for either of them to ever have another happy day.

A peal of laughter from the front of the store distracted him, and he glanced back to see two men leaning against the counter, jawing with the storekeeper.

"Mm-mm, just look at that."

"She's a sweet thing, sure 'nuff. I'd like to get me some of that."

"Don't let her daddy hear you talking like that," the storekeeper warned them. "I heard McDonnell took a whip to the last man he heard talking about her."

At the mention of the name McDonnell, Will turned his full attention on their conversation. He glanced out the store window, expecting to see

Caitlin walking down the street, but there were only a few stragglers outside the store.

"Well, *somebody's* had it."

At that, all three men gave way to boyish snickers, and Will turned his back to them, still listening intently. They went on to discuss a couple of other women in town and the need for rain in the area. At last the pair of loafers left the store, and Will made his way to the counter. "Just need cigarette makin's."

The storekeeper nodded and turned to gather the tobacco and rolling papers. Will glanced out the window once more, puzzled. He was sure those hayseeds had been talking about Caitlin, but there was no sign of her.

"Here you are, mister. Anything else?"

"I reckon not." Will turned back to the storekeeper and caught sight of a folded newspaper lying on the counter. Smack dab on the front page, Caitlin's picture stared up at him, and he nearly dropped the coins he withdrew from his pocket. "You sell newspapers?"

The man shook his head. "No, but you can have that one. It's a week old, but it'll do for something to read."

Will nodded and pocketed the cigarette makings. He reached for the paper and said, "Much obliged."

Once outside the store, he slipped into the alley and scanned the newsprint. He'd learned to read in prison, and it was paying off already. The article referred to Caitlin as "Miss McDonnell" and said nothing about a husband. Just as he'd predicted, she'd left Cole behind and returned to her rich-girl life. She'd even turned into one of those full-time do-gooders, traveling all over Texas-speaking up for orphans.

He read all about her plans for a new orphans' home not too far from Eden. Will was positive he knew just where the place was, and he wouldn't have to wait very long before Caitlin McDonnell would be traveling over open country on her little mission.

Will smiled to himself and made his way to the end of the alley and slipped behind the row of buildings where he'd left his horse. He tucked the newspaper inside his saddlebag and slipped out of town unnoticed.

"Only generosity and compassion will spare the destitute children of this state needless suffering and offer them hope for a better future."

The audience applauded appreciatively, and Caitlin carefully cut the ribbon barring the doors to the children's home. Uncle Cam stepped forward, opened the doors, and turned to those gathered at the foot of the steps.

Always the master of any occasion, he waited until the applause lessened and said, "May the good people of Texas never let these doors be closed to any child."

The applause increased, and everyone filed inside for the reception. Potential patrons were invited to view the modern facility that could offer medical care, schooling, and living quarters for the orphaned and the abandoned.

Jamie ran ahead, his new shoes clattering on the freshly polished floors, and Caitlin hurried after him. She barely caught up with the child before he collided with one of the resident doctors.

"Settle down, young man," she scolded, taking firm hold of his hand. "What did I tell you about coming with me today?"

He wouldn't look at her, and she pressed. "What did Mommy say?"

"I haf' to be a gent-a-man," he repeated her instructions in a sulking voice. "No running indoors."

"I dare say these floors will see their fair share of heel marks before long. One more little boy won't do any harm."

Caitlin and Jamie both turned toward the boy's unexpected ally, the doctor he'd nearly bowled over moments ago. He ruffled Jamie's hair and suggested, "Perhaps you and I can have a race after everyone has gone home."

Jamie glanced up doubtfully at Caitlin. "Mommy won't 'low me."

"Let me talk to her," he said in a conspiratorial tone and winked. He straightened up and smiled at Caitlin. "I'm Dr. Randall."

"I believe we met at one of the board meetings last month," she said, returning his smile. "How nice to see you again. We were just on our way to the reception."

"I was going there myself. May I escort you?"

Caitlin hesitated, but when he didn't offer his arm she accepted what she hoped was a mere show of good manners. He led them toward the spacious room that would eventually seat two hundred children for meals, all the while detailing his hopes for the future of the institution.

"This is one of the finest facilities I've ever worked in, but there is still much we won't be able to do." He glanced at her. "I mean no disrespect, of course, but the plight of poor and abused children is barely even acknowledged by society, let alone the medical community."

"There's no need to defend yourself. If you weren't passionate about your work, you wouldn't be suited for what we hope to accomplish."

They joined the assembly in the dining hall, shaking hands and exchanging pleasantries. Dr. Randall discreetly led Caitlin and Jamie outside to a lovely garden with benches on either side of a brick walkway.

"How lovely," she remarked. "Surely the children will need a larger playground. This is a bit formal, don't you think?"

"This won't be for playtime," he assured her. "Many of the children are too ill to play, but they need a quiet place to enjoy the outdoors. Also, this will provide a place to visit, should a child have visitors."

"Visitors? You mean their families?"

"Not all orphans are without parents." He shook his head sadly. "Many children are placed in institutions because their family can't or won't care for them."

"How terrible."

He smiled in understanding. "I used to think so, too. But only a selfish parent would keep a child in a situation where their welfare was in jeopardy. I've seen children half starved, beaten, and worse. Their mothers sneak them away and hand them over to strangers rather than have them go on suffering. Can you even imagine seeing your child in such a plight?"

Caitlin glanced at Jamie and shuddered at the thought. A happy child, he had never known a moment of fear or hunger, and she realized how easy it was to take such things for granted.

At last, the carriage pulled away from the orphanage, and Cam sank back against the padded leather seat. "I didn't think that would ever be over. My fingers are swollen from shaking so many hands."

Caitlin laughed. "It's your own fault for being so charming."

"Remind me to restrain myself next time." He paused thoughtfully. "You seem to have made your fair share of lasting impressions today. That Dr. Randall followed you around like a lost puppy today."

"He was only being kind," she insisted, threading her fingers through Jamie's hair as he settled beside her on the seat. "He knew Jamie was fidgety, so he offered a tour of the grounds."

Curling her arm around the boy, Caitlin urged him to lean against her in hopes he would drift off to sleep. He had been too excited for a morning nap and needed to rest after such a busy day.

Jamie yawned wide, rubbing his eyes. "He said to come back anytime we want."

"That might be a good idea."

Caitlin ignored the mischievous glint in her uncle's eyes. "As if I had the time to spare."

"What does take up so much of your time, Caity?" He didn't wait for an answer before running down his own list. "Garden clubs, church functions, and you serve on every charitable committee in Texas. Do you enjoy any of it, or are you just keeping yourself busy?"

Taken aback, she didn't know how to answer such a blunt question. To tell the truth, she didn't know the answer, so she pointed out the obvious. "I have a child to raise. That keeps me busy enough."

"That's not what I asked."

She knew better than trying to be vague with an attorney, especially one as crafty as Uncle Cam. "I'm happy with the way things are. Peaceful."

He smiled as if he understood and leaned his head back against the plushly upholstered seat, closing his eyes. Caitlin glanced down at Jamie, grateful to find him dozing against her breast, and let herself relax for the first time since leaving home this morning.

The carriage suddenly lurched to the right, and

the pace became unbalanced. Cam was instantly alert and leaned toward the open window. "What's going on, driver?"

"One of the horses done gone lame." The driver's voice held more irritation than concern, and Caitlin hoped the problem could be remedied. "We'll have to cut him loose. There's a way station 'bout a mile up ahead, and they'll have a fresh horse for us."

Caitlin groaned. No doubt the stop and commotion of changing horses would serve only to awaken Jamie and prolong their return trip. Glancing toward the horizon, she tried to gauge how much daylight they had left, and she convinced herself that they could make up the lost time and still arrive at home before nightfall. She knew the driver would not travel after dark, and the thought of spending the night in a shabby rest station made her shudder.

She had not slept away from home in three years, and no one suspected it was because she was haunted by fears of not being able to return. She often dreamed of being trapped in a strange room, of beating on a bolted door and begging to go home. It was silly, she knew, but she always made excuses when invited to visit relatives or travel with a friend.

The afflicted horse was unhitched from the coach and picketed near a copse of slender saplings. The driver explained that someone from the rest area would be back later to claim him. Caitlin knew the practice was commonplace, but she couldn't help looking back as the coach resumed its trek. The gelding watched them ride away, and she wondered if he understood that someone would be coming for him. An uneasy feeling settled inside her, and she couldn't forget the hopelessness in the poor beast's eyes.

The way station came into view, and the coach lumbered to a stop in the scraggly clearing that stood before a sturdy, new building. Jamie slept peacefully, and she hated to disturb him by getting out of the stage. Uncle Cam stepped down and held his hand up to her. "Might as well stretch our legs before the rest of—"

Whatever he said after that was lost in an explosion of gunfire. The driver began swearing and scrambling for a rifle, and Cam hauled Caitlin and Jamie out of the stage. "We have to get inside!" he shouted. "Hurry!"

Jamie struggled against the viselike hold Caitlin had on him, but her strength was greater than his. Once they were safely inside the building, bullets began shattering the windowpanes and showering them with shards of glass. Cam toppled the long plank table on its side, and Caitlin huddled behind the makeshift fortress. She could barely hear men shouting above the gunfire, and she shrank from the agonized cries of the wounded, all the while shielding Jamie's body with her own.

Silence fell like a net, far more sinister than the explosive gunfire. Caitlin held Jamie tight, his tiny fingers gripping the sleeve of her dress. She glanced over to see her uncle slumped against the wall and the sleeve of his tan jacket dark with blood.

"Uncle Cam!" she cried, scrambling to his side. "Let me see."

She pried his fingers away from the wound and breathed a sigh of relief to see that the injury was not serious. Jerking a length of cotton material from her petticoat, she applied pressure to the wound to stop the bleeding. Jamie sat staring wide-eyed at the bloodstains beneath his uncle's jacket, and Caitlin gasped at the sight of a far more serious wound in his abdomen.

Suddenly, the door burst open, and Caitlin blanched at the sight of two armed men ducking inside the station. She pulled Jamie beside his uncle, and Cam held the boy to his uninjured side.

"I know you're in here, Caitlin," one bandit spoke at last, his voice muffled behind the bandanna covering his face. "Come on out. You can't hide forever."

She recognized the voice, even before Will Thornton removed the dusty bandanna. All the blood rushed from her head, and she fought against the panic and shock of seeing someone she thought was long dead. Every reassurance she'd taken over the past few years vanished, and she scrambled to garner her best defense. Above all else, she had to keep him from seeing Jamie.

Caitlin heard boot heels scrape across the plank floor and the soft jingle of spurs. She might as well be right out in the open, as it was useless to remain crouched behind the table. Her only hope was to keep him distracted long enough for help to arrive.

Rising to her feet, she made her way around the fallen table to face her nemesis. "What do you want?"

He laughed. "Now is that any way to talk to your kin?"

"You're no kin of mine," she seethed, hating him more than she thought possible.

"You and I have some unfinished business." He handed his rifle over to his helper and advanced on Caitlin, his hands urgently tugging at his belt buckle. "I've waited a long time for this, and you're going to regret every day."

He lunged for her, but she anticipated his move and scrambled out of his reach. She tried to maintain the distance between them, but he caught her arm and twisted it cruelly. Her cry of pain brought a smile to his lips. "That's nothing, sugar. I'm going to hurt you so many ways you'll thank me for killing you."

"Mommy!" Jamie tore loose from Cam's weakened grip. "Mommy, no!"

Stunned, Will turned loose her arm and stared as she knelt to enfold the little boy in her arms.

"Mommy?" he repeated, taking in Jamie's dark hair and blue eyes, the child's features the very image of his father. "Well, I'll be damned."

"Leave us alone, Will," she pleaded, turning Jamie's face away from him. "You've no cause to hate me."

"No cause?" he sneered down at her. "I spent

three years rotting in prison because of you. I'd say that's cause enough."

"Prison is where you belong. If it weren't for you, Cole would still be alive."

A startled look flashed in his eyes, and the malevolence in his voice was chilling when he said, "Cole's not dead. Not yet, anyway."

"He died in the stage holdup just outside of Santa Fe," she insisted, refusing to let him shake her. "You know that as well as I do."

"That was a setup. Cole led us all into an ambush to save his own skin." Will regarded her with a twisted sort of amusement. "Looks like he screwed us both, honey. In more ways than one."

Without warning, Will backhanded her across the face and sent her sprawling backward to the hard-packed dirt floor. The impact knocked the breath out of her and her hold on Jamie slipped just for an instant but long enough for Will to snatch him up by the collar.

The child screamed hysterically, and Caitlin struggled to her feet despite the ringing in her ears. She reached for her son but Will knocked her down and turned for the door. No sooner than he cleared the exit, she was after him.

"Give him back to me!" she screamed. "Give him back!"

"Mommy! Mommy!" Jamie was crying out in terror. "Mommy, please!"

Before she could reach them, Will handed the boy up to a mounted rider waiting with their horses. Jamie was crying hysterically, desperately struggling against the rough hands that held him, and Caitlin feared he would be thrown to the ground and trampled by the horses. She wasted no time, charging after Will just as he vaulted into the saddle, and the horse turned at his command. Caitlin managed to catch hold of the reins, but Will Thornton anticipated her actions and leveled his pistol with Jamie's head.

"Please, Will, please give him back to me," she begged, desperation evident in her voice. "I'll leave him with my uncle and go with you, instead."

"Too late, sweetheart." He laughed and shook his head. "You tell Cole I'm looking for him."

When she didn't drop the reins immediately, he cocked the revolver for emphasis, and Caitlin felt her heart stop beating. "You bring the son-of-a-bitch to me or the boy here pays the price."

Will spurred his mount and jerked the reins, and the others followed suit. Caitlin ran after them, knowing she had no chance against such fast horses, and she cried out, "I don't even know where he is!"

Will turned his mount for a moment as the others flew past him. "Then you'd better start looking."

He laughed and hurried after his band, leaving behind a cloud of dust and the fading cries of a terrified child.

"Don't come back without my grandson!" Duncan McDonnell's rage filled the tiny way station. "And bring Thornton back to me *alive.*"

Soldiers from nearby Fort Griffin had been assembled to search for the stolen child, but Duncan wasn't going to settle for anything less than vindication.

He had arrived within hours of the attack to find his brother fighting for his life and his daughter in a stupor of grief and terror. Immediately, he took charge of the situation and vowed retribution for the attack on his family. A doctor was still working with Cam, but the bleeding had stopped and the wound was clean.

One of the troopers cleared his throat and his voiced squeaked when he asked, "Alive? What good will that do?"

"I'm going to cut his heart out." Duncan crossed the dusty lot and looked down at the lanky young man. "I want him to feel every inch of the blade."

The soldier's face turned white, and their sergeant began barking orders for them to move out on the double. The need to ride with them was overwhelming. The very thought of his innocent grandson at the mercy of that bastard infuriated him, and Duncan knew a fear unlike any he'd felt before. Even when Caitlin was missing, he never feared for her life. Perhaps he hadn't let himself, but this time he couldn't deny the very real possibility that Jamie might already be dead.

He turned back inside the bullet-riddled building and felt helpless for the first time in his life. He'd clawed his way out of the slums, fought Indians and Mexicans, and paid for every acre of his land with blood and sweat. He knew how to deal with anyone who crossed him, but nothing could undo the damage done by this unforseen, senseless violence.

The doctor had finished bandaging Cam's shoulder and began placing his instruments back into his bag. Duncan crossed the room and knelt beside his brother, gripping his hand.

"Don't you die on me, brother," he said, alarmed at how pale Cam was. He could barely return Duncan's grip. "I'll need a good lawyer if they try me for killing these bastards."

Cam's usual wry humor was gone. "It's my fault, all my fault. I should have been wearing a gun. I should have—"

"You can't help getting shot." Duncan repented silently for thinking the exact same thing until he saw how badly his brother had been wounded. Still, he would always wonder how different the outcome would have been if he'd been there instead of Cameron. "I won't have you blaming yourself."

"You're going to need plenty of rest." The doctor had returned to stand over them. "Do you have someone to keep those bandages changed?"

"He'll be taken care of," Duncan assured them both. "I appreciate everything you've done, doctor."

He nodded and glanced once more at his patient. "You're a lucky man, Mr. McDonnell."

Cameron looked as if the man had spit on him.

"You rest for now," Duncan ordered, cutting in before Cam could further berate himself. "I'll have you home soon."

He rose and made his way to the back of the room where Caitlin had taken a seat by the window. She stared out toward the road, but the blank look on her face made him wonder if she was really seeing anything.

At first, the stage driver was positive Caitlin had been taken along with her son, but a couple of soldiers found her over a mile from the station, lying facedown on the road. At first, they thought she was dead but soon realized she'd collapsed from running after the outlaws. Both troopers were mortified by Duncan's blunt questions, but they assured him that Caitlin's clothes were intact and nothing suggested she had been violated.

Duncan took in the ugly bruise along one side of her face, the torn clothes, and the bloody scabs on her palms, and the thought of his beautiful daughter crawling in the dirt sickened him. She hadn't said a word since his arrival, and he wasn't sure what to do to help her.

"Caitlin, honey, can you hear me?"

"Hello, Papa." She turned at the sound of his voice, smiling up at him. "Will you please tell Jamie it's time to come inside for supper?"

Panic shot through his heart. "Honey, don't you understand what's happened?"

"I let him go outside to play," she answered. "But I told him not to wander off because supper was almost ready."

My God, she'd lost her mind. Duncan knelt before

her, gently clasping her hands. "Do you remember what happened after the stage stopped?"

"Jamie's going to be just like his daddy," she continued, brushing a snarled lock of hair away from her face. "Did I ever tell you about the time—"

"Caitlin, you've got to listen to me," he broke in. The last thing Duncan wanted to hear was any reminiscence about Cole Thornton.

She wasn't listening. Caitlin glanced down and gasped in surprise at the sight of her torn and dirty dress. "Just look at me. I'm a mess, and here we have company coming for dinner."

She fiddled with the ripped bodice to no avail. "I told him not to . . ."

The voice trailed off, and she met her father's grief-stricken eyes. "Oh, Papa, I told him not to . . . I told him to leave us alone."

A sob rose in her throat, and Duncan barely caught her before she bolted to her feet. "Let go of me!" she cried out in anguish. "He took my baby!"

"I know, honey, I know." Duncan held her tight, even as she struggled. "We'll get him back, I swear it."

She shook her head. "You don't know Will Thornton. He's a monster. He'll kill him just for spite."

"I've already sent telegrams to the governor, the Rangers, and the U.S. Marshal. Every lawman in Texas will be looking for him by morning. He won't find a place to hide."

"He said I had to find Cole, but how?" Seemingly

unaware of the tears streaming down her face, Caitlin asked the one question Duncan didn't want to answer. "How can I find someone I thought was dead?"

Eight

Things were finally going well.

For the first time since he could remember, Cole felt a sense of hope without the threat of having it all snatched away by a whim of nature or twist of fate. He was careful to keep his stance relaxed and his expression unreadable as the herd of mustangs thundered into the livery's corral.

Dust swirled in their wake and the grit stung his eyes, but Cole didn't look away. He watched for any sign of panic as the gate was closed, and the horses realized they were confined. The stallion made a great show of objecting to being penned up by tossing his head and circling the wary mares.

Already, a crowd was gathering and excitement rippled through the throng of people. Mostly greenhorns and mail-order cowboys, amazed to learn such horses existed, let alone could be bought for a reasonable price. Cole scanned their eager expressions and could almost feel the weight of their money in his pocket.

"Easy pickins, Thornton." Joe Hollis stood beside him, nodding his head in approval. "Easy pickins. Hell, they'll be fighting each other to give you their money."

Cole only shrugged. "I can't please everybody."

Hollis laughed. "I swear, but you got the luck. If you fell in a fifty-foot well, you'd land on a feather bed."

Luck had nothing to do with it, but Cole didn't bother to point that out. Instead, he turned away from the corral and made his way toward the saloon. The auction wouldn't start for several hours, but he wanted those horses where buyers could get a good look at them.

If he had his way, he would do nothing but breed and sell horses and never look at another cow. Horses, however, were a luxury and cattle paid the bills. Someday, though, he would be able to hire enough hands to tend the ranch and be free to devote all of his time to the wild mustangs.

Once the gate to the corral was securely fastened and the number of horses verified with the auctioneer, Cole walked away so the crowd could inspect the horses and speculate on the prices.

Hollis followed him inside the saloon and joined him at the bar. He'd met Joe working on a cattle drive and considered him as much of a friend as he allowed himself. When Cole had acquired a place of his own, Joe appointed himself foreman.

"Whiskey." Joe waved two fingers at the bartender. He glanced around the smoke-filled room and needlessly observed, "Crowded in here, for the middle of the day. Auctions and hangings always draw the crowds."

Cole let his gaze follow Joe's around the barroom and saw more unfamiliar faces than ever before. Aside from the usual wranglers and cowhands, the ragtag assembly consisted of gamblers, teamsters, and a myriad of drifters whose motives were impossible to fathom.

Towns meant money and money always meant trouble. He knew only too well that nothing drew outlaws and vultures quicker than the promise of easy money. It was only a matter of time before gunfights and holdups became everyday occurrences.

The swinging doors burst open, and a kid no more than twelve shot inside, calling out, "Mr. Thornton! Mr. Thornton, you got a telegram."

Cole whipped around and recognized the son of the freight driver who passed through town twice a week. Breathless, the boy could barely get the words out, but he managed to explain, "They barely caught us before we pulled out! It just came . . . from Texas!"

The room fell silent, and Cole snatched the wrinkled paper from the kid's sweaty hand. Christ Almighty, who would send him a wire from Texas? The nearest telegraph wire was thirty miles away, and Cole couldn't imagine anyone being that determined to reach him. Only the locals knew of today's auctions, and even his mustangs wouldn't warrant interest from that far away.

Everyone was looking on, as if he were going to read the damn thing out loud. Cole downed his whiskey and made his way out of the saloon, clutching the telegram in his fist.

Once he was certain the crowd from the saloon wasn't going to follow him into the street, he slowed his pace and paused in front of the general store. Nothing good would be coming from Texas, he knew that, and he was tempted to toss the telegram into an ashcan.

Slowly, he unfolded the slip of paper and scanned the brief message.

Will Thornton has your son. The boy will die if you do not return to Texas.

His eyes flew to the remittance: *Duncan McDonnell.*

Twice more, he reread the cryptic message as if it were written in some foreign language he had surely misunderstood, but the meaning was clear.

His son.

Cole slumped against the rough-hewn building, feeling as if a mule had just kicked him in the gut. He would like to think this was some bastard's idea of a joke, but no one in Texas would dare use Duncan McDonnell's name for any such purpose.

His son.

The words buzzed around his brain like mosquitoes, drawing blood every time they landed, and his mind reeled from the rush of long-dead emotions. Elation, yes. He had a child. A child Caitlin had hidden from him all these years, but the rage he wanted to feel about that quickly turned to alarm. He knew exactly what Will was capable of doing, and he braced himself for the very real possibility that Caitlin might already be dead.

He reread the telegram, assuring himself that McDonnell wouldn't fail to mention something that monumental.

How in the hell had Will gotten his ass out of prison so soon in the first place? He wasn't cunning enough to escape, and Yeager had sworn he would do ten years, at least.

Cole swore silently, barely resisting the urge to smash his fist into something. Anything. He'd nearly killed himself trying to put the past behind him. Now, one telegram had brought everything back. Caitlin, his family, the ugly memories, and now a son he knew nothing about.

At least one thing was certain. Now he knew. He knew why Caitlin ran.

Sally Jessup had given up on a lot of things in her life, and, in the last three years, she wanted to believe she'd given up on Will Thornton. He was a thief, a liar, and she always ended up sorry and vowing to never let him use her again.

Even knowing all of that didn't stop the elation she felt at the sight of him riding toward the saloon. From the window of her tiny upstairs room, she peered down at him and decided the past few years hadn't been any better for him than they had been for her.

Two men rode with him, and she forced herself not to run downstairs and meet him out front.

When she thought he'd had time to secure his horse, Sally opened the door to her room and listened for the bartender's greeting. "What'll it be, gents?"

She made her way to the top of the stairs and watched him duck inside the empty saloon. The place never did much business before nightfall, and his companions went straight to the bar and ordered beer. She heard Will ask for her and whiskey in the same sentence.

Cautiously, she descended the first two steps and leaned against the railing. "I'm right here."

"Well, hello, Sally." He whirled around and smiled up at her. "Aren't you glad to see me?"

She nodded slowly. "For how long, I wonder."

He laughed and she noticed for the first time he was carrying a heavy bundle against his chest. "Get on down here and look what I brought for you to see."

Cautiously, she made her way down the stairs, not liking the shit-eating grin on his face one bit. He was up to something, and she would probably end up right smack-dab in the middle of whatever trouble he was in this time. She stopped dead in her tracks as he placed the bundle, a sleepy toddler, in a chair at a nearby table.

"Wake up, boy," he said. "There's a lady here to meet you."

The child blinked and glanced around the room before shaking his head. "No, no. I want Mo-mmy."

Will frowned. "This is Sally, boy. You be nice to her."

Sally slipped into a chair beside the child and studied him closely. Gently, she cupped his face and gazed into the saddest blue eyes she'd ever seen. "My God, he looks just like Cole did when he was a boy."

"I reckon he does." Will plopped down beside her and tossed his hat on the table. "That's Cole's boy."

Stunned, she turned back to Will, who was helping himself to the bottle of whiskey the bartender had brought over. Sally had wondered whatever became of Cole after he left Santa Fe. Bounty hunters had hauled Caitlin out of town, and as far as Sally knew, Cole never came back to ask what happened to her. No doubt, Caitlin was the boy's mother, but what had happened to her?

So many questions flew through her mind she couldn't pick just one to ask. Finally, she just asked, "What on earth is he doing with you?"

"I'm looking out for Cole's interest." Will downed a shot of whiskey and poured himself another. "He doesn't even know about the kid."

"But you did?"

"Quite by accident," he assured her. "I ran into Miss High and Mighty."

Sally didn't ask who he meant. It irked her to know Will still had it in his craw that Caitlin wouldn't lie down for him. "You took her kid?"

"Hell, no." He swallowed. "Her family was going to get rid of him, put him in an orphans' home."

"Get rid of him?"

Sally couldn't believe anyone wouldn't want this

sweet little boy. She knew Caitlin's father was some important cattleman who had more money than God. No doubt, the whole bunch considered Cole little more than trash and had no use for his kid.

"I can't believe Caitlin wanted you to take care of him." She couldn't resist adding, "The way I remember things, she couldn't stand the sight of you."

Will's eyes narrowed slightly. "It doesn't matter what she wants."

The flash of anger on Will's face gave her an uneasy feeling, and the situation was sounding more and more farfetched. Sally decided to ask one more question, one she hoped wouldn't aggravate him any more. "Do you think Cole will really come after him?"

To her surprise, Will smiled. "I'm positive about that."

Still, she wondered. Once Caitlin had gone back to her family, had Cole just forgotten about her? She turned back to the child and thought how undeniable his resemblance to Cole was. Cole couldn't deny the boy but would he want to raise a kid? "What's your name, sweetie?"

The little fella's lip trembled when he whispered, "Jamie."

His eyes were bright with tears and she couldn't help but notice the moisture clinging to his long eyelashes. Sally knew nothing about children, but something tugged at her insides, and she responded to an urge to make those tears go away. "Are you hungry? Would you like something to eat?"

He nodded earnestly, and she rose to take him to the kitchen that adjoined the saloon and the restaurant. The smell of fried chicken was already filling the air, and she hoped Mardi would have hot biscuits and honey.

"I wouldn't mind some dinner, myself!" Will called after her, but she paid him no mind.

Jamie's little fingers held tight to her hand, and he huddled against her skirt as the sound of voices and clanging pots rose from the kitchen.

Mardi turned from the stove, and her dark face lit up when she saw the little boy. "What'cha got there?"

"This is Jamie." Sally helped him into one of the kitchen chairs and sat down beside him. "He's come a long way to visit me, and he's hungry."

Mardi laughed, reaching for a plate. "Little boys stay hungry."

Sally poured a glass of milk for him, and he soon had his hands and face sticky from a biscuit Mardi had slathered with butter and jelly. Sally glanced up to see Will lounging in the doorway, wearing a sly grin.

"Haven't you fed this child?"

"Sally, I don't know anything about taking care of kids." Will seated himself at the table. "You know that."

A pregnable silence followed, punctuated only by the clanging of a pot and Mardi asking Jamie if he liked snap beans.

"I need you to help me." Will leaned forward,

but she didn't search his eyes for sincerity. "Help me take care of him until Cole shows up."

This wasn't the first time Will Thornton had claimed to need her, and it wasn't the first time she'd known better. She didn't answer right away, and Mardi provided a handy distraction by setting a plate of food in front of the child. Sally concentrated on helping the little fella with his dinner. He managed well enough with a spoon to eat the mashed potatoes and snap beans by himself, but she pulled bite-size pieces of chicken off the bone for him.

Jamie had just about cleaned his plate before she glanced up at Will. He was grinning at her as if he already knew what her answer would be.

The little boy crawled into her lap and let his head fall against her shoulder, and Sally felt something unfurl inside herself. Something good and vulnerable. Her arms closed around his tiny body, and she combed her fingers through his hair. Will didn't need anyone. A little boy with nowhere to turn did.

Cole gazed down on the McDonnell ranch, his horse shifting restlessly beneath him. The lot in front of the house looked like a military post, and he wouldn't have been surprised if the governor of the state of Texas showed up. Duncan McDonnell had only to snap his fingers and men jumped.

He grimaced at the thought. These men were here to do McDonnell's bidding; he was here to save his son. Resentment surged through him at the thought of all the so-called lawmen gathered around like children at a picnic when they should be out following Will's tracks.

It had been easy enough to check up on Will's parole and when he left prison. After that, however, it was as if he had disappeared from the face of the earth. Cole wasn't discouraged by that. Will wasn't man enough to face him outright and called himself making Cole come to him.

He would hunt Will down and make him pay not only for taking the child but for every misery he'd caused Cole in the past three years. Experience had taught him it wasn't enough to strike back at an enemy, an enemy had to be destroyed. Completely.

Once again, he scanned the folks milling about but caught no sight of Caitlin. She was nowhere in sight, and he pushed back any thought of her being harmed or worse. She wasn't the reason he was here. He told himself over and over again, he was here for the child she had hidden from him.

Caitlin had never seen so many lawmen in her life. Texas Rangers, United States Marshals, deputies, and soldiers all milled around, waiting for any word of ransom demands or rescue opportunity.

Mostly, they stood around devouring the food brought by worried neighbors. News of the attack on the stage had spread like wildfire, prompting shock and curiosity, and the outpouring of concern was manifested in the form of covered dishes taking up every available space in the kitchen and being served to those gathered at the house. It all reminded Caitlin of a wake, and she fled to her room.

Her frustration mounted, and she couldn't believe her father was allowing those lawmen to remain idle when they should be out looking for Jamie.

"Caitlin, honey, you're going to drive yourself crazy staring out that window."

Letting the curtain fall back into place, Caitlin turned around and tried to smile. "I don't have far to go."

The expression on Lily Faulkner's face professed the pity and concern she'd been trying so hard to conceal. Her best friend since grade school, Lily had all but taken up residence at the McDonnell ranch since learning of Jamie's abduction. Shielding Caitlin from the suffocating concern of well-meaning friends, Lily delighted in dodging their nosy questions and piquing their curiosity all at the same time.

Even Dr. Carroll's insistence on seeing Caitlin out of concern for her health was politely but firmly denied. Lily kept Caitlin busy, sewing a new dress and scouring the Montgomery Ward catalog for shoes to match. Without her, Caitlin would no doubt have gone mad with despair.

"I have no idea what I've done wrong." Lily resumed her matter-of-fact optimistic facade, constantly assuring Caitlin everything would be all right, and turned her attention to the dress neither one of them would wear. "This sleeve just will not set right."

Caitlin moved to sit on the bed beside her friend and covered Lily's hand with her own. "You don't have to keep pretending. It helps, actually, to know I'm not alone in being worried."

Lily let the dress fall to the floor. "Well, you most certainly aren't alone, but mostly I'm angry. You never did anything to those people to deserve something like this."

"Will thinks he's hurting Cole by doing this, but Cole never knew about Jamie." Her throat tightened. Caitlin was finding it almost impossible to speak of Cole in the present tense. "Obviously, he doesn't care about me."

"Oh, honey, you were both so young." Lily was the only person Caitlin had ever spoken freely to about Cole. "If things had been different—"

"Things are different now," she pointed out. "He never tried to contact me. Not once."

"Maybe he couldn't." Lily thought for a moment. "The uncle said he'd been in prison, Cole probably was, too."

Caitlin had considered the possibility herself, but that wouldn't explain the vendetta Will had against Cole or how any of it involved her. Cole had, after all, chosen his family over her. If Will felt cheated, he needn't bother blaming her.

A timid knock came at the door.

"Missy Cay-lan."

Lily opened the door, and Caitlin recognized the cook's little boy standing in the hallway. As soon as the door was opened, he bounded into the room, his dark eyes wide with excitement. "Missy Cay-lan!"

Lily caught him gently by the arm. "Not now, sweetie. Miss Caitlin doesn't feel good."

Shaking his head, Pedro stood his ground. "I have to give something to Missy Cay-lan!"

"What is it, Pedro?" Caitlin managed to smile at the child and motioned for him to come to her. "What did you bring me?"

"A letter," he said in a conspiratorial tone. "A secret letter."

Caitlin felt every drop of blood rush from her head, and she barely managed to get to her feet. With shaking fingers, she reached for the folded paper, afraid to read whatever it said.

Meet me tonight. Come alone or I'll leave town.

She glanced up to find Lily watching her with anxious eyes. When Caitlin offered no explanation, Lily smiled down at the child and asked, "Who gave you that letter, honey?"

The little boy's eyes widened in alarm. "I can't tell. He said not to tell."

"It's all right." Caitlin stood on shaky legs. "I know who sent it."

Lily's eyes widened, and she hurried Pedro out of the room, assuring him that he had done just fine. When she turned around, her eyes were still wide with excitement. "It's from Cole. He's here, isn't he?"

Caitlin nodded. "He wants to see me."

"See there. He does care about you. He wouldn't be here if he didn't."

"If he cared about me, he would have been here three years ago." Caitlin drew a deep breath and folded the note. "This is about Will and whatever bad blood fell between them."

"This is about your son, Caitlin McDonnell," Lily snapped, slamming her hands on her hips. "And you had better remind Cole Thornton of that as well."

The night air held an unexpected chill, and Caitlin contemplated turning back to the house for the tenth time. At first, she'd vowed to make Cole Thornton come to her, but as sunset neared she wouldn't risk having him take whatever chance she had of saving Jamie away from her. No doubt, Cole wouldn't set one foot in the house without her father killing him, and she would never find her son.

At last, she neared the stream, picking her way along the overgrown path, and realized how difficult finding the place would have been without the benefit of the full moon. She hadn't been near this spot since the fateful night she'd run away, filled with foolish notions about love and adventure. The trees had grown tall and close, and the branches overhead formed a canopy of rustling leaves. Caitlin hesitated, reluctant to be swallowed up by the darkness waiting inside the grove of cottonwoods. She started at the sound of footsteps and her breath caught at the sight of Cole Thornton emerging from the shadows.

At first, they could only stare at one another, and Caitlin knew from his expression how much he thought she had changed. He, on the other hand, could have passed her on the street, and she wouldn't have known him. The boyish smile and eyes filled with youthful idealism were nowhere to be found in those cold, forbidding features, and it was all she could do not to look away and betray the qualms she had over seeing him again.

At last he said, "I didn't think you'd come."

It was what he had said to her that day, that first day they had met here, and the significance was not lost on her. Still holding his gaze, she replied, "I didn't have a choice this time."

His only reaction was the slightest lift of his eyebrows, barely noticeable except that she was entranced with every nuance of his appearance. His hair was longer than she remembered, and several days' worth of stubble darkened his jaw and sharpened the menacing gleam in his eyes. In three years, he had aged ten, and it frightened her to think what he might have been through in those years. Stifling her concern for Cole or his hardships, Caitlin schooled her thoughts to the matter at hand.

"Your bastard uncle has my child. What do you intend to do about it?"

"Your child?"

She swallowed. "You know what I mean."

"Do I?"

He was trying to provoke her, and he was succeeding. "I didn't come here to match wits with you, Cole Thornton. Unless you're here to help us bring Jamie home, I have no use for you."

Her counterattack was more successful than she had hoped, and she felt her bravado slip as he approached her, his eyes narrowed in anger.

"I'm not here for you to use, Caitlin McDonnell." He stared down at her for a moment, and then a taunting smile sharpened his features. "I'm sure you already have another man for that job."

She could feel hot color rush to her cheeks, but she refused to give him the satisfaction of embarrassing her. Instead, she regarded him as she would a stable hand. "Don't be vulgar."

He wasn't going to let the subject go. "So, there's been no one?" She shivered as his eyes traveled the length of her prim costume. "No one but me?"

"I will not discuss such matters with you."

"No one but me," he concluded, and she could neither deny nor confirm the assumption without condemning herself. "Daddy must be keeping you on a leash."

"No, he hasn't had to." She turned away from his intense stare. "I have no intention of making the same mistake twice."

She barely felt him take hold of her arm before she was roughly hauled into his embrace, colliding against the solid wall of his chest. The impact knocked the breath out of her, and she struggled to form a protest. Her mistake was looking up into his eyes. For an instant, she saw a glimpse of the young man she'd loved so desperately, and a strangled cry escaped her lips as the sinister stranger took his place.

Cole slid his hands to her bottom and drew her solidly against him, grinding his hips against hers. He lowered his head, and his mouth found the tender flesh at the base of her throat. She gasped at the feel of his beard scraping her skin, and her legs yielded instinctively against his thigh.

He cupped the back of her head in his palm, digging his fingers into her scalp, and raised her face to his. Her eyes drifted open, and she found him staring down at her, studying her like a wolf contemplating a fresh kill.

Reality poured over her like bucketfuls of cold water, and she twisted out of his arms, putting a good deal of distance between them. She brushed the wrinkles from her skirt and glared at him. "How dare you try to take advantage of me under these circumstances?"

A sneer marred his features when he replied, "Don't act so high and mighty, Miss McDonnell. As I recall, you were always ready for a quick tumble."

Caitlin nodded, as if he hadn't insulted her. "Yes, I was very foolish in those days, but I learned my lesson."

"It was a pleasure teaching you."

That made her angry, and she glared at him. "What are you doing here? If you're not here because of Jamie, then why?"

He advanced on her by several steps. "Maybe I

was curious to find out why you never let me know about the boy before now."

Warily, she retreated and backed into a tree trunk. "I thought you were dead."

"Then why did you send for me?"

She hesitated. "What do you mean?"

"Your father sent for me." He fingered his shirt pocket and produced a crumpled telegram. "At first I thought it was someone's idea of a joke, but—"

"Let me see that." She snatched the paper from his hand and read the cryptic message. "We all thought you were dead. How did he know where to find you?"

"Dead?"

"It was in the newspaper." She glanced up at him. "The Thornton gang was slaughtered."

"I'm sure you were heartbroken."

She nodded. "I was."

His eyes narrowed, and she hastily added, "And glad I'd come home."

"So am I."

His voice held no anger, and once again she felt a pang of anxiety to think of the hardships he'd faced in the past few years. She noticed a small scar over one of his eyes, and his build was leaner than she remembered.

She took a step toward him, praying he still cared for her a little. "Do you know where he is? Will, I mean."

He shook his head. "I've a pretty good idea, but he could be anywhere."

"You've got to find him." She sounded desperate, and she was. "You'll have to track him down."

"That may be just what Will wants me to do."

Her breath caught at the reluctance in his voice. "Jamie is your son! You have to go after him!"

His eyes narrowed. "What proof do I have the boy is mine?"

He said something else, but her brain was ringing with such fury she feared her eardrums would burst. The resolve she had fought so hard to hold on to shattered and she lunged at him, her fists flailing against his chest. Startled, he caught her by the arms, momentarily restraining her, but she kicked and struggled against him with a ferocity neither of them anticipated.

"Caitlin!"

She heard her name, but nothing registered except desperation. Why wouldn't someone help her?

"Mommy! Mommy, please!"

She could still hear Jamie's terrified screams, the scene playing over and over in her mind. No matter how fast she ran, she couldn't reach her child. She sank to her knees as the fight drained out of her and she rocked back and forth, her face buried in her hands.

"Caitlin?"

This time the voice was a whisper. He dropped to one knee beside her, and she felt strong hands on her shoulders. The urge to lean into his embrace was overwhelming, but she resisted even though his grip was the only thing keeping her from collapsing facedown on the ground.

"Caitlin, look at me."

She did, but his image blurred. "Oh, Cole, he's just a baby."

His arms closed around her, and she let her face fall against his shoulder. The tears she'd held back for the sake of her father's grief, her uncle's guilt over being unable to protect them, and her own tenuous hold on sanity came in a flood of anguish and helplessness. Her child was somewhere needing her, calling for her, and wondering why she didn't come for him.

Cole never let go of her. She felt his hands stroking the length of her back, and his touch soothed her as nothing else had done. Slowly, her sobs subsided into mute, shuddering gasps for breath. He moved one hand to raise her face to his, and she didn't think to stop him when he lowered his mouth to hers.

The kiss was slow and gentle, like a dream they were both sharing, and she felt limp as his mouth left hers and traced the line of her jaw. The heat of his breath feathered against her throat, and she knew she should resist him while she still had the strength. The first heated touch of his lips on her skin banished such thoughts, and she dug her fingers into his shoulders and held on for dear life.

She needn't have worried. Cole wasn't letting go. His hold tightened, and she hung in his arms. All thoughts of blame and betrayal were swept away in the sweet rush of forgotten passion.

He held her firmly against him as he lowered the two of them to the ground and leaned over

her, his face taut with desire. She raised her palm
to his face, wanting to erase the bitterness, but he
wanted nothing to do with comfort.

He wanted surrender.

Caitlin knew she wasn't submitting to Cole, but to
herself, instead. For too long she'd denied the love
and the need she felt for him, but she wouldn't
squander what might be her only chance to relive
the memories locked in her heart. She had tried so
hard to forget, only to be frightened when she
couldn't remember what it was to give herself to
someone she loved.

She felt his hands slide under her skirt and then
the cool night air on her bare skin. Somehow he
shed his own clothes as easily and settled himself
above her, nudging her thighs open with his own.
He reached between them and touched her gently,
reawakening the anticipation for more.

Caitlin gasped as he thrust deep inside her, and
her eyes flew open just in time to see the look of
arrogant satisfaction on his face. She tried to look
away, but he lowered his mouth to hers and kissed
her until she was limp in his arms. He lowered his
mouth to her breast, and she arched against him,
twining her legs around his hips.

He began to move within her, hurling her to the
edge of pleasure but pulling her back each time
ecstasy was within her grasp. With maddening control, he ignored her pleas and pinned her hands
above her head when she tried to hold him close.
The move further parted her gaping blouse and
exposed her breasts fully to his searching mouth.

"Please, Cole," she whimpered, hating the aching need in her voice. "Please."

When he finally released her hands, she was helpless to do little more than cling to him as her body trembled beneath his. She heard his deep groan of pleasure and felt the slightest contact of his teeth against her collarbone, but everything else was lost to the mindless ecstasy that swept over her.

When they lay spent and weak from release, Caitlin wound her arms around his neck and gently combed her fingers through the silky length of his hair. She felt him shudder in her arms and pressed her lips against the pulse at his throat. He eased onto his back and gently drew her with him, pillowing her head on his chest, and, for a long time, neither one of them spoke.

Caitlin listened to the strong beat of his heart and breathed in his familiar scent. It was as if no time had passed and they were young lovers once again, stealing time together and savoring every moment. The evening breeze picked up, causing her to shiver, and his arms tightened around her.

The simple gesture of affection warmed her heart, and her voice caught when she spoke. "Why didn't you contact me while you were in jail?"

His whole body tensed, and, too late, she thought he might not want to talk about the past few years. She hurried to explain her reasons for asking. "My family could have helped you, Cole, and I wouldn't have thought any less of you for being in prison."

A vile curse escaped his lips, and he pushed her out of his arms and rose to his feet, angrily tucking in his shirttails and buttoning his pants. His anger frightened her, and she couldn't believe he thought to keep secrets from her. "Cole, please, don't be upset. I told you, it doesn't matter, I—"

"Yeah, I know, you wouldn't think any less of me." He reached for his hat that had fallen to the ground and slapped it on his head. "I don't give a damn what you think of me, lady. I haven't for a long time."

Caitlin's fingers were shaking, and she fumbled to button her blouse. He turned away from her, but the darkness did nothing to lessen the humiliation of groping for her underclothes and hurrying to pull them on under her wrinkled skirt. She was barely on her feet when he turned around, and she resisted the urge to smooth back any errant strands of hair.

"I don't know why my father sent for you." Managing the cold, haughty tone of voice gave her some comfort. "But I don't want your help. I don't want anything from you."

Nine

Cole slammed the door to his hotel room hard enough to rattle the windowpanes, and he seriously considered putting his fist through the wall. He'd intended to set Caitlin straight about a few things, especially keeping silent about his son all these years, but the mere sight of her tear-streaked face and the desperate catch in her voice had transformed him into the lovesick fool she'd led around by the nose all those years ago.

He could still see the horror on her face when he first touched her, and he should have turned around and left right then. Instead, he let his temper get the better of him only to weaken when he pushed her to tears. Kissing her felt so natural, and lust took over after that.

A bottle of whiskey was waiting on the dresser, and he hesitated before reaching for it. He knew a couple of drinks wouldn't be enough to take the edge off his anger, and he'd already made a big enough fool of himself without getting drunk at the crack of dawn.

Before he could uncork the bottle, Cole caught the unmistakable sound of boots hurrying up the stairs and vanishing on the carpeted hallway. He returned the bottle to the dresser and let his hand rest on the handle of his pistol. Without waiting for the courtesy of a knock, he jerked the door open to the surprise of the three men assembled just outside his room.

"What do you want?"

"You Cole Thornton?"

"You wouldn't be standing outside this room if I weren't," he sneered. "Who the hell are you?"

"Adam Troxler, town marshal." When Cole offered no reaction, he nodded toward his lackeys and finished the introduction. "These are my deputies, Powell and Nichols."

Each man nodded slightly and offered only the slightest acknowledgment. "Thornton."

He leaned against the doorjamb and made no attempt to disguise his disdain for their show of strength in numbers. "I know this isn't a social call, so state your business."

"Can't we come inside? Troxler insisted. "This is a private matter."

Cole almost laughed out loud. "Yeah, right, I'm going to put myself behind closed doors with three small-town lawmen looking to prove their mettle."

The man called Powell leaned forward, taking the bait. "If you're not wanted for anything, what's there to be afraid of?"

"You know damn well I'm not wanted for anything." He paused thoughtfully. "Not in Texas, anyway."

Powell swallowed hard, infuriated by the insinuation that a state line could restrain his authority. His eyes narrowed slightly and he grinned. "Say, Marshal, don't you think he looks a lot like his pa?"

"Yeah, he does," Nichols piped up before Troxler could answer. "Course his pa weren't in the best of health last time I seen him."

The deputies snickered at their own joke, but Cole wouldn't be baited into defending Sean Thornton. He knew what his father was, but also recognized Powell and Nichols for what they were. "Hard to tell what a man looks like when you shoot him in the back."

Troxler looked peeved and quickly changed the subject. "We came here to find out what you know about that low-down uncle of yours."

"I don't know where he is, if that's what you mean, but it's for damn sure he's not going to ride into that little gathering you've got going at McDonnell's ranch and give himself up."

They exchanged looks of surprise and Cole only shrugged. "I rode out there yesterday evening and had a look around. It seems foolish to have that many lawmen sitting around twiddling their thumbs when they should be out looking for that boy."

"We figure the kidnapper will be contacting the family with his demands." Troxler's eyes narrowed. "Unless that's why you're here."

"Why I'm here is none of your business. I already know what his demands are, and I'm pretty sure I know where to find him."

"Then tell us, damn you."

"So you can ride in on him with an army of men?" Cole shook his head at their stupidity. "He'll kill the boy the minute he sees you, and don't think he won't be looking over his shoulder."

"Why would he be looking over his shoulder?" Troxler exchanged a knowing look with his comrades. "Unless you tip him off."

"*I'm* the reason he's looking over his shoulder."

Cole shut the door before Troxler could reply, but he could hear the string of oaths trailing after them as they stomped off down the hall.

Caitlin tried to steady herself as she turned from the washbasin, but her legs were like water. She reached for the bedpost and let her forehead fall against her trembling hands. Her stomach was sore from the effort of heaving over and over until there was nothing left but blood and bile. When she felt certain she wouldn't be sick again, Caitlin sank to the bed and shuddered, drained of tears.

If she lived to be a hundred, she would never forgive herself for what she had allowed to transpire between herself and Cole the night before. How could she accept comfort from the man who was the cause of her misery? Yet, she had given only a token protest when he took her in his arms and demanded what should have been unthinkable. Instead, she'd responded with an insatiable passion, as if they had never been apart.

He would be long gone by now, and she should be thankful. His only motive for returning was to flaunt the fact that he'd done well without her. He didn't even care about Jamie. Except for the one snide comment about not knowing if the boy was really his, Cole hadn't asked anything about their child. If he could just see that sweet little face one time, there would be no doubt.

She retrieved her father's crumpled telegram and reread the cryptic message. There was no doubt Duncan McDonnell had sent it, but Caitlin wanted to know how her father had known where to find Cole. The telegram was dated the very day Jamie had been taken, so there hadn't been much of a search.

They had not spoken of Cole since before Jamie was born, and she didn't want to believe that her father had known of his whereabouts all these years and kept the knowledge from her. Neither did she want to think what she might have done had she known. Would she have contacted him about the baby?

No, not at first. She had been devastated and tried to convince herself that she couldn't possibly be pregnant, but the gradual changes in her body soon became obvious and undeniable. Papa had been so good to her, refusing to hear any talk of shame or disgrace. That was his grandchild, he reminded her, his heir, and anyone who maligned the child would bear the brunt of Duncan's wrath.

Perhaps Papa had feared Cole would someday come to claim his family and take them away. Caitlin knew now that there was no chance of that.

Still, Papa should have allowed her to make the

decision. If she had known Cole was still alive, she would have known about Will and the threat of revenge that included her and Jamie, as well.

She made her way down the stairs, desperation giving her the determination she needed to confront her father, but just as she reached the door to his study she heard angry voices inside and froze.

"I don't care! You should have brought him back here in chains."

"Be reasonable, McDonnell." Caitlin recognized Marshal Troxler's voice. "He doesn't know where Will Thornton is, and if he did he wouldn't tell us."

"Why wouldn't he?"

"It seems Thornton has reasons of his own to find his uncle."

"You keep watch on him, and I guarantee he'll lead you right to his uncle." Duncan's voice held such malevolence Caitlin shuddered. "Do whatever it takes to save the child, but I want Cole Thornton destroyed along with his useless kinfolk."

"You have our word on that."

Caitlin heard the scrape of boots on the floor and dashed back upstairs before the men emerged from the library. They shook hands with her father and assured him that they would be watching and ready to follow Cole the minute he left town.

She was torn between elation and despair knowing Cole intended to go after Jamie. If anyone could find Will, it would be Cole, but what would become of Jamie then? Will wanted revenge, and Cole would have to kill him first in order to save the child. She knew Cole would do what had to be done, but the unexpected entourage of lawmen would severely compromise Jamie's safety.

Her father closed the front door, and Caitlin hurried to the bottom of the stairs. Before she lost her nerve, Caitlin drew a deep breath and asked, "Papa, why didn't you tell me Cole was alive?"

Duncan spun around. "What are you talking about?"

"I know Cole Thornton is alive." She held on to the bannister, forcing herself to stand straight. "You've known all this time, and you never told me."

"Caitlin, don't upset yourself. I'm taking care of everything."

"By killing him?" she wailed. "By killing my baby's father?"

"He doesn't deserve to be Jamie's father."

Caitlin didn't miss the loathing in his voice, partially concealed beneath a gentle understanding tone of voice. She shook her head. "He *is* Jamie's father. Even killing him won't change that."

"No, but at least I'll be able to rest, knowing he can't hurt you anymore."

"Or take me away?" The guilty look in her father's eyes was all the confirmation she needed. "That's why you lied to me about him being killed?"

"I never lied to you!" His control snapped, and his face flushed with anger. "I didn't know until a year or so after . . . you came home. A horse trader in Abilene mentioned his name, and I started asking questions."

"And you never told me?"

"So you could take Jamie and run after him?" he demanded. "No, I didn't tell you. I haven't forgotten the way you looked standing on that depot platform. Skinny as a rail and dressed in rags. I'll kill him myself before I let him put you through that again."

"You had no right to keep this from me." Her voice was a whisper, and she swallowed hard before saying, "I don't know what I would have done, but it was killing me to think someone I cared about was dead."

"You were better off not knowing."

"If I had known about Cole, I would have known Will Thornton was out there somewhere, looking for me and Jamie." She drew a ragged breath. "This is all your fault."

"Caitlin! Don't say that!"

"It's the truth, and I can only pray that Cole can undo the damage you've done."

"Miss Caitlin, I can't go along with a thing like this."

"Please, Zeke, you're the only one who can help me."

Zeke Carpenter had worked for her father as long as she could remember, and she knew he was the one person she could trust completely. He was soft-hearted enough to want to help her, and so terrified of Duncan McDonnell that he would never betray her secret.

"Your Pa won't like it one bit," he pointed out, but not even her father's fury could keep her from going after Jamie. "Not one bit."

"You won't be blamed," she assured him. "If we succeed, he can't complain, and if not I'll swear that I tricked you."

That wouldn't be hard to do. Poor Zeke was a simple thinker, Papa always said, but he could track an ant across a flat rock. He wasn't stupid, but he didn't believe in wasting time studying things that didn't concern him.

His brows knitted together, and he winced as if weighing the situation was too much of a strain. Desperation pushed her, and she begged, "Please, Zeke, if those lawmen catch up with Cole before I do, little Jamie won't have a chance."

She didn't mean to cry, but her son's name on her lips cut deep and drew tears. He turned away from her, as if he'd seen something he shouldn't, and resumed currying the mule. "I figure we'd best leave at sunup, but you do the explaining to your Pa. Tell him what you think is best, but I won't have him thinking you run off again."

There was nothing Caitlin felt she needed to explain to her father. She knew he would be hurt and angry, but she couldn't trust him not to stop her. She couldn't trust him at all. She resisted the urge to hug Zeke for fear he would die of embarrassment but squeezed his arm and thanked him before hurrying out of the barn.

In the end, she told Lily that she was traveling to visit her aunt. Her friend agreed that being away from all the constant reminders would be good for her. Once she was gone, Papa might question Lily, but he wouldn't learn the truth.

Guilt nagged at Caitlin, knowing that Papa would take comfort in thinking that she was traveling in the opposite direction as Cole, when she was, in fact, determined to catch up with him and foil her father's scheme.

They rode in silence for almost an hour, and Caitlin knew she would only fluster Zeke with any attempt at conversation. From time to time, she would see him studying a pile of brush or a grassy clearing and couldn't imagine what he might be looking for or what he saw. She didn't ask for fear he would think she wasn't confident in his ability.

Twice they stopped to water the horses, and Caitlin was beginning to doubt her stamina. She hadn't ridden in years, not like this, and the muscles in her back and legs were protesting loudly. To her surprise, she glanced over to find Zeke regarding her with open amusement. "You'd best walk for a while, or I'll have to pry you off that mare with a crowbar."

She could imagine the picture she presented and smiled, wondering how many times Cole had thought the same thing. She had been no less determined in those days, but she was caught up in the euphoria of adolescent infatuation and would have walked through fire for Cole. Desperation now fueled her strength; she would reach Jamie or die trying.

When the horses were well rested, they resumed their journey on foot. Caitlin knew Zeke was slowing his pace to spare her, but she feared any delay would allow too much distance to fall between them and Cole.

At last, she suggested, "We'd better get a move on or we'll lose him before sunset."

Zeke stopped and let the mule's reins fall to the ground. Without a word he scanned the horizon and then glanced over his shoulder. He took a deep breath and said, "Ain't no use, Miss Caitlin."

"What do you mean no use?"

"He knows we're following him." He shrugged and hung his head, ashamed. "I should have seen before now. He's been leading us in circles for the last two hours."

She couldn't believe it. "He's playing *games* with us?"

Caitlin turned, looking in every direction and swore to make Cole pay for this. He knew how urgent it was that they find Jamie! God only knew what Will Thornton was capable of doing, and here Cole was wasting precious daylight and taunting her, besides.

"Son-of-a-bitch," she said, loud enough for Zeke to hear her and blush to the tops of his ears. She wanted to say a lot more, a lot worse, but she knew it was useless. Instead, she seated herself on a large rock amidst a rugged outcropping and removed her hat. "Why is he doing this?"

A troubled expression crossed Zeke's face, and she quickly assured him that she didn't expect him to answer that question. She withdrew a handkerchief from her pocket and mopped her forehead where damp tendrils were clinging.

"It's too late to turn back now." Zeke was grasping for a solution. "Don't you think we'd best make camp for the night and decide what to do in the morning?"

Caitlin only nodded, sickened by the futility of their trek. Time was fast slipping away, and with each passing hour, her chances of finding Jamie alive lessened. She bit her lip and tried not to cry in front of the simple man who'd tried to help her. It was wrong to involve him, and she feared he would blame himself for not getting her to Jamie in time.

If anyone was to blame, it was Cole. He knew what kind of monster his uncle was, and still he remained loyal to him, leaving her behind to wait while he played outlaw. It had been more than three years ago, but her hurt and resentment were still fresh. Her eyes began to sting, and she squeezed them shut even as the tears slid down her face.

She hurried out of sight, leaving Zeke to assume that she needed privacy and gave in to her misery. Why, after so much time had passed, did it still hurt to know he didn't love her? She'd told herself over and over that her feelings for him had been nothing more than youthful infatuation, but that didn't ease the pain of knowing she had never meant anything to him.

She made her way back to the stream and found

that Zeke had already set up a neat campsite and had coffee brewing and beans simmering in a skillet. He was busy tending their horses, and she saw that he had already spread out their bedrolls, at least thirty feet apart.

She was physically and emotionally drained, and she sank gratefully to the pallet near the fire. Zeke finished with the horses and returned to the campsite, anxiously stirring the beans.

"They burn a mite easy sometimes." Caitlin only nodded and he went on to say, "I'd rather eat beans cold out of the can than burnt ones."

He used a folded bandanna to lift the coffeepot from the fire and filled two cups. She thanked him as she accepted the steaming cup. "It smells wonderful."

He grinned at the compliment. "Yes'm. Can't get along without good coffee."

Caitlin had no appetite, but she wouldn't hurt his feelings by refusing his cooking. She tasted a few bites and pushed the beans around on the tin plate. When he went to retrieve cigarette makings from his saddlebag, she dumped the remains of her dinner on the ground at the far edge of the campsite. She made an excuse of being tired and settled down on her bedroll, but she knew she wouldn't sleep a wink tonight.

She did lie awake for the longest time, praying that Jamie was all right and telling herself that they would find him. At some point, she dozed off and slept for what seemed like only minutes before awaking with a start. Something wasn't right.

The moon was partially blocked by a thin patch of clouds, but she still had a clear view of the camp. Zeke stood with his back to her and his rifle slung over his arm, staring toward the creek. He cocked his head to one side and his back visibly tensed. One of the horses snorted loudly, and Caitlin heard the uneasy pawing of hooves against the dirt.

"Zeke?" she called softly, causing him to round on her as if she'd screamed bloody murder.

"Shh!" he warned. "Keep quiet."

She wanted to tell him that it might be Cole. Perhaps he had decided to join their camp, and she hated the rush of anticipation she felt at the prospect. At any rate, she'd better get up so she could recognize him and keep Zeke from blowing his head off.

She was barely on her feet before Zeke shoved a pistol into her hands. The look in his eyes frightened her, and she could only nod when asked, "You know how to use this thing?"

The horses were growing more agitated, and Caitlin froze at the sound of horses in the distance, growing nearer. Gunfire erupted and Zeke shoved her to the ground. "Get down! Get down!"

She did, almost dropping the pistol, and her fingers were shaking so hard the gun was likely to go off whether she intended it to or not.

"All we want is the horses and yer woman!" A sinister voice cut through the night. "Ain't no use in getting yerself killed."

* * *

Cole swore out loud.

He'd wasted the better part of the day trying to lose Caitlin and her guide, thinking they would soon give up and go home. It was nearly dark before the damn fool had figured out they weren't going anywhere, and then he'd started making camp instead of getting Caitlin back home.

Instead, he'd made a fire, boiled coffee, and attracted the attention of a ragged band of desperados, looking to steal anything they could trade for whiskey. Cole waited to see what the man would do before he acted.

The thieves weren't willing to bargain, and as they neared the campsite Cole realized the idiot was going to open fire when he was outnumbered and in plain sight. Shots were returned, and Caitlin screamed, spurring Cole to take action.

From his vantage point, he was able to pick off the two riding lead but not before a shotgun blast knocked Caitlin's guide to the ground. He made his way down the rocky slope and fired at the one wielding the shotgun. The man's horse reared, and he landed hard and didn't move. Two were left, but they were quick to abandon the fight.

Silence returned and something tightened in Cole's gut. Why wasn't Caitlin screaming or calling his name? He hurried the rest of the way down the slope and scanned the campsite, now littered with bodies.

"Caitlin!" he shouted.

There was no reply.

"Dammit, I know you're still here!" He waited,

catching the faint sound of her ragged breath. "Answer me!"

With the toe of his boot he turned one of the fallen raiders onto his back and swore out loud. "Caitlin, these men are renegade Apaches. Two got away, but they'll be back for their dead, unless they find some whiskey. I'm not waiting around to see. Get out here right now, or I'll leave you to deal with them yourself."

The ragged breathing grew louder, choked back a sob, and she slowly emerged from behind a jagged boulder. She was terrified and her eyes were wide as dinner plates, gaping at him. The sight of her so frightened made him want to take her in his arms and vow to protect her, and he stifled any such softheaded ideas.

Instead, he crossed the distance between them and took her, none too gently, by the arm. "Come on, let's get out of here."

He gathered their two horses and led them back to his own mount. Without a word, he reached to lift her onto his horse, not trusting her to ride alone. His hands had barely settled around her waist when she threw her arms around him and held tight. She was shaking uncontrollably, and he couldn't stop himself from gathering her close and trying to comfort her.

It brought back memories, memories he'd tried to bury beneath anger and bitterness, and he ached with the need to have her love him again. Making love to her had only opened old wounds and put more distance between them than ever before. Even now he knew it was fear that made her reach for him, but he couldn't push her away.

She tried to say something, but the words wouldn't come, and when they did they were lost in a rush of choking sobs. The top of her head barely met his shoulder and he buried his lips in her silky hair. "Caitlin, we have to get out of here."

"What about Zeke?" she asked, looking up at him. "We can't just leave him here."

"There's nothing we can do for him now." She started shaking her head, but Cole brushed his fingers over her lips, silencing her. "I won't risk getting you killed."

"It's all my fault. I practically forced him to bring me out here."

He started to tell her that it sure as hell was her fault because she should have kept her butt at home. Instead, he held her close and said, "No, it's not your fault."

She shuddered, and her arms tightened around his waist. Steeling himself, he set her away from him and hoisted her up into the saddle. He climbed up before her, and her arms immediately circled his waist. Another miscalculation.

He had sworn never to touch her again, but the feel of her soft body nestled against his back and her thighs splayed around his hips was just about more than he could stand. The fact that they would have to find shelter for the night only complicated matters.

Ten

Caitlin held tight to Cole, but her fear wouldn't go away. The awful bloody scene had been swift and deadly, and she couldn't escape the fact that Zeke had died only because he'd been willing to help her.

Zeke's a good man, but he can't decide whether to spit up or down without somebody telling him what's best.

How many times had she heard her father say something along those lines about the man who'd worked for him for so long? Zeke always consulted someone on every minor detail and always did exactly as he was told. Caitlin had no right to put him in a position where the wrong decision could be deadly.

She tried to justify her actions by reminding herself that Jamie's life hung in the balance, but she could have found a way that didn't involve deceiving her father and leading a good-hearted man to his death.

By the time Cole brought their horses to a halt, she was exhausted. So exhausted she nearly collapsed when he lifted her down from the horse.

Her legs were like water and he caught her roughly when she collapsed against him.

He led her to the edge of a rocky slope and let her sink to a grassy patch of ground. "Don't move."

As if she could.

Caitlin could hear him swearing under his breath, and she knew she would have to contend with his anger. It was obvious he didn't want her along, but leading them in circles and wasting time was uncalled for. If anything, what happened tonight was as much his fault as hers.

At last, he returned to stand over her. "I'm waiting for an explanation."

Forcing herself to look at him, she tried to decide on the best answer. She didn't dare tell him about her father having him followed and risk having him abandon the search altogether. "I have every right to participate in the search for my child."

"What makes you think that's what I'm doing?"

A chill shot through her. She hadn't considered any other possibility, but she couldn't very well tell him that she'd overheard lawmen promising her father to follow him and cut him down the moment he led them to Will. He would never help her if he knew that.

"I'm taking you back to your father tomorrow," he said when she didn't answer. Her mouth fell open, but he cut her off before she could protest. "You had no damned business coming after me!"

"I had to!" she cried before she could stop herself. His eyes narrowed, and she groped for an explanation. "Jamie needs me, and I want to be there when you find him."

"Will isn't planning a family reunion, Caitlin."

"Neither am I." She decided on a different tactic. "Cole, you're the only one who can help me, but if you waste another day taking me home, we might not ever find Jamie."

"Are you prepared for finding the boy . . . but not saving him?"

She wasn't. She refused to consider the possibility, but she managed an answer. "If Jamie is dead, nothing else matters. I won't care what happens."

He turned away from her, and she heard another muttered oath. At last he returned and stood over her, his hand extended. "Come on, Caitlin. You won't be able to ride tomorrow if you don't get some sleep."

He led her to the bedroll he'd spread out neatly and she sank down on the ground. She'd barely stretched out on the pallet before he settled himself beside her. She started and looked over her shoulder, not certain what to expect.

"I have only the one bedroll." His arm slipped around her waist and drew her snug against his chest. "I didn't plan on anyone coming along."

She let her head fall against his arm, and in a quiet voice she asked, "You *were* going after Jamie, weren't you?"

He hesitated. "Yeah, I was."

He could feel the tension drain out of her, and she turned her face against his shoulder. Her hair felt like silk against his chin, and he couldn't resist brushing his lips against her temple. She smelled so sweet, and he hated to think how many times he'd dreamed of breathing in the warm scent of her body only to awaken alone and aching at the very thought of her.

Her arm slipped around his neck, and her body drew closer to his. His mouth lingered on her skin, but he knew touching her even slightly was dangerous. Steeling his control, he raised his head and tried to untangle their limbs. A soft moan of protest escaped her lips, and her arm tightened around his neck.

"Please, Cole," she whispered. "Hold me, don't let me go."

Letting go was the last thing he wanted to do, but it was what he had to do. Gently, he cupped her elbow and drew her arm from around his shoulder. "Caitlin, you're frightened and you don't know what you're saying."

Her palm slid over his jaw, and she combed her fingers through his hair. "I'm not frightened. Not when I'm with you."

Her lips brushed against his, and he was lost. His arms closed around her, and he deepened the kiss, raising his hand to the nape of her neck. Her mouth yielded beneath his and welcomed the invasion of his tongue, but she was impatient and met his passion with sweet strokes of her own.

Rolling onto his back, Cole dragged Caitlin along with him and slid his hands under her skirt until the material bunched around her hips and spilled over his arms. She squirmed slightly when his hands cupped her bottom, but he pulled her down for a long, hard kiss while settling her atop his aching groin.

She gasped at the feel of his arousal straining against the thin fabric of her underclothes, and he reached between them to stroke her to an urgency that matched his own. Her hands trembled when he placed them on the front of his jeans, and she hesitated only a moment before working the buttons.

He groaned at her awkward touch but he wanted the seduction to be hers, her desire to rival his, and the pleasure to be mutual. She bent to kiss him, and he found the fastening of her drawers and slid them down over her hips. When she raised her head, he saw uncertainty in her eyes, and he knew she was waiting for him to take over. She tugged at the waistband of his jeans, and the only assistance he offered was a slight shift of his weight.

A brazen confidence shone in her eyes when he was naked beneath her, and he took full advantage of her newfound boldness, grasping her hips and guiding her onto his throbbing arousal. A strangled cry escaped her lips, but she was soon moving against him, driving herself to madness and taking him with her.

Her head fell back and he felt her shudder, but he didn't relent. She barely recovered from the first shuddering climax before he drove her over the edge again, this time going with her.

"I love you," she whispered as she wilted against his chest. "I've always loved you."

He poured himself inside her, and held her close. Until she'd spoken those words, Cole hadn't realized how desperately he needed to hear them.

Caitlin lay frozen on the bedroll, pretending to be asleep, but she knew it would be only a matter of minutes before Cole would be ready to leave. She'd been awake long before he rose from their makeshift bed and began building a small fire, but she remained huddled beneath the blanket, uncertain what to do or say next.

Once again, she'd given herself to him without hesitation or giving thought to the consequences. He had even tried to dissuade her, albeit halfheartedly, but she had arched against him like a cat, eager and willing.

Cole, I love you. I've always loved you.

The words were like nails driven into her heart, and she cringed to think of him throwing them back in her face. Even now, he was probably laughing to himself at how easy it had been to get under her skirt. Without even the pretense of remorse or guilt over the past.

And he had yet to ask her anything about Jamie.

She couldn't believe he wasn't the least bit curious about his son. How stupid she was to believe he cared, yet she had found pleasure and comfort in his arms, as if saving her child was only a second thought.

She tensed at the sound of his boots crunching in the rocky soil, moving in her direction, and she couldn't help flinching at the feel of his hand on her shoulder.

"Caitlin?" he murmured. When she didn't answer, he brushed a strand of hair away from her face. "Caitlin, wake up."

She sat up warily and drew the blanket around her shoulders. The pins holding her hair had been lost and several locks of hair fell over her eyes. He reached to smooth them away, and she recoiled from his touch. A shadow crossed his face.

"We need to leave as soon as you can get ready."

That was all he had to say, and she hurried to her feet. She sought her privacy and did the best she could to straighten her clothes and braid her hair. She was glad she didn't have a mirror, imagining the wretched sight she must be.

At last, she made herself return to the makeshift camp only to find that he had already packed everything away. The horses were saddled and ready, and he was waiting.

She straightened her shoulders and crossed the distance between them. "I'm ready if you are."

He only nodded. She reached to hoist herself into the saddle only to freeze at the feel of his hands on her waist. Deliberately, he let his knuckles graze the underside of her breast, and she twisted away from him.

Tears sprang to her eyes and clogged her throat, making her voice tremble. "Please, just don't touch me."

She turned away from him and covered her mouth with one hand, as if she could stifle her strangling sobs. She bit her lips, but tears slipped down her cheeks, and she tried to wipe them away with her bare hand. Oh, God, if anything happened to Jamie, she would never forgive herself.

"Caitlin, we're never going to find the boy if you go on a crying jag every time I touch you."

She stiffened at the sound of his voice, so low and solemn, and she turned to find him watching her with a grim expression.

"I can't help it," she whispered. "You don't know what he means to me."

Cole flinched as if she'd slapped him, and she would have given anything to take back those words. "I'm sorry. I didn't mean that the way it sounded."

"Why not? It's the truth."

His bleak expression tore at her insides, and she wished he would get mad. She could deal with his anger a thousand times easier than she could seeing him hurt.

"I *don't* know," he went on to say. "I don't know anything about my own son. At least you have memories of him. If we don't find him—"

"Don't say that!" She turned away from him, not wanting to hear anymore. She didn't want to even consider losing Jamie, and she didn't want to feel guilty over Cole's sorrow. "I did the best I could, and you're the last person who should judge me."

"You're the one who left me," he reminded her. "You didn't want me to even know about the baby, so I do hold you accountable for what's happened to him."

Caitlin couldn't believe her ears. She drew a deep breath and slowly turned around, stunned by the accusing glare he fixed on her. "I didn't know I was pregnant. Not until later, weeks after I'd been home. By then, I had already read about the ambush in the newspaper and thought you were dead."

"And that was proof enough for you? One newspaper article and you count me dead and gone?"

"What about you? You *knew* I was alive, and you knew where I was. Why didn't you ever contact me?"

"Did you want me to?"

She swallowed back the truth, not willing to bare her soul when he hadn't shown the slightest inclination to make amends with her. "I worried about you and prayed for your safety."

A cynical smile touched his lips. "You should have stayed with me, for your own safety, and the boy's."

She gaped at him. "How safe would we be tagging along after an outlaw?"

He pushed past her and swung himself up into the saddle. "You ought to remember your scorn for outlaws, Caitlin, *before* you lie down with one."

He might as well have slapped her. She flinched, not from what he said but from the truth of his words. He had turned her life upside down when she was too young to understand what was happening, left her with a child to raise, yet she had professed her love to him without hesitation.

Without a word or a backward glance, he turned his horse, leaving her to mount her own and ride after him. She didn't know which made her angrier—the fact that he didn't wait to see if she would follow him or the fact that he knew she would. Any qualms she might have had about deceiving him vanished, and she understood that there had never been any truth between them.

All that day and the next they rode in stony silence. Cole could feel the daggers she stared into his back, and he hadn't failed to notice the lengths she went to avoid the slightest physical contact with him. If she wanted to pout, he'd let her pout.

He made no attempt at conversation and offered as little assistance as his conscience would allow. He saddled and unsaddled her horse, but left her to mount and dismount on her own. He slept, using his saddle for a pillow, leaving the bedroll for her to unroll and put back together. The first night she slept with her back to him as if she wanted nothing to do with him. But last night, he knew he hadn't imagined the flicker of disappointment in her eyes when he bedded down on the opposite side of their campfire.

He knew her well enough not to believe she was sorry. Her pride was badly bruised, and she needed to believe her rejection mattered to him. He needed to believe it didn't.

After all this time, he didn't believe she could do any more damage, but she could. First, she had pushed him away with all her talk of him being in jail, and he'd tried to resist the sweet passion she offered. Even as she slept in his arms, he told himself she might regret their lovemaking once her fear had passed.

The moment he touched her, he knew. She was angry with him, angry with herself, and mortified that she had responded to him. He knew now that she saw him only as a means to an end. She wanted to find the child, but so did he. The only difference was that she wanted him gone once she had the boy.

By late afternoon, her frustration was unmistakable. He stopped to water the horses, and her eyes were filled with questions. They were less than an hour's ride from a ragtag little town where Sally had lived on several occasions, but he volunteered nothing. He knew she was worried, but she refused to speak to him, even to ask where they were going.

At last the town came into sight, and her eyes widened in anticipation. She looked his way and asked, "Where are we?"

"I don't think this town has a name."

She waited for him to elaborate.

"This is where Sally usually ends up when she and Will are on the outs."

Caitlin's eyes widened in horror. "I'm not going anywhere near that woman!"

"You don't have to. If she's here, I intend to ask her a few questions and then we'll be on our way."

"And if she's not, we've wasted a lot of time."

"If she's not here, someone might know where she is . . . and who she's with."

Her face paled visibly, and Caitlin nodded in agreement. "I don't know what to hope for."

"Hope the boy is with them wherever they are. And that we find them."

The town was nothing more than a row of ramshackle buildings—saloons mostly—and Caitlin recoiled from the open interest of several men gathered outside of a faro house. If Cole noticed their stares and raunchy laughter, he didn't let on.

They rode to the end of the street and stopped just outside of a large frame building bearing an ornate sign that read THE RED APPLE INN. Unlike the other structures, the inn was freshly painted and all the shutters hung securely in place. Caitlin suspected it was the nicest place in town, and not likely to be where they would find Sally.

Cole tied their horses to the post outside, and she followed him up the stairs and inside. The lobby was nearly dark from the heavy blinds closed against the afternoon sun, but she noted a cozy grouping of chairs where several guests were chatting pleasantly.

"My wife and I need a room for the night."

At the sound of Cole's voice, Caitlin's head whipped around in time to see him sign the register and produce several bills from his pocket. He glanced over his shoulder and gave her a warning look.

The clerk handed over a key and openly studied Caitlin. "Anything for the little lady?"

"How soon can you have a hot bath brought to the room?"

"It costs extra," the clerk warned. "Fifty cents."

Cole placed a silver dollar on the counter. "Make sure it's hot and send plenty of towels."

"Yes, sir. Right away."

Cole gestured for her to follow him upstairs, and she considered holding her objections until after she'd had that hot bath, even if he meant to watch her. Once inside the room, however, her brazenness failed at the sight of the double bed wedged beneath the window.

He tossed one of the saddlebags onto the floor and crossed the room to peer out the window. "I'm going to take the horses to the livery and do some looking around."

"Before you go, I think I should tell you . . ." The words stuck in her throat, and she tried again to think of the right way to broach the subject. "I heard you tell the clerk that we're married. . . . I just don't want there to be any misunderstandings between us."

An arrogant smile touched his lips, and he shook his head as if he felt sorry for her. "Don't worry, Miss McDonnell. I have no intention of demanding any husbandly rights."

"Then why did you say that? Why did you insist on one room?"

"How long do you think it would take for word to get around town that there was an unmarried woman alone in a hotel room?" He crossed the room and let his hand fall on the doorknob. "Once they bring up your bath, lock this door and keep it locked."

"Where are you going?"

"I told you. I need to see about the horses, and then I'm going to do some asking around." He grinned over his shoulder. "I'll be back before you start missing me too bad."

The minute the door closed behind him, she rushed to turn the lock. Nothing in this town was more of a danger to her than Cole.

"Sally Jessup? Can't say the name is familiar, but that don't mean nothing."

Cole never looked away from the shaving mirror, watching the man empty a kettle of steaming water into a copper bathtub. He waited to see if he would elaborate.

"Names aren't important with women like that."

Cole finished shaving and let the subject drop. He restricted himself to asking as few questions as possible, displaying only a passing interest in Sally. After all, why would a man with a beautiful wife tucked away in a hotel room be asking about an aging whore?

He ducked his head and rinsed the soap from his face and stared at his own reflection, deciding he was the biggest fool on the face of the Earth. He couldn't forget the pale look of horror on her face as she looked at that bed and contemplated sharing it with him.

Making inquiries about Sally had been a weak excuse for coming to the bathhouse. He intended to return to that room clean-shaven and wearing clean clothes. He wasn't going to give her any excuse to reject him other than the truth. He couldn't help but hope he also returned with news of Sally and the boy's whereabouts. Caitlin might not want him, but she needed him, and he wasn't above reminding her of that.

The general store yielded only the basic necessities and less information. He stopped in two low-rent hotels and a faro house, but no one knew anything about Sally. At last he ducked inside one of the seedier-looking saloons and ordered whiskey at the bar. Without a word the bartender uncorked a bottle and waited for Cole to lay his money down before filling the glass. Raising the glass to his lips, Cole barely tasted the drink before slapping his hand over the coin just as the man reached to claim it.

"I said whiskey, not kerosene."

The bartender's eyes narrowed, but he ducked under the bar and produced an unopened bottle. The sound of female laughter startled him, and Cole turned to see a scroungy-looking woman seated at a table against the wall.

"Mister, most men that come in this place don't know the difference."

"That's enough out of you, Florence." The bartender poured a miserly portion into a new glass. "Lucky for you our regular customers aren't so choosy."

Cole caught hold of the bottle just as the man

moved to put it away. "No point in you having to go to so much trouble when I want a refill."

He took the bottle and made his way to the table where the woman called Florence was seated. She looked up at him, and he cringed at the wariness in her eyes. Reluctantly, she motioned for him to be seated.

He slid the bottle across the table, and she didn't hesitate to pour herself a generous amount. She studied him with unabashed skepticism. "So which is it, mister? Are you the law or a bounty hunter?"

He leaned back in his chair. "What makes you ask?"

"I've done this kind of work long enough to tell when a man just wants to ask questions." She downed the whiskey and grinned. "Maybe I could change your mind about that."

"I'm not the law or a bounty hunter." He drained his own glass and looked her straight in the eye. "But all I want is a few answers."

She shrugged. "Go ahead."

"I need to know if you ever heard of a woman named Sally Jessup."

The immediate loathing in her eyes was all the confirmation Cole needed, and he prayed she would be willing to talk.

"Yeah, I'm sorry to say I do." Florence helped herself to another glass of whiskey. "Me and her worked at a place up the street. It was a nice place . . . well, you know, compared to some."

"Is she still there?"

Florence shook her head. "No, she took off about a week ago."

Cole struggled to sound only mildly interested. "By herself?"

"No, not Sally. Some old beau of hers showed up and she took off with him."

"Did she say where they were going?"

Florence shook her head. "I didn't know nothing about it, until she was gone . . . along with all the money I had stashed out back."

Her face flushed slightly, and Cole knew she was fighting against tears. "Did anyone see if they had a kid with them?"

"A kid?" Surprise registered on her face.

"A little boy . . . not quite three years old."

She shook her head. "She was gone before I knew what was going on."

Cole was certain Sally had taken off with Will, but he wondered how far they would be able to go. "How much money did she take?"

"Forty-six dollars," Florence said, as if it were a fortune. "I been saving up for six months, but it still wasn't enough for a train ticket."

"A train ticket?"

"Back to Tennessee." She shrugged. "My ma still lives there . . . she don't know about . . . this."

He didn't bother to ask what "this" was. Unwittingly, a picture of Sally came to mind. He couldn't have been more than thirteen the first time he met Sally, and he remembered thinking how pretty she was. He recoiled from the thought of what might have happened to Caitlin if she hadn't had a rich family to come to her rescue.

It occurred to him for the first time that Caitlin had every reason to run. A woman alone, uncertain of his return, and scared out of her mind. He sure as hell wouldn't have wanted her to end up in a grungy saloon drinking whiskey with strangers.

He rose from the table and thanked her for her time. Turning away from the bartender's view, Cole dug into his pocket and withdrew one hundred dollars. He placed it on the table and waited, but she didn't reach for it.

"Don't waste your life hoping things will get better." He pushed the money toward her. "You buy that train ticket and go home while you still can."

Eleven

No matter how hard she tried, Caitlin could not keep her eyes open. She'd made the mistake of lying down just to rest and fell right to sleep. She had no idea how long she'd been asleep, but she knew she needed to get herself together before Cole returned. She would be mortified for him to see her curled on the bed with nothing but a towel wrapped around her.

The innkeeper's wife had offered to take Caitlin's clothes to be laundered, and she had gratefully accepted. She knew Cole had paid extra for the laundry service, just as he had for the bath and the food that had been delivered to the room. She tried not to think about where he got the money, but it worried her that Cole held fast to his outlaw ways.

Did he still believe every time would be the last?

She forced herself to rise from the bed and find someway of putting herself together. Her hair was still damp, and she had to find some way to comb out the tangles before it dried into a snarled mess. Cole's saddlebag lay in the corner, and she knelt to search for anything she could use.

He carried little in the bag. A couple of shirts, a pair of jeans, and extra socks, and she found it odd that he carried no personal items such as a razor or hairbrush. Despite the rugged changes in his looks, Cole still took care in his appearance, and she was reminded that hardship had chiseled the lines around his eyes and erased the smiles that used to come so easily.

Caitlin did the best she could to comb her hair with her fingers, but she knew it would be a sight. She crossed the room and peered out the window, taking a good look at the town for the first time. Before, she'd been too leery of attracting unwanted attention to herself by openly scrutinizing the town for any sign of Sally Jessup.

She glanced down the row of dance halls, gambling houses, and saloons. Any one would offer sanctuary to a woman like Sally, who plied her favors so easily. The last time Caitlin saw Sally was in Santa Fe, the day Caitlin checked out of the hotel and headed for the stage. Sally had chased her down the hall, warning her that Cole and Will had deserted them, and she was a fool if she expected Cole to come after her.

Any doubt Sally meant to plant in Caitlin's mind dissolved when a man, clad only in long johns, stepped out of her hotel room and demanded that Sally return immediately. He offered to double the price if she brought Caitlin back with her, and Caitlin bolted for the stairs, almost feeling sorry for Sally.

She didn't know whether to hope Sally was with

Will or not. Sally was no angel, but she was a thousand times better than Will Thornton. At least, Sally might offer the child a little kindness, but Caitlin cringed at the thought of her sweet baby in the company of whores and drunkards.

She caught sight of a woman wearing a gaudy dress that bared her arms and most of her legs step outside a saloon onto the sidewalk. A man followed her, and they stopped just outside the entrance. He turned slightly, and Caitlin was horrified to recognize Cole as the man speaking to her so earnestly.

Trembling with anger, Caitlin gripped the windowsill and looked on as the woman smiled up at Cole. Without warning, the woman lunged and threw her arms around his neck, planting a kiss right on his mouth. He placed his hands on either side of her waist, but he wasn't pushing her away. Finally, she peeled herself off of him, and he smiled!

Caitlin couldn't believe it. He actually smiled down at that hussy! He turned to make his way across the street, leaving the woman staring after him with a dreamy look on her face.

Caitlin bolted from the window when she realized he was heading toward the hotel. Damn him! He was supposed to be looking for her baby, not wallowing in bed with a whore! The very idea hurt so bad she stumbled and barely caught hold of the iron bedstead, steadying herself.

She glanced down at the bedspread, now wrinkled from her nap, and seethed at the prospect of him actually thinking he would share that bed with her! She snatched one of the shirts from his saddlebag and hurried to put it on. Thankfully, it fell to her knees and covered her decently enough.

The doorknob rattled and she vowed hell would freeze over before she unlocked that door. She didn't have to. The knob turned and he stepped inside, pocketing the key he hadn't bothered to tell her he had. The idea of him barging in at any time while she bathed or slept pushed her past all control.

"Don't you know to knock before barging in on a lady?"

His eyes narrowed, but she didn't relent. "Or has it been so long since you've lived around decent people, you just don't remember?"

He slammed the door. "I remember a lot of things about sharing a hotel room with a lady."

"I trusted you!" She was too furious to be insulted. He let the saddlebag slung over his shoulder fall to the floor, and she noticed his change of clothes and clean shave. "Don't even think you're staying in this room tonight."

He advanced on her and caught her by the arm. "Settle down, lady, before everyone in town thinks you're crazy."

"I don't care what they think!" She twisted away from his grip. "I must be crazy to think you cared even a little about your own child."

A muscle ticked in his jaw and a warning sounded in the back of her mind. If she wasn't careful, she would push him too far, but hadn't she been pushed too far?

She snatched the saddlebag from the floor and scooped up the one lying in the corner and turned toward the window. "I've been sitting on pins and needles waiting to know what you found out about Jamie. And where have you been? Rolling around with a slut!"

She managed to get the window open before he could stop her, and she struggled against his hold on her shoulder. "If that's the kind of woman you like, go to her! And *leave me alone!*"

He caught her by the arms and hauled her roughly away from the window before she could dump his belongings into the street below. She braced herself, unafraid, for whatever defense she would need to muster against him. Instead, he laughed, and she could only gape up at him in surprise.

"What's the matter, Miss McDonnell?" he taunted. "Don't tell me you're jealous."

She was stunned. Nothing had prepared her for him to laugh at her. She dropped the saddlebags to the floor and slapped him across the face. Pain shot right up her arm but he didn't flinch. He didn't move. The only reaction she could see was the humor rapidly drain from his eyes, replaced by something deeper than anger.

Defeat.

He released her and turned away, looking out the window. Caitlin was still breathing hard, and she wasn't ready to give up the fight. "I trusted you. You said you would help me find my child."

"Your child," he said more to himself, never

looking in her direction. "I suppose he is yours. You sure as hell never meant for me to know anything about him."

"I thought you were—"

"Dead? Yeah, I know." He did look at her then. "You didn't even give him my name, Caitlin. Are you going to tell me that was because you thought I was dead?"

She didn't know how to answer that, and silence hung between them.

"The woman you saw me talking to worked with Sally up until last week. Sally left town last week . . . with a man who showed up unexpected." He turned back to the window and braced his hands on the sill. "She didn't see who he was, but I'm sure it was Will."

Suddenly, Caitlin was ashamed of herself for hitting him, for what she said. She could see where her palm had left a faint mark on his freshly shaven jaw. Mostly she was ashamed that she had never even considered his feelings regarding their child. She had wanted . . . demanded that he help her rescue Jamie, but then what?

She'd built her entire life around Jamie, and the thought of sharing him with someone frightened her. Especially someone to whom she was so vulnerable. Could she share her child with Cole without losing herself to him as well?

"There's a place not too far from here that Will and my . . . that we used as a hideout. Two, maybe three, days' ride." He wouldn't look at her.

"Cole, I'm sorry." She moved to stand beside

him, not knowing what to say. "I just didn't know what else to think."

"You thought the worst. You always thought the worst of me." He turned away from her. "I just don't care anymore. Think what you like and walk out . . . like you did before."

"I didn't walk out on you," she countered. "I just couldn't go on living like that."

His shoulders tensed visibly.

"Besides, what would have happened to me when you went to jail?"

"I didn't go to jail," he told her. "I came back and found you gone."

"Will went to prison and you didn't?"

"It doesn't matter now."

A chill ran up her spine. "What doesn't matter?"

"None of it matters," he said. "It's all in the past."

She caught his arm. "Tell me."

He did. He told her about getting thrown in jail, Yeager's threats, the fake telegram, and the shoot-out between Jess Martin's gang and the stage full of marshals.

Caitlin was overwhelmed. "Why didn't you tell me what you were planning?"

"I couldn't risk anyone knowing about it. Not even you." He sat down on the edge of the bed and leaned forward, bracing his forearms on his thighs. "If anything went wrong, Yeager would've hung me himself. I didn't want you to be involved."

"But Cole, my father could have—"

"Your father would have strung me up quicker

than Yeager." He spared her an impatient look. "Don't bother to deny it."

"Papa loves me, Cole." She didn't know how to make him understand. "I know he can be harsh, but he only wants to protect me."

"From me?"

"From getting hurt."

"I never hurt you," he insisted. "You left to keep me from knowing about the baby."

"N-no." She shook her head. "I didn't know about the—"

"You expect me to believe that?"

She knelt before him and clasped his hands. "I was afraid, Cole. Afraid you wouldn't be able to come back for me, afraid to stay there alone, and mostly afraid you'd joined up with Will again and would want to take me along."

He looked skeptical.

"I didn't know about the baby until after I'd been home a good while. By that time, I thought you had been killed. . . ." Her voice trailed off. She knew he didn't want to hear that again. "For a long time, I wished I were dead. The first time I felt the baby move, I realized how lucky I was to still have part of you with me."

She felt his hands settle on her shoulders, and she shuddered at the feel of his thumbs slipping inside the collar of the borrowed shirt. Gently, he traced the line of her collarbone and lowered his head to kiss the top of hers.

Swallowing back her tears, Caitlin looked up at him. "Cole, I'm so sorry. I should have—"

He brushed his fingers against her lips, silencing her. "No, I'm the one who's sorry. You had every reason to be afraid, and I should've come after you."

Pulling her onto the bed, Cole rolled her beneath him and brushed a gentle kiss against her lips. With a wry smile, he removed his own shirt from her body, and she felt herself blush under his intense gaze. Twice already they had made love, but the darkness had hidden her nakedness from his eyes.

"You're staring," she finally said when his eyes lingered on the fullness of her breasts and traveled the line of her belly and gently rounded hips. "Having a baby changes a woman."

"Only for the better," he whispered lowering his mouth, and her nipple pebbled beneath the heat of his breath. "My baby made you even more beautiful."

Her reply was lost in a gasp of pleasure as he explored every difference of her body with his mouth and his hands. He had never been more tender, more passionate, and she knew her heart was already lost.

Afterward, he held her close, and she listened to the rhythm of his heart beating. When he spoke, she felt his breath catch.

"Tell me about . . . Jamie."

It was the first time Cole had spoken his son's name out loud, and Caitlin didn't miss the husky tone of his voice.

"He's an angel," she whispered, and then she smiled. "When he wants to be."

Cole grinned slightly. "That's what Ma always said about me."

"He looks just like you." Caitlin could easily imagine Cole as a little boy. She traced the strong line of his jaw, and her thoughts turned grim. "Will took one look at him, and he knew."

She felt Cole tense, but she couldn't keep from asking, "Do you think he would . . . hurt Jamie?"

He hesitated, and Caitlin felt her heart sinking. "He wouldn't have come for Sally if he'd harmed the boy. No doubt, he told her some cock-and-bull story and got her to go along with him."

Caitlin wanted to believe that.

"Was it hard on you . . . having the baby?"

"The doctor said I had an easy time, but I don't know how he can be the judge of something like that." He brushed a kiss against her forehead. "My aunt came from Dallas to be with me, but I was so scared."

"I wish I'd been with you."

"So do I." She smiled. "I wasn't due for another month, and I knew babies who come early don't always live."

"What did you do?"

"There wasn't much I could do." She shuddered, remembering the ordeal. "My aunt tried giving me paregoric, but all it did was make me so sick I couldn't hold my head up. The pains started before daylight, and it was nearly midnight before he was born."

His hand slipped to the flat plane of her belly, and he traced the line of her navel with his index finger. "And here I've gone and put you at risk all over again."

Caitlin drew a deep breath, wishing she could deny the possibility. "Would that be so . . . so awful?"

"For you, maybe." He rolled over and pressed her down on the bed, kissing her gently. "I don't intend to let you go this time."

"What's so awful about that?" She smiled up at him, but his expression remained solemn.

"Let's get married, Caitlin."

She was stunned, and her sharp intake of breath betrayed her astonishment.

"We can get married right here in town." He went on before she could answer. "There's a justice of the peace, and he can give us a license and perform the ceremony."

He did love her! Tears stung her eyes as he kissed her, but she shook her head. "No, we can't get married here."

"Why not?"

"I want to wait until Jamie can be with us," she whispered. "I know it sounds silly, but—"

"But what?"

"There's a story I read to him—*The Three Bears.*" She hesitated at the uncertainty in Cole's eyes. "It's a story about a family of bears. There's a mama bear, a baby bear, and a papa bear."

It sounded foolish to her own ears, but she knew how much the story meant to Jamie. She drew a breath and went on. "He always points to the pages and says, 'Papa Bear . . . Papa Bear.'"

"You're going to tell him I'm Papa Bear?"

Caitlin couldn't help laughing at the doubtful expression on Cole's face. "No, but he should be a part of the wedding. It affects him as much as it does us."

"Will he understand that I'm his father? Not just some man you're marrying?"

"He will, if you're the one who explains it to him."

Cameron drained the brandy from his glass and stared into the fireplace. Despite Dr. Carroll's warnings, he felt well enough to be out of bed, and he had depleted his personal stash of liquor upstairs and badly needed a drink. For days, the whole house was glutted with lawmen and a constant stream of concerned friends and neighbors, but today things were quiet at last.

All people knew to say to him was how lucky he was to be alive and that there was nothing he could have done. Nothing *he* could have done.

He gritted his teeth and reached for the brandy decanter, cursing the pain that shot through his arm. He refilled his glass and downed half of the liquor in one gulp. His brother would be checking in on him soon, and he hoped to pass out before then.

Duncan meant well, but Cam was tired of hearing about all that was being done while he lay useless, waiting for his body to mend.

Not that he would be any more use then. His whole life he'd stayed behind where it was safe. He stayed home with his mother while his brother worked in the coal mines. When they came to America, he went to school while his brother scoured the boweries for work, and later he'd gone away to college while Duncan established himself in Texas. Always, he had it easy while Duncan carried the load.

His law practice thrived, but most of his clients were Duncan's friends and business associates. Not that anyone less would be welcome. Cameron was known for his fierce loyalty to his brother, and now that loyalty was eating at him.

He'd sworn on his life never to betray his brother again, and in doing so he'd betrayed the niece he loved as his own daughter. He remembered the genuine fear on Duncan's face when Cameron had sworn never to reveal what his brother had learned about Cole Thornton. So many times, he'd seen Caitlin lost in thought with tears in her eyes, but he had remained silent.

"I wish I had better news for you, McDonnell."

Cameron turned at the sound of voices in the foyer. He didn't recognize the first man's voice, but there was no mistaking Duncan's sharp response.

"By God, I want answers! You should be out looking for my daughter!"

Dread crept along Cameron's spine, and he stepped into the foyer. "Something has happened to Caitlin?"

"No!" Duncan shook his head. "They just haven't found her."

"Found her? Who is this man?"

"This is Captain Del Raymond." With a grim expression, he explained, "I contacted the Rangers. They've been searching for Caitlin."

"Duncan." Cameron groaned aloud. "Her friend told you that Caitlin just wanted to get away for a few days."

"To visit her aunt, I know. Just to be sure, I sent a telegram, and they haven't seen or heard from Caitlin."

"So you sent the Texas Rangers to track her down?"

"There's no doubt in my mind that she went running after Cole Thornton. He slipped out of town without anyone knowing it, and Caitlin wasn't far behind him."

Cameron shook his head and sadly concluded, "And whoever finds Caitlin finds Cole."

"That's what I hoped." Duncan hung his head. "I'm afraid the captain has brought us bad news."

Raymond cleared his throat. "We found a small campsite that had been attacked by renegades. There were three dead men and what appeared to be a woman's satchel. Inside, we found items that clearly belonged to Miss McDonnell."

Cameron suddenly felt light-headed, and he leaned against the doorjamb. "And you think she's been abducted by the renegades."

"I don't believe it." Duncan pushed past his brother into the parlor and headed straight for the brandy decanter. He poured himself a generous amount and downed it in one swallow "She's with Thornton. I'll stake my life on it."

Raymond grudgingly followed him, declining the offer of a drink. "It's unlikely she would have left her personal belongings behind if she went with someone of her own will."

"Then he forced her!" Duncan shouted. "You were supposed to find her. If you'd done your job, we would know where she is . . . where they both are."

"Tracking your daughter wasn't a problem. That's how we found the campsite." Raymond tapped his Stetson against his thigh. "You told me yourself they were at least three days ahead of us."

Duncan's shoulders slumped, and he looked much older. "If I'd had any idea what she was up to, I would have—"

"Locked her in her room?" Cam suggested, pitying his brother's desperation at the thought of losing Caitlin. "You can't make her a prisoner here."

"Damn it, that's not what I meant!" Duncan glared at him but just as quickly bit back his anger, and Cameron knew it was because his brother considered him a weakling. "I just want her home. All I ask is that Caitlin and Jamie are returned safely."

"Whoever attacked the campsite took your daughter's horse." Raymond replaced his hat on his head and took a few backward steps toward the exit. "I sent my sergeant on after them, and I came back to let you know what's happened."

When Duncan offered no gratitude, he continued. "Weldon is the best man I have. If your daughter's alive, he'll find her."

"Thank you, Captain," Cameron said, offering the man a gracious escape. "We'll be anxious to know what you learn."

With a brusque nod, he left, and Duncan rounded on Cameron. "How dare you accuse me of mistreating my daughter?"

"I didn't say you mistreated her," he countered. "If anything, you've been too good to her. She depends on you for everything."

"She's my daughter!"

"But she's not a child." Cam shook his head sadly. "Let her go, Duncan. If you don't, she'll end up a helpless old maid with no life of her own."

"How can you say that?"

Cameron crossed the room and refilled both their glasses and let his clink against his brother's in a macabre salute. "Just look how I turned out."

Twelve

The town was so dead Will didn't think he could stand it much longer. It was just like prison. The days dragged by and the nights were even longer. Leaning against a post on the back porch, he wondered why he'd let Sally talk him into coming back here.

He knew her reasons. She liked having him stuck in this jerkwater little town where she was the best-looking woman for thirty miles. The closest thing to a saloon was the back corner of the general store where old men gathered to play checkers and drink corn liquor. If he raised any hell about it, she started in about how she was going throw *him* out of *her* house.

He'd forgotten how contrary that woman could be, and he would be glad to be rid of her as well. He was sorely tempted to pack his gear and take off for Mexico. To hell with her and Cole!

He still wanted his revenge on Cole, and his anger hadn't lessened one bit. He just hadn't counted on having to do so much waiting, and he had already waited too long.

He wished now he'd just taken Caitlin and left

the kid behind. Cole would've still come running, and Will wouldn't have to put up with a whining kid and Sally's mouth. Instead, he'd be passing the time easing himself within Caitlin's body, and his revenge on Cole would be double.

That was what he really wanted. Lots of uninterrupted time alone with Caitlin. He could take his time and have her every way he could think of, and he already had a few good ones in mind. Even if Cole didn't come after her, her daddy would fork over enough money to get her back that Will could live easy the rest of his life. In Mexico, maybe even Brazil.

He cringed at the sound of Sally's gleeful laughter and glanced over his shoulder to see her and the kid making their way back to the house. The boy scrambled ahead of her and plucked a dandelion from the parched ground. He presented the flower to Sally, who oohed and ahhed like it was a bunch of roses.

Shit.

He stomped back inside the house and snatched a bottle of whiskey from the table. He drank deeply, shuddering as the cheap liquor scorched his gut and burned a hole in his anger. He drew a few steadying breaths and wiped his mouth with the back of his hand.

No. No, he wouldn't be cheated. Cole had it coming to him. They all did, but Cole especially. The son-of-a-bitch was going to pay for turning on him, and he was going to pay in spades. Will raised the bottle to his lips and drained what remained of the rotgut he'd drunk all his life while everyone else enjoyed fine bourbon. He swallowed the last drop and threw the bottle, smashing it against the wall.

"What the hell's the matter with you?" Sally burst into the kitchen. "Have you lost your mind?"

"I'm getting the hell out of here."

He snatched one of his discarded shirts from the floor and didn't bother to button it before grabbing his hat and saddlebag.

"What do you mean, you're out of here?" Sally gawked at him as if she didn't understand English. "Where are you going?"

"Where I damn well please," he snarled, reaching for the back door. "I'll be back when it suits me."

"What am I supposed to do?" she demanded. "What about Jamie?"

"What about him?" Will was sick of the whole business. "You can manage without me for a few days."

"Will Thornton, I've been managing without you my whole life!"

He stormed outside and slammed the door behind him. He didn't give a damn what Sally did with the kid. He was tired of waiting on Cole, and the next best thing to killing Cole would be getting his hands on Caitlin.

"Daddy! Daddy, carry me!"
Caitlin smiled as Cole swung Jamie onto his shoulders

*and the child laughed out loud. In a field of wildflowers,
she ran ahead of them, swinging a picnic basket in one
hand and trying to keep her straw hat in place with the
other. Everything was perfect. The sky was clear, a warm
breeze was blowing, and she was with the two people she
loved most in all the world.*

*Anxious to reach the picnic spot, she turned to see
what was keeping them. The sun was in her eyes, and
she could make out only the tall figure of a man coming
toward her. She smiled and held out her hand, startled
by the vicious grip that seized her arm, and she tried
desperately to pull away.*

"Cole!" she cried. "Help me!"

*"He can't help you. No one can." Will Thornton's
sneering features came into focus. "You owe me, remember?"*

*The sky overhead grew dark, and heavy rain droplets
pelted her face. "Where's my baby! Give him back to me
and I'll do anything you like."*

*"That's more like it." He pointed behind her. "There's
your boy. Go get him."*

*She whirled around and gasped at the sight of Jamie
standing far off, dirty and bedraggled. She hurried to
reach him, but he backed away from her outstretched
hand.*

*"Why didn't you come for me?" he asked, his tiny features
contorted with anguish. "Why didn't you save me?"*

*"I tried, sweetie, I tried." She gulped for air and
reached for him again. "I tried so hard."*

*He shook his head, backing away from her still. "It's
too late."*

"No! Your daddy and I are here to save you."

"It's too late, Caitlin."

She froze at the sound of her mother's voice. Emerging from the shadows, her mother swept Jamie into her arms as Caitlin watched in horror. "I'm taking him with me."

"No!" Caitlin cried, but her voice was lost in the rumble of thunder overhead. "Please give him back!"

Mama shook her head sadly. "It's too late, Caitlin."

Blackness swirled around them, and her mother turned from her and faded into the shadows, taking her child away forever.

"Cole," she sobbed. "Where are you? Why won't you help me?"

Caitlin bolted upright in the bed. Her heart was slamming against her chest and she could scarcely draw a breath. The room was still dark, and she realized she was in bed alone. A movement in the shadows caught her eye, and she turned to see Cole, fully dressed, buckling his gunbelt around his waist.

"W-what are you doing?" she asked. Her hand was shaking as she pushed the hair out of her eyes. "What time is it?"

"An hour or so before sunup."

"What are you doing?" she repeated.

He neared the bed and reached out to stroke her cheek. "I'm going to get our son."

"Now?" She scrambled out of bed, dragging the sheet along with her. She tried to wrap it around her shoulders, but her feet became tangled in the length pooling on the floor. "Why didn't you wake me up?"

"I was going to tell you goodbye."

"Goodbye?" She clutched the makeshift robe around herself and shook her head. "You're not going without me."

"It's too dangerous, Caitlin."

She hobbled across the room and groped to light the lamp on a table. With the third match, she had given up trying to preserve her modesty and let the wrinkled cotton slip to her waist. The room flooded with light, and she turned toward him, gathering her precious sheet around her.

"You can't go after him alone," she insisted. "I need to be there so he won't be afraid. He won't understand."

"All I plan to tell him is that I'm bringing him back to his mother."

If he's still alive. If I make it back.

The words lingered in the air like smoke from a dying candle, and Caitlin rushed into Cole's embrace as soon as he opened his arms. She squeezed her eyes shut against the burning sting of tears. "Please, please take me with you."

He held her tight and stroked the back of her head, smoothing her tousled hair. "No, sweetheart, I won't risk anything happening to you."

She forgot all about being brave and started to cry. She couldn't help it. The dream was all too vivid in her mind, and she couldn't shake the overwhelming sense of dread she felt. "If you go, I'll never see you again."

She sounded ridiculous. Like a child, but she

wasn't going to try and explain a nightmare about her mother's ghost taking away her child.

"You know better than that." His voice was low and soothing. "I always came back for you before."

His words held no accusation, but still they stung. What would have happened if she had waited for him? She wouldn't let herself contemplate the hundreds of scenarios that would never be. Here and now was all that mattered. And Jamie.

A sob rose in her throat. She couldn't bear the thought of what Cole might find, but could she stand not being there when he did find her child? She would sell her soul to hold Jamie just once more and let him have no doubt that she loved him.

Cole silenced her renewed pleas with a gentle kiss. He cupped her face in his palms and searched her eyes. "Promise me. Promise you'll wait for me."

She nodded. "Promise you'll come back."

Caitlin didn't leave the room all day. Meals were brought up to her, and she occupied her time altering two skirts a woman had left behind some time ago. They were too small for Mrs. Hadley, the innkeeper's wife, so she gave them to Caitlin. Each one had to be rehemmed and taken in several inches at the waist.

She tried to read a book someone had discarded, but she couldn't concentrate. She jumped at every sound and ran to the window whenever she heard the rattle of a wagon passing by or a rider stopping near the hotel. School let out, and she was shocked at the number of children streaming out of the one-room building.

Even sleep eluded her, and she lay awake all that night.

By midmorning she could stand it no longer. She had to get out of that room before she suffocated from worry. Mrs. Hadley had shopping to do that afternoon, and Caitlin invited herself to go along. She made her way down the stairs and caught sight of the pleasant woman behind the front desk.

She saw Caitlin and waved before turning back to a guest at the counter. "No, sir, we don't charge lawmen . . . especially a Texas Ranger."

Caitlin froze in place.

"You're mighty kind, ma'am."

"We're happy to oblige." Mrs. Hadley handed him the key to his room. "Come on down, Caitlin. I'll be ready to leave in just a minute."

He turned at the mention of her name, and Caitlin faltered on the stairs. Fleeing to her room would only create suspicion where there should be none. She had done nothing wrong, and there was no reason the law would be looking for her.

"Caitlin?" He grinned slightly. "Caitlin McDonnell, I'll just bet."

Damn you, Papa.

"*Mrs.* Thornton," their host corrected.

"Well, well, won't your pa be surprised to hear that?"

"Mrs. Hadley, I've changed my mind about going out. Perhaps tomorrow."

"That'll give us a chance to have a little talk." He neared the staircase, and Caitlin saw the badge pinned to his vest. "I'm Sergeant Weldon, Texas Ranger."

"Since I am a law-abiding citizen, I can only assume your invitation is of a personal nature and very improper."

He wasn't the least bit put off by her haughtiness and even chuckled out loud. "With all due respect, Miss McDonnell, I believe you've waited too late in the game to get choosy about the company you keep."

"Humph." She turned and hurried back upstairs.

"You can't get rid of me that easy, ma'am," he called out, and the warning was clear despite his good-natured manners. "I'll be waiting for you every time you come down these steps."

The afternoon wore on, and Caitlin's nerves were frazzled. At last, she decided hiding wasn't a solution, and the best she could hope for was that he would leave town once she answered his questions.

"Well, good evenin', ma'am." He rose to his feet when she entered the small parlor that led into the dining room. "You certainly look lovely."

"I could say the same for you." She noticed that he had shaved and changed his clothes since that morning, and it irked her to know he hadn't been camped out at the bottom of the staircase as he had threatened. At least, not all afternoon.

He ran a hand along his clean-shaven jaw. "I

thought you might be more willing to talk with me if I looked halfway decent."

His confident smile made Caitlin suspect he considered his appearance more than halfway decent. His pale hair and light eyes were striking in contrast with his tanned features, and women probably did find him handsome. There was, however, a ruthless determination in his gaze, and Caitlin remained leery. "I simply don't see what we have to talk about."

"Your son."

She swallowed, sinking onto the sofa. "Jamie? What do you know about him?"

"Just that you're anxious to find him."

She nodded.

"Then we just might be able to help one another."

"How?"

He sat across from her and leaned forward, balancing an elbow on one knee. "You take me to Thornton, and I'll see that your boy is returned safe and sound."

"My father sent you, didn't he?" Caitlin gripped the arm of the couch. This time Papa had gone too far, as if he hadn't done enough damage already. Thank God, Weldon found her before he found Cole. "Sergeant, I assure you Cole Thornton has done nothing wrong. I was not kidnapped. In fact, Cole isn't even here. He left yesterday morning."

"And you're waiting for him to return." When

she didn't deny his conclusion, Weldon leaned forward and added, "With your boy, you hope?"

Caitlin hesitated. There was no way she could speak nonchalantly of Jamie.

"Will Thornton is a desperate man, Miss McDonnell. He won't hand over that child without a fight."

"He escaped from prison, didn't he?"

"No, some softhearted folks got to believing criminals like him could be rehabilitated . . . put back into society. Will Thornton received early parole at the urging of the prison warden. A week later, they found the old man dead in his own bed. His throat had been cut."

Caitlin gasped, but he continued. "Will hadn't been out of jail a month when he took your boy."

"How can I take you to him?"

"Did Cole tell you where he was going when he left here?"

She shook her head. "Just that he would be riding through rough country."

"I'm offering to help you find your son. Isn't that what matters?"

"Of course it is." She hesitated, weighing her words carefully. "I don't understand why you're looking for Cole."

"Your son's life is hanging on the hope that Cole isn't riding into an ambush. Do you really think he can take on a whole gang of outlaws and come out unscathed?"

"What gang?"

"Will Thornton didn't attack that way station alone.

What makes you think he's man enough to face
Cole on his own?"

Promise you'll wait for me this time.
I did come back for you and you were gone.
Cole's words rang over and over again in her
mind, and Caitlin doubted he would ever understand her reasons for going along with Weldon.
She wasn't sure she understood them too well herself. Weldon had done a lot of fast talking about
finding Cole, outsmarting Will, and saving Jamie.
She *had* believed Weldon would send her home,
bound over to another Ranger, if she refused to
cooperate, and she hated him for using her child
against her.

"Let's get moving, Miss McDonnell." Weldon's
voice startled her, and she hurried to finish washing her hands and face in the cool stream. "I don't
want to lose him."

Caitlin dried her hands on the hem of her skirt
and turned to find Weldon waiting with the horses.
She allowed him to help her into the saddle before
asking, "You're certain we're on his trail?"

"Yes, ma'am." He mounted his own horse and
turned the big mare toward the narrow path that
had started out as a respectable road. "I can find
any man's trail, no matter how hard he tries to
cover it up."

"Is Cole trying to hide his tracks?"

Weldon glanced over his shoulder, a little startled. "Not exactly."

Caitlin held her tongue. Weldon's arrogance was exasperating, but she could gouge his pride only so deep.

They rode on for several hours with little spoken between them. Without warning, he turned his horse and rode into a narrow ravine. Caitlin followed, but her patience was wearing thin. She wanted to know what he expected to find in a washed-out gully besides rocks and snakes.

"I suppose this will be as good a place as any to stop for the night."

Caitlin glanced toward the west, trying to gauge the time. "It's a little early in the day, don't you think?"

"Perhaps, but I doubt we'll find a better spot than this before nightfall."

He swung down from the saddle and made his way over to help her do the same. She watched as he led the horses to the tiny water hole and admitted to herself she was tired, but she was anxious to find Cole and go after Jamie.

"I hope you're not stopping on my account," she offered when he returned. "I'm doing fine, and we should put as many miles behind us as we can."

"We're making good time," he assured her. "You let me worry about such things. Right now, I'm going to find something decent for dinner. Do you like jackrabbit, Miss McDonnell?"

Not especially, but she nodded anyway.

"Then I'd better fetch two of 'em. I sleep better on a full stomach."

He retrieved his rifle from his saddle and nimbly made his way up a narrow rise. Glancing back once more, he grinned slightly and disappeared over the slope.

Caitlin sighed and sank to the ground. When this was all over, she would never ride a horse again or spend another night outdoors. She wore a lacy chemise under her blouse, and the thin garment caught and clung where perspiration pooled between her breasts and trickled down her back.

The tiny water hole looked muddy, shallow, and inviting. Just to splash a little water on her arms and throat would be heaven, but she didn't dare remove her blouse with Weldon likely to return at any moment. Glancing over her shoulder, she saw no sign of him and hurried to remove her shoes and stockings.

She tested the water with one bare toe, disappointed to find it lukewarm, but it was better than nothing. Bunching her skirt around her knees she stepped in and grimaced at the feel of mud between her toes. The water barely topped her calves and she bent over to dip one hand in the water and rinse the sticky film of sweat from her legs.

Just as she moved to straighten up a hand clamped hard over her mouth and an arm caught her roughly around the waist, hauling her out of the water.

"What the hell are you doing out here?"

She squirmed but Cole held tight. "Didn't I tell you to keep your ass put in that hotel?"

He loosened his fingers over her mouth and she gasped for air. "Listen to me!"

"No, you listen to me!" His palm flattened against her lips. "You're lucky you haven't already gotten yourself killed."

"Turn her loose, Thornton."

Caitlin's struggles ceased, and she felt every muscle in Cole's body tense at the sound of a rifle being cocked.

"Do it now, or I'll blow your head off. You want the little lady to share a bullet with you?"

Without warning, Cole released his hold on Caitlin and she tumbled to the ground, landing hard on one knee. She scrambled to her feet and stood gaping at the sight of Shane Weldon shoving the barrel of his rifle firmly between Cole's shoulder blades.

"What are you doing?" she demanded.

"My job, lady. You sit over there and be quiet." Weldon's attention returned to Cole. "Unbuckle that gunbelt. Now."

Cole glared at Caitlin with such malevolence her insides turned cold. She stumbled backward and sank to the ground, watching helplessly as Weldon took Cole's gunbelt and tossed it at her muddy feet. There was no mistaking the sound of handcuffs being fastened around Cole's wrists. He barely flinched, but she knew too well how the irons bit into your flesh with every move.

Weldon searched Cole's pockets and relieved him of another pistol and a knife strapped inside his boot. "You didn't come to play, did you, boy?"

Cole said nothing, and his eyes never left Caitlin. She hung her head, too ashamed to look at him.

She stared at the pistols tucked inside the holster, but she didn't doubt for a second that any false move on her part would get Cole killed.

"Where's your horse?" When he received no response, Weldon casually replied, "It's your choice. You can ride your own horse, or I'll tie you like a dog and drag you behind mine."

"No!" Caitlin cried out before she could stop herself. "Let him ride my horse!"

"Now there's an idea." Weldon twisted Cole's arms and forced him to his knees. "You can ride the buckskin, and the little woman can ride with me, all snug and cozy like."

"Please, Cole," she begged. "Please, just tell him where your horse is."

He wouldn't even look at her now and she feared he would refuse. Suddenly, he jerked his head toward a copse of trees peeking over the ravine, and the rage on his face broke Caitlin's heart. He hated her now, and she couldn't blame him.

"You're smarter than you look." Weldon scooped Cole's gunbelt from the ground and grinned at Caitlin before turning to gather their horses. "We need to get as many miles behind us as we can."

Caitlin winced upon hearing her own words thrown back at her, calling her a fool. She risked a glance at Cole, and further risked saying, "Cole, he tricked me, I swear."

"Save it for someone else."

"Please, I promise you I didn't—"

"I'm not interested in your explanations."

Weldon hauled Cole to his feet and shoved him

forward, and Caitlin followed, carrying her shoes and stockings. There was nothing else she could do. She didn't trust Weldon, and she couldn't expect Cole to trust her. Yet both men held the only hope she had of finding her child, and she couldn't trust either one of them not to use that hope against her.

Thirteen

Weldon was no fool. He was a bastard and a liar, but he was no fool.

Caitlin had no choice but to ride beside him, refusing to speak to him or look at him. Unfortunately, her only alternative was to stare right at Cole's back. Weldon had Cole ride ahead of them where he could watch every move his prisoner made. The handcuffs made handling the reins awkward, but Cole managed better than expected.

Twice, Cole's horse faltered, and Weldon drew his gun without hesitation and nearly scared Caitlin to death. The only hope lay in the lengthening shadows, and the chance Cole could get away in the dark. She tried not to think about her dwindling chances of finding Jamie.

They pressed on until a farmhouse loomed in the distance, and Weldon was counting on the family's hospitality. He wasn't disappointed.

"Anything for a Texas Ranger," the man said as if it were an honor. "You can put your prisoner in the barn."

Caitlin's heart sank.

His red-haired wife hefted a crying toddler onto

her hip and nodded her head toward Caitlin. "What about her?"

Weldon offered a hasty explanation. "I'm seeing that she is safely returned to her family."

The introductions were made, and Rebecca Stanton invited Caitlin inside while her husband, Harley, offered to help Weldon with his prisoner. Caitlin had never felt so hopeless as she did watching Cole disappear inside that barn. She jumped at the touch of Rebecca's hand on her arm.

"Bless your heart, honey. I didn't mean to scare you."

Caitlin shook her head and tried to smile. "I'm all right. Just tired."

"I reckon so."

Rebecca ushered Caitlin inside the house, but the heady aroma of baking bread and simmering apples alone would have led Caitlin to the kitchen. Two red-haired little girls were busy at the table shaping scraps of pie crust into tiny figures.

"That ain't no cow!"

"Is so!"

"Then where's its horns?"

"Hush your squabbling, girls. We have company."

They gaped at Caitlin as if she had two heads, and the toddler cried for his mother to put him down. "Lordy, these young'uns are going to run me to death."

The little one could barely reach the tabletop, but he managed to seize a fair share of the pastry dough.

"Ma! Make John Taylor leave us alone, *please.*"

Ignoring her daughter's complaint, Mrs. Stanton motioned for Caitlin to take a seat at the far end of the table, near to the iron stove. She peered into the oven and stirred a large pot on top of the stove, satisfied that her dinner was coming along just fine. "Just call me Becky, everyone does."

Caitlin gratefully accepted the glass of water Becky held out to her. "I can't tell you how sorry I am to impose on you like this."

"Impose!" She laughed and shook her head. "Lord, do you know how glad I am to have someone to talk to besides the young'uns?"

Caitlin managed a weak smile and listened as her hostess went on to tell how she and her husband had moved to Texas five years ago and what things were like back in Kansas. Caitlin wondered if Becky Stanton had any idea how lucky she was.

The kitchen was so homey and peaceful, filled with children's voices and comfort. Everywhere Caitlin looked, the room bore signs of the family's pride in their home. She was certain Becky had made the gingham curtains herself, and the girls had picked the colorful bouquet of wildflowers poked in a Mason jar of water.

"So, what about you?" Becky brushed her hands together, ridding them of flour, and studied her guest. "How'd you come to be mixed up with that outlaw?"

Caitlin looked down. "He's not an outlaw."

"Honey, I'm not trying be nosy, but that's not how it looks to me."

John Taylor toddled over to Caitlin and presented her with a piece of wadded-up pie crust. With his sandy hair and brown eyes, he looked nothing like Jamie, but Caitlin longed to put her arms around him and hold him close. Instead, she whispered a feeble "thank you" and squeezed the dough in her palm.

He giggled in delight and scrunched his lips into a pucker, craning his neck toward her. She leaned forward, and the feel of his drooling mouth on her cheek undid her. A sob tore from her throat, and she buried her face in her hands, helpless to stop the tears.

Oh, God, please, just let me see my baby one more time.

John Taylor began to cry, and one of the girls asked softly, "What's wrong with her, Ma?"

"Girls, take your brother and go play in the front room." Chairs scooted across the floor, and more whispered questions went unanswered as Becky hurried them out of the kitchen. "Don't let him break anything."

A gentle hand settled on Caitlin's shoulder, and Becky offered her a damp dishtowel. The cloth was cool against Caitlin's tear-streaked face, and she shuddered with the effort to stop crying. "I'm so sorry. I didn't mean to upset your children."

"You haven't upset anyone."

She drew a deep breath against another wave of tears. "I'll be fine now."

Becky slid into a chair beside Caitlin. "Is it something you want to talk about?"

Caitlin shook her head. "I wouldn't know where to begin."

Work-worn hands covered Caitlin's. "Where's your baby?"

"I don't know." She shook her head. "I've been trying to find him, but—"

She tried not to cry, but she couldn't finish the explanation, and Becky's arms closed around her. The truth was Caitlin had just about given up hope, and the hopeful reassurances of a stranger did nothing to lessen her despair.

Dinner was a miserable ordeal. The two girls kept their eyes peeled on Caitlin as if she might explode at any moment, and John Taylor fussed the whole time. Caitlin barely tasted her food, and it was killing her to know that Cole was fastened up in the barn like an animal. Sergeant Weldon and Mr. Stanton took no notice of the somber faces around the table and talked at length about cattle and railroads and the price of land in Montana.

At last, they rose from the table and asked the ladies to excuse them while they went out on the front porch for a smoke. Becky began clearing the table, and Caitlin moved to help her.

"I'll do this. Here." She shoved a clean plate into Caitlin's hands and said, "Take him something to eat, honey. Slip right out that back door and they'll never know you're gone."

Caitlin nodded and felt fresh tears welling up.

"Hurry up. If you get started bawlin' again, he'll starve to death."

Caitlin smiled, and she did hurry. The latch on the barn door was heavy, but she managed to get inside without any trouble. The barn was dark, and she caught the sweet scent of freshly cut hay. Her eyes slowly adjusted to the light, and she was able to make out a silhouette of Cole seated against the wall.

She barely stopped herself from calling out his name and hurried to kneel beside him. "Cole, I'm so sorry."

He didn't bother to look at her. "Get out."

"Don't be angry with me," she begged. "I brought you some dinner, and—"

"I don't want it." His voice was cold and distant.

"Cole, you have to believe me. I didn't know—"

"I did believe you. Look what it got me."

Caitlin closed her hands in tight fists to keep from reaching out to him. He had every right to be angry with her, but she was shocked that he would think she deliberately betrayed him like this.

"I thought he wanted to help us."

"Why would the law want to help someone named Thornton?"

"You're not an outlaw, Cole. You never were."

The barn door swung open and light from a lantern flooded the interior. Caitlin bolted to her feet and faced Shane Weldon. His eyes went from her face to the plate of food she had placed beside Cole and back to her face again.

"Aren't you the thoughtful little thing?"

Caitlin ignored his sarcasm and returned to Cole's side, taking advantage of the light to see if he was injured. His face bore no bruises, but there were bloody marks on his wrists from the handcuffs that fettered him to a post. Instinctively, she raised her hand to his face, and he turned his head away from her touch.

"Now, I thought you were a right smart man, Thornton, and here you go turning away from a pretty lady."

"Leave him alone." Caitlin glared up at Weldon. "Just go away and leave us alone."

"Can't do that, ma'am. He might try and take advantage of that tender heart of yours."

There was so much she needed to say to Cole, but nothing she wanted Weldon to hear. He reached down and took hold of her upper arm, gently pulling her to her feet. Cole never turned his head in her direction, even as Weldon hauled her out of the barn and fastened the door.

Once outside, she tore away from his hold. "You lied to me. My father may have sent you after me, but that gave you no right to use me as bait for a trap."

She braced herself for one of his snide retorts, but instead his face grew somber. "I'm sorry, ma'am, but there was no other way."

"You have no reason to arrest him. He was exonerated by the U.S. Marshal."

"In New Mexico territory," he countered. "The Thorntons are still wanted in Texas for bank robbery."

"That was years ago, and he took no part in the robbery."

"That's for a judge to decide. My job is to see that he's brought in to answer the charges."

"You said you'd help us save Jamie."

"That was the truth. I'll go after Will Thornton and bring your son back to you."

"I'm going with you."

"Oh, no. No, you're not. In the morning, Stanton is going to fetch the sheriff to lock Cole up in the county jail. You can either wait for me here or in a cell."

Caitlin's stomach twisted into a knot. Will would kill Jamie at the very sight of a lawman. She followed him back to the house, and her despair sharpened into desperation.

Weldon opened the back door and escorted her inside the kitchen, keeping a firm hold on her elbow. Harley Stanton turned at the sound of the door closing, and Caitlin could see Becky leaning against his shoulder. Becky's eyes were bright and her face a little flushed, and her husband looked sheepish at being caught comforting his wife.

"Everything all right, Sergeant?" The pitying look he gave Caitlin left little doubt what his wife had been telling him about. "Miss McDonnell, are you all right?"

"Fine, thank you."

"I've made up the spare room for you, Sergeant Weldon," Becky said. "Caitlin, the girls are going to sleep on a pallet in our room, and you can have their bed."

Caitlin nodded.

"If you folks don't mind, Miss McDonnell and I have some things to talk over."

The Stantons both looked to Caitlin for confirmation and she nodded.

"Then we'll say good night and see you in the morning." Harley Stanton turned toward the narrow staircase that led up to the bedrooms. "Just call out if you need anything."

"There's coffee on the stove," Becky offered. "Just needs warming up, if you'd like some."

Once they were gone, Caitlin backed away from Weldon, putting the kitchen table between them. "Say what you have to say."

"Caitlin, I'm not your enemy." The sincerity in his eyes was convincing, but she stood wary. "Please, let's talk about this."

He didn't move in her direction, and she finally nodded and sat down. He slid into the chair across from her and folded his arms on the tabletop, weighing his words carefully. "I wish there was something I could do to make this easier for you."

"Take me to my son."

"I wish I could do that, too," he assured her. "By my orders are to see that you and your son are returned home safely. I can't risk your life by dragging you into a gunfight."

"But you're willing to put Jamie right in the middle of one?"

"Of course not. I hope to slip in unnoticed and eliminate Thornton without a fight."

"That's a lot to hope for."

He nodded and the conversation lulled. He leaned back in the chair. "Why don't we have some of that coffee?"

"I'll get it." Caitlin rose from the table, grateful for the diversion.

She crossed the kitchen and placed the coffeepot on the stove to heat. There had to be some way to reason with him, to make him see that there was more at stake than bringing outlaws to justice.

She heard his chair scrape away from the table, and she turned around with a start at the sound of his boots on the floor.

"Relax," he said, insulted by her wariness. "I'm just going out on the porch for a smoke while the coffee heats up."

The screen door closed behind him, and Caitlin turned to search for the cups and searched another cupboard for the sugar bowl. Becky Stanton's kitchen was well stocked and neat as a pin. Caitlin was amazed at the assortment of medicinal items on hand. The woman had everything. Tonics, elixirs, and jars of dried herbs. There were a few items Caitlin recognized: castor oil, paregoric, and stomach bitters.

She opened another cabinet, shuddering at the memory of how sick she'd been after taking paregoric. She found the sugar bowl and dumped a spoonful into Weldon's cup. The coffee was warm enough now, and she filled their cups. Her eyes wandered back to the shelf of medicine, and her hand stilled over his cup.

He wasn't going to listen to her, she knew. If anything, Weldon intended to make her see his side of things and gain her cooperation with more threats. The only chance Jamie had was Cole reaching him before anyone else. Weldon had to be stopped.

She reached for the laudanum but drew back. That would only ensure he had a good night's sleep, and too much could kill him. Caitlin had no idea how much was too much. She scanned the row of bottles and smiled when she remembered the paregoric. If it made Weldon only half as sick as it had made her, he wouldn't be able to do much more than hang his head over a bucket.

She reached for the bottle and tried to remember how much Aunt Nell had given her. She heard his boots on the porch and acted quickly, pouring the medicine in the coffee. There wasn't time to measure and more came out than she meant.

The hinges on the back door sounded, and Caitlin replaced the bottle and shut the cabinet. She returned to the table and placed his coffee on the table, sipping her own once she was seated. He joined her and she caught the lingering scent of tobacco smoke on his clothes.

"One sugar, right?"

"You noticed." He smiled, and she recognized the cunning charm he meant to use on her. "It's a rare treat to have a lady fuss over me . . . even just a little."

"I find that hard to believe." She returned a little charm of her own and smiled coyly as he took the first drink of coffee. "I would think a gallant man in uniform would be very popular with the ladies."

"The rangers don't wear uniforms."

"Oh." She smiled sheepishly. "Surely, there's someone you consider special."

He shrugged. "I don't give much thought to settling down, anyway. I spend too much time chasing outlaws to be a family man."

Her smile fell at the comment. He tried to apologize, but she dismissed the remark. "Don't worry, Sergeant, I know you're just doing your job."

He relaxed visibly upon hearing her admission. "I'm doing what's best . . . for everyone."

She hid her reaction behind her coffee cup, and he took her silence as concurrence. He raised his cup and drank nearly half the tainted brew.

"I'm glad you understand. Can I trust you to wait here with the Stantons until I return?"

"I'd rather not."

He was surprised by her answer. "You'd rather go into town? I thought you and Mrs. Stanton were enjoying your visit."

"She's very nice, but she has three children and a house to run." Caitlin bit her lips and hoped she looked dismayed. "You wouldn't really lock me up in a jail cell, would you?"

"I'm responsible for your welfare. If you were to—"

"All I want to do is go home," she assured him. "I can catch a stage back to Eden, and you can pay the driver to point a shotgun at me the whole way."

He grinned. "I doubt that would be necessary."

"Not at all." She forced herself to return his smile. "So, we'll leave first thing tomorrow?"

He nodded. "I'd like to get going by daylight, so we'd better turn in for the night."

"A good night's sleep is just what I need." She rose from the table and claimed his empty cup. "I'll just wash these up first. Good night."

He turned toward the stairs, and Caitlin waited until he was out of sight. She rinsed out their cups and turned to make her way up the stairs. Her hands were sweating, and she prayed that God would forgive what she had done but allow it to work.

She slipped inside the Stanton girls' bedroom and contemplated not changing into her nightgown. She could lie down on the bed, fully dressed, and be ready to leave at a moment's notice. However, the moment might not come, and she would only arouse unwanted suspicion. She compromised by removing only her shoes, skirt, and blouse and slipping her nightgown over her underclothes.

Wide awake, Caitlin lay straining to hear any sound. John Taylor cried, and Becky sang in a hushed tone that nearly lulled Caitlin to sleep. She blinked hard against sleep and against tears, and she weighed her pitifully limited options. Her only real hope was Weldon being too ill to travel at daylight, allowing her a few precious unguarded moments in which she could free Cole and see that he escaped unnoticed.

She turned on her side and hugged the feather pillow tight against her chest, slowly rocking back and forth in time with the muffled lullaby. Gradually, the song faded, and Caitlin could picture Becky placing the sleeping child in his crib for the night. How many times had she gone through the same ritual, taking for granted she would have so much time with Jamie.

At least you have memories of him.

Cole's words droned in her mind, deepening the ache she felt inside. She hated thinking of him out there in the barn—cold, tired, and hungry—and it hurt even more to know he wanted no comfort from her.

At some point, she drifted off to sleep. The sound of heavy footsteps on the stairs jolted her awake, and she panicked at the thought of Weldon taking Cole and leaving her behind. She rushed to the window, relieved to find the sun barely beginning to rise, and shucked out of the nightgown and dashed downstairs as soon as she was dressed.

Becky was alone in the kitchen, feeding wood into the stove, and Caitlin tried to sound at ease when she said, "Good morning."

The woman's surprise at seeing Caitlin was obvious. "Well, good morning!"

"You're up early."

"Early?" Becky shook her head. "I should've had biscuits in the oven by now, and the coffee's just now perking."

Hopeful, Caitlin asked, "No one's had breakfast then?"

"Harley went to get started with the chores, and

I was going let you sleep until I had the food on the table."

Caitlin nodded and asked what she could do to help with the meal. Given the easy task of setting the table, she kept her eyes on the staircase as she doled out plates, cups, and silverware. A door opened and shut, and she caught sight of Shane Weldon moving slowly down the stairs, leaning heavily on the railing.

He looked miserable and hope began to rise within her. Keeping her eyes on the task before her, she said, "Good morning, Sergeant Weldon."

His reply was unintelligible, barely more than a groan.

Becky gasped out loud. "Mercy, Sergeant, you're plumb green around the gills!"

A fork slipped from Caitlin's fingers and clattered to the floor, and she bent to pick it up before risking another look at Weldon. "My goodness, what's wrong?"

He shook his head. "I don't know, but I've never been so sick in my life."

Caitlin bit the inside of her mouth and swallowed back her guilt, remembering how miserable Cole must be out in that barn. "Here, sit down and let me get you some coffee."

He groaned at the thought and sank into a chair at the table, propping his forehead in his upraised hand.

"Coffee's the last thing he needs on a queasy stomach." Becky stood at the counter, rolling out biscuit dough, and nodded toward the coffer of medicinal supplies. "Caitlin, I've got some stomach bitters in that cabinet yonder. Put a few drops in a glass of water for him, will you?"

"Of course." She nodded and made her way to the cabinet and pretended to search for the right bottle. Caitlin tried not to think about how deceitful she was becoming and plucked the paregoric bottle from the shelf. Weldon gratefully accepted the concoction he thought would make him feel better. "You'll probably feel fine after a day of rest."

"Can't spare the time," he insisted, handing her the empty glass. "We're riding out of here this morning if I have to strap myself in the saddle."

Caitlin decided that might just be the best suggestion she'd heard in days.

Cole didn't resist when Weldon ordered him to mount his own horse or when the son-of-a-bitch replaced the handcuffs on his wrists. In all the years he lived on the wrong side of the law, Cole had never worn irons, and he vowed to find a way to use the ones he wore now to strangle Weldon. He would take the first opportunity that came along and leave Weldon lying on the side of the road, wearing his own handcuffs and missing a few teeth.

He tried not to look at Caitlin, riding calmly beside Weldon. He tried to ignore her altogether, but she wasn't making it very easy. She chattered on about what nice people the Stantons were, how clear the sky was, and how badly folks needed rain.

Weldon didn't seem to pay much attention to her or anything else. They hadn't gone two miles that morning before he stopped his horse and stumbled toward a clump of bushes, retching like a dog. Cole couldn't even enjoy the bastard's misery for Caitlin rushing to his side to offer a canteen of water, assuring him a cool drink would make him feel better.

Instead, he got worse and worse, and Caitlin fussed over him like a sick calf.

"How much farther to the town?" she asked, when they stopped again.

He shook his head and groaned. "Not sure. Stanton said about . . . about twenty miles."

"Cole, how far do you think we've traveled?"

He couldn't believe she was asking him the distance as if they were traveling to a barn raising. Sparing her only a moment's glance, he glared at her without saying a word. Impervious to his fury, she urged Weldon to sit down and rest for a few minutes. "Once we get to town, we'll find a doctor, and you'll be fine."

Weldon nodded and sagged down on a low boulder, hanging his head. Caitlin helped him slip out of his jacket, suggesting that he might be too warm. She folded the garment and laid it across her saddle, turning toward Cole without a trace of the sweet-natured concern he'd seen earlier.

Her expression was grim and, facing him with steely determination, he couldn't miss the silent plea in her eyes for him to trust her. Before he could refuse, her hand slid along his thigh and covered his hand resting on the pommel of his saddle. A cold bit of metal dug into his palm, and he glanced down to see her press a tiny key into his palm. Her fingers lingered just a moment before she turned back to Weldon.

Cole unlocked the handcuffs and slipped the key in the pocket of his shirt, never taking his eyes off of Caitlin. He couldn't imagine what in the hell she was up to, but he wasn't going anywhere without his rifle and gunbelt.

"We'd better get going, Sergeant," she cooed over Weldon's shoulder, hooking her arm under his. He staggered to his feet and tried not to lean on her. "Are you sure you can make it?"

He nodded, and she released his arm. He managed a few stumbling steps and crumpled to the ground. Caitlin motioned for Cole to wait where he was and gingerly shook Weldon by the shoulder. "Sergeant? Sergeant, are you all right?"

He made no reply and Caitlin's eyes flew to Cole. "Bring me those handcuffs! Quick!"

Cole swung down from his horse and handed her the irons, glad to be rid of them, and knelt to help her roll Weldon onto his back. She snapped the handcuffs on his wrists. "Let's get him to his feet."

"What the hell for?" Cole demanded. "He stays right here, and you can stay with him if you're so concerned about him."

"If we leave him, he could die," she countered. "If someone does find him, they'll be after us before sundown."

"What do you want to do then?"

"We leave him where he'll be taken care of and kept off our trail."

"Where?"

"The jail in the next town." She smiled slyly and retrieved Weldon's coat from her horse. "Congratulations, you've just been promoted to sergeant in the Texas Rangers."

Caitlin swallowed hard but her heart was in her throat as they rode into town. Cole had sworn she was going to get them both hung, but she had more faith than he did. This was her only chance of reaching Jamie, and God wouldn't punish her for taking the only road.

She glanced over at Shane Weldon, slumped forward on his horse, and prayed she hadn't overdone things with her concoction of paregoric, laudanum, and sugar water. She'd barely stopped Cole before he turned up the canteen and doped himself but good. The disbelief in his eyes was all the confirmation Caitlin needed that her actions could've had deadly results, but she caught the smile he tried to hide as they turned the horses toward town.

They didn't speak the remainder of the trek, but Caitlin suspected he was no longer furious with her. She hated to think that he believed she'd turn him into the law so easily. If he had any doubts, surely her actions had convinced him otherwise.

The town was small but not deserted. Wagons rolled down the main street, and Caitlin noticed a steady stream of folks coming and going from different shops and stores. A few people turned their heads to stare at the odd-looking trio, but most were too engrossed in their own affairs to notice.

Bold as daylight, they rode up to the sheriff's office, and Cole gave her one last warning look, silently reminding her of her promise to let him do the talking. He slid down from his saddle, and she did the same while he dragged Weldon from his horse. With a jerk of his head, Cole directed her toward the door ahead of him.

Before she could reach for the latch, the plank door swung open, and a young man stepped out to meet them. He smiled pleasantly, and Caitlin thought he looked more like a preacher than a lawman.

"Howdy, folks." He tipped his hat toward Caitlin before turning to Cole. "What's the trouble?"

"Are you the sheriff?"

"I'm McBride, his deputy." His eyes traveled to Weldon's slouched form. "Is he drunk?"

"He's sick." Cole went on to explain. "He's wanted by the Texas Rangers, and I need to leave him with you until they can claim him."

The young deputy took in the expensive leather jacket Cole was wearing and the badge pinned to the front. "You're a Ranger? Why don't you just take him in?"

Cole nodded his head toward Caitlin. "I got to take the woman back to her family."

McBride hesitated, and Cole grew impatient. "Look, he's getting heavy. Can we talk about this inside?"

"Of course." McBride scurried aside, and Cole hauled Weldon inside the law office. The deputy wasted no time unlocking a cell and helped Cole deposit Weldon onto a narrow cot in the corner. "Who is he?"

"One of the Thorntons." Cole emerged from the cell and calmly crossed the room to help himself to a cup of coffee. "I'm sure you know all about them."

McBride looked puzzled but squared his shoulders and said, "Oh, sure. We've been watching for them for days. Don't recall any mention of a woman."

"Thornton kidnapped her." Cole grinned at Caitlin over his coffee cup, looking all the world like the cat who ate the canary. "I caught him trying to sell her to a whorehouse in a mining camp."

Caitlin gasped and barely stifled an indignant denial. Deputy McBride, however, blushed to the tops of his ears, and Caitlin feared he would faint. Not certain she could curb her reaction, she turned her back to them and stared out the window.

"That bastard," she heard McBride mutter.

"Oh, there was no harm done." Cole was enjoying this. "She's too damn mean for anything like that. I'm not even sure why her pa wants her back home, but that's his problem."

"What about the prisoner?"

"Just send a wire to the Rangers, and they'll come after him."

"I don't know if I should do that." McBride cleared his throat and admitted, "The sheriff usually makes those decisions, and he won't be back until day after tomorrow."

Cole didn't miss a beat. "You keep him here for me, and I'll come back this way after taking her home. If no one's come to claim him, I'll take him back myself."

Caitlin glanced over her shoulder to see a deep frown of deliberation on the deputy's face. At last, he nodded his head. "All right, I'll do it. Can't hurt nothing to keep him locked up a spell. And you promise to come back for him?"

Cole extended his hand and spoke reverently. "You have my word. You haven't seen the last of Shane Weldon."

Fourteen

Caitlin couldn't believe Cole was laughing. After all that had happened, he was laughing so hard he'd couldn't speak. She turned away from him and knelt to wash her face in the stream.

"I wish I knew what you think is so funny."

"The look on your face in that sheriff's office."

They had left Weldon in the diligent care of Deputy McBride and rode out of town as if they didn't have a care in the world. Once the town was well behind them and the silhouette of buildings was no longer visible, they took off as if the devil himself was on their heels. Only for the sake of the horses did they stop to rest at a stream partially hidden behind a grouping of boulders.

Guilt nagged at Caitlin's conscience leaving Weldon in jail, even knowing he would have done the same to them. They had taken his weapons but not his money or his horse. Cole explained to the deputy that the horse belonged to the Rangers, and they would need it to transport him back to San Antonio. Caitlin vowed to return Weldon's gunbelt and rifle once this nightmare was over.

She glanced over her shoulder to see Cole settling down on the ground, leaning back on his elbows. He had doubted her plan but could think of nothing more practical, and she refused to leave Weldon for the buzzards. However, he did take to the role with surprising enthusiasm, and she suggested that he had missed his calling.

"Me? A lawman?" he'd asked doubtfully.

With smug delight, she said, "No, an actor."

Even now, she thought he looked rather pleased with himself, but she wasn't sure if he was savoring jailing Weldon or embarrassing her.

"Had I known you would enjoy my little charade so much, I wouldn't have suggested it. Surely, you could have thought of something a little more respectable to say about me."

"It's the truth," he insisted. The smile on his face was absolutely wicked. "Any woman who would poison a Texas Ranger is too mean to work in a whorehouse."

Caitlin felt a smile threaten her own lips, and she splashed Cole with her dripping hands. He caught her gently by the arm and pulled her down beside him. She found herself staring up at him. He was no longer laughing, but his eyes were bright with merriment and a smile lingered on his lips.

She swallowed. "Do you forgive me?"

He stroked his knuckles along her cheek. "Forgive you?"

"For letting Weldon talk me into following you," she explained. "I should have waited for you."

His lips followed the path of his knuckles. "Did he give you a choice?"

"No, not really," she admitted. She thought for a moment and regarded him openly. "That really didn't matter to you, did it?"

He shook his head. "No, it didn't. I should have listened to you."

Caitlin cupped his cheek and smiled. "You can't believe that I would really turn you in to the law. You know I love you, Cole."

"Yeah, I know that." Sadness flickered in his eyes. "Do you know that you're the only person who ever loved me?"

She fingered the dark hair at his temple, her heart aching for him. "I can't believe that. What about your mother?"

"She cared about me," he replied without hesitation. "But she thought having a child would fix everything and make Sean into a decent family man. When that didn't happen, she felt like I let her down."

Caitlin squeezed her eyes against the sudden rush of tears. She hated the thought of a little boy feeling so unloved, and she suddenly felt no better than his family. She had professed to love Cole but walked away from him when her faith in him was challenged.

"I never meant to hurt you," she swore. "I was just so afraid—"

"Shh, don't cry." He brushed his lips over hers. "You were raised to run to your father when you were frightened. I was raised to be frightened of my father more than anything else."

"I wish your father had been more like mine."

He grinned at the thought. "I can't even imagine that."

Later that afternoon, Caitlin awoke so stiff and sore she groaned aloud at the effort to sit up on the bedroll. She glanced around and caught sight of Cole staring in the direction of the rising sun. More than once, she'd caught him gazing off into the distance, and she wondered what he hoped was out there.

As quietly as she could, Caitlin stole across the clearing and let her gaze follow his. The sky was thinly veiled by clouds, but the sun shone through, promising a clear day.

"Stay back. We can't let anyone see us."

Her heart lurched in her chest. "Are we there?"

"Almost."

She squinted against the sunlight and could just barely make out the cluster of buildings springing up from the flat expanse of grassland.

"Don't you recognize it?"

Caitlin looked at him, puzzled. "Have we been here before?"

He grinned and the answer dawned on her. "This is where Sally was living when we first left Eden!"

"Yeah. Some old geezer left her that house, and she hangs on to it just to have a place to go when she needs one." His expression grew serious. "Or when she needs a place to hide someone out."

Caitlin frowned. "Will."

"I've never known her to turn him down."

Hope sprang up inside Caitlin. "Let's go."

"Whoa, wait a minute." Cole caught her by the arm and led her down a narrow path that led to a cliff overlooking the town. "I'm not going in there until I know who all is there."

Caitlin bit her lip and tried to understand, but her doubt was clear. Cole pinned her with a look so dire she shivered. "The last thing we want is to ride in there and find ourselves surrounded by Will and a bunch of thugs."

Lying flat on their stomachs, Cole and Caitlin peered over the edge of the cliff. A row of weathered buildings stood in a barren clearing, and the place looked deserted. Panic knifed through Caitlin's heart. What if they were too late?

Will Thornton often bragged about not being a patient man, and Caitlin had no doubt what would happen to her child when Will tired of waiting for them. She glanced over at Cole, and his face gave no indication that he was worried.

A light breeze passed over Caitlin's face and she heard distant voices and the faint laughter of a child. Cole's hand on her shoulder barely stopped her before she scrambled to her feet. Desperately, she scanned the row of buildings and the overgrown lot before spotting two figures walking down the hill at the far end of the town.

She still had to squint against the sun, but she could see him. It was Jamie, scrambling downhill, holding the hand of a woman Caitlin immediately

recognized as Sally, and laughing. He was all right.
He was all right.

She was barely able to drag enough air into her
lungs before Cole's hand clamped over her mouth.
She struggled and gestured toward the child, but
he shook his head adamantly.

"We can't let them know we're here."

She tugged at his arm and pleaded with her eyes.
She had been patient, she had trusted him, and now
he wouldn't let her claim her child. Tears spilled
down her face and over his fingers, and she could
only watch as Sally led Jamie by the hand into the
house.

Her chest was heaving with stifled sobs, and her
legs buckled beneath her weight when Cole gingerly pulled her to her feet. Without complaint, he
scooped her into his arms and carried her to their
hidden campsite. He sat her down gently, but she
toppled over like a rag doll without enough stuff-
ing.

She huddled into a ball on the fragrant carpet
of pine needles and tried to understand the need
to wait. Barreling into town now would be disastrous, she knew that, but she was devastated to
know her precious baby was so close and not be
able to reach him.

The feel of Cole's hand on her shoulder startled
her, and she tensed. Rather than pull away, he
eased her into his arms and rocked her gently.

"Everything is going to be fine," he murmured
against her ear. "He's not hurt, and we'll slip in
as soon as I know exactly what we're up against."

She nodded against his shoulder and swallowed back another sob. Cole wouldn't take chances with a crying female tagging along, signaling their arrival like an army bugler. She drew a deep calming breath but lingered in his arms a little longer.

The minutes dragged like hours, and Caitlin began to believe Cole would never be satisfied with the situation. He patiently inspected his rifle and cleaned and reloaded the pistols, all the while Caitlin's nerves grew taut as piano wire. For all they knew, the ideal moment might not ever arrive.

They built no fire and twilight brought a chill to the air. Cole checked the horses one last time and at last came to stand over Caitlin. "Are you sure you can go through with this?"

She took his hand and rose to her feet. "Whatever happens, I have to be there, and Jamie has to know I came for him."

"I haven't seen any sign of Will, but that doesn't mean he's not here." Cole paused while she considered the possibility of facing Will's intent on revenge. "If he's not there, the less said to Sally the better."

"What are you going to tell her?"

"Nothing. I'm going to let her tell me what she thinks is going on and go along with her." Cole put his arms around her and stroked her back. "No matter what, we won't leave without him."

They rode silently into town, and Caitlin thought things looked more desolate than they had the first time she had been here. She recognized Sally's house right away and wondered what was keeping it from collapsing down around the woman's ears. They left their horses a short distance away and stole quietly along the back lot and slipped unnoticed onto the sagging back porch.

Caitlin held her breath as Cole raised his fist and pounded on the door. Inside, they could hear a chair scooting across the floor and the clatter of dishes, but no voices. Cole knocked again.

"Hold your horses!" Sally's voice accompanied her footsteps, and the door suddenly burst open. "What do you want—Cole! My God, I didn't think you'd be here for another week."

"You were expecting me?"

"Of course, I was expecting—" Sally caught sight of Caitlin and started to close the door, but Cole blocked the entrance with his shoulder. "What's she doing here?"

"I want my—"

Cole caught hold of Caitlin's arm and jerked her back behind him. "I'm looking for Will, Sally. Have you seen him?"

"He ain't here now," she informed them. "Took off two days ago, the son-of-a-bitch."

"Can we come in?" he asked. "I need to talk with you."

Cole stepped inside the kitchen and seated himself in a chair at the table. Caitlin was frantic. She wanted to know where Jamie was, and she wanted him back right now. She held her tongue, but only because Cole pinned her with a look that warned her to keep quiet.

A bottle of whiskey was sitting on the table, and

Sally filled her own glass and another one for him. "So, you came for the kid, I suppose."

Cole heard the strangled cry of alarm escape Caitlin's throat, but she didn't say anything. Instead, he felt her slump forward, catching herself on the back of his chair. Cole shrugged. "I came to find out what this is really all about."

"Don't ask me," Sally told him over her glass. "Ask her. She's the one trying to get rid of him."

"What are you talking about?" Caitlin's control snapped. "If you don't give me—"

"Shut up, Caitlin!" She froze, and he grabbed her arm and shoved her into the chair beside him. Cole suspected Sally didn't have a clue about Will abducting the child, and he couldn't let Caitlin say anything otherwise. Sally would balk at anything that might go against what Will wanted, right or wrong.

He glared at Caitlin and hoped she would forgive him. "Don't say another word you hear me?"

She nodded slowly, staring up at him as if he were a stranger.

Sally seemed pleased by the exchange, but nothing else was said until she lit a thin cigar and tossed the match into a forgotten coffee cup. "He's a good kid, Cole. I can't imagine anybody not wantin' him."

Cole nodded. "Caitlin and I have come to an understanding on a few matters, and she sees how wrong she was."

"I figured her family was behind most of it."

"They were," he agreed. "But she understands

now that I'm her family. Me and the boy, and things will be different from now on."

"Mommy?"

Caitlin shot out of her chair at the sound of the sleepy voice and ran toward the tiny figure standing in the doorway of the kitchen, rubbing his eyes. She dropped to her knees and scooped him into her arms. "Hello, sweetie."

His little arms found their way around her neck, and she buried her face in his dark hair, "Oh, baby, Mommy missed you so much."

Cole downed the liquor in his glass to burn away the knot forming in his throat. The boy's face was buried against Caitlin's throat, and Cole couldn't see what he looked like. The knot in his throat gave way to a tight ache in his chest, and he turned back to Sally and asked, "What did you tell him?"

She frowned. "About what?"

"Why he was here . . . with you?"

"Oh, that," she said as if it were a minor point. "I didn't tell him anything. Will was positive you'd come for him, but I wasn't so sure . . . seeing as how you didn't know anything about him. I didn't want him waiting on somebody who wasn't going to show up."

"He thinks he was just here for a visit?"

She nodded. "I had no idea you'd be showing up with her."

Cole glanced back at Caitlin. She was still holding the boy, and Cole heard her sniffle and choke back tears. "We're working things out," he finally

said, reaching for the bottle and refilling his glass.
"It's a complicated situation."

"Cole, I never believe more than half of what
Will tells me, that son-of-a-bitch." Sally ground the
stub of her cigar into a saucer. "But if there's even
the slightest chance her family wants to do away
with that child—"

"Her family's got nothing to do with it now."

She nodded and downed a big swallow of whiskey. "I'll take your word, Cole, but if I find out
different you'll be sorry."

Cole was puzzled. He'd never known Sally to
care about anyone to the point of threatening revenge, and he wondered what she would do if she
knew the truth behind Will's lies about Caitlin's
family. "He'll be all right. I promise."

Sally glanced over his shoulder, and he turned
around to see Caitlin sitting on the floor with the
child in her lap. She was whispering something in
his ear, and he started giggling and let his head
fall back against her shoulder. Cole felt everything
inside him twist into knots, and he could only stare
at the tiny face that did look so much like his.

The boy's dark hair was mussed from sleep and
fell in his eyes the way Cole's always did, and his
sleepy smile revealed white baby teeth and the dim-
ple Cole had hated growing up.

Cole had to force his attention back to Sally's
lecture on parenting.

"I don't want you two playing fast and loose with
his feelings," she warned. "Don't promise him things
you can't deliver."

Cole's eyes narrowed. "What do you mean?"

She leaned forward and lowered her voice. "I mean, don't you fill him up with a lot of talk about having a pa and then turn out just like Sean Thornton."

Cole tossed another stick of wood on the fire and stirred the glowing embers until the warmth filled the shallow cave. He stared into the dancing flames for a long time, trying not to think about what Sally had told him.

He looked up at Caitlin sitting across from him with the boy in her lap. She was trying to rock him to sleep but his eyes were wide open, peering over at Cole. When he realized Cole had caught him staring, he buried his face against Caitlin's shoulder. She combed her fingers through his hair and urged him to go to sleep.

"You need some rest yourself," Cole told her.

She looked up. "Yes, I'm exhausted."

"About the things I said back there . . . at Sally's, you know I didn't mean—"

"I understand." Caitlin brushed a kiss against Jamie's forehead. "As long as we got out of there, I won't complain."

Indeed, that had taken some fast talking on Cole's part. Sally had insisted that they stay the night, and Cole feared she would become suspicious when they refused. A midnight encounter with Will would be disastrous, at best, and Cole wouldn't risk their lives on the chance that Will might not show up at three in the morning drunk and looking for a fight. He offered the only excuse he knew Sally would accept.

Caitlin's family, he told her, had the Texas Rangers hunting them, and he didn't want to have the law coming for them at her house and risk getting Will thrown back in prison. Sally agreed wholeheartedly and sent them on their way.

He made his way around the fire and helped Caitlin to her feet. Jamie's body hung in her arms, and he started to cry when she placed him on the bedroll. She dropped down beside him, and he quieted immediately and snuggled close to her.

"Mommy, who's at man?"

"Shh," she murmured. "You go to sleep and I'll tell you all about him in the morning."

For a long time, Cole watched them sleeping. The fire died down, and he added more wood to keep the darkness from hiding them from his eyes. The boy was curled up with his back against Caitlin, and her arm was draped over his chest.

He tried to find some satisfaction in saving his son, but he couldn't escape the ugly fact that he was the reason for the boy being in jeopardy in the first place. He had condemned Caitlin for not giving the child his name, but how many times had he wished his name wasn't Thornton?

He thought of all the times he'd awakened in the night and prayed his father wouldn't return. For a while he tried to believe his mother when she assured him that Sean really did love them and couldn't help being mean when he drank. Cole glanced back at Caitlin and Jamie. He rarely got drunk, but he did take a drink when he wanted one . . . what if—

He stopped himself right there. He refused to believe that whiskey alone could ever make him hurt Caitlin or his son.

The life he'd made was nothing to offer a woman and a child: a two-room house, some land, and cattle. He wouldn't be offering them anything, but taking away everything Duncan McDonnell could give them. The last thing he wanted was for his son to grow up wishing for more of a father.

Caitlin tried to sit up, but her arm had fallen asleep from the weight of Jamie's head pillowed in the crook of her elbow. She reached out and gently cradled his head and moved him over just enough to free her arm. The feeling rushed back into her arm like a thousand needles pricking her skin, and she brushed a kiss against his cheek before rising to her feet.

Feeling as if she'd been beaten, Caitlin stretched her aching muscles and brushed her hair out of her face. Cole was nowhere in sight, but a fire was already burning and the horses were saddled and waiting. No doubt, he'd gone to find something for their breakfast. She started toward the stream to fill the coffeepot but stopped when she realized she would be going out of sight from Jamie.

The last thing she wanted was for him to wake up and find himself alone. She could wait for coffee and settled beside the fire where she could watch

Jamie while he slept. She must have woken up at least a dozen times during the night, needing to reassure herself that Jamie was still with her and still safe. That finding him wasn't a wonderful dream that would end and leave her aching for her child.

Caitlin started shaking, suddenly overwhelmed with relief that it was all over. She hugged herself and rubbed her arms hoping to warm herself, but the chill was coming from inside.

"What's wrong?"

She turned at the sound of Cole's voice and shook her head. "Nothing. It just struck me how close I really did come to losing him. I was worried sick before, but I wouldn't let myself think about living without him."

"Well, you have him back now. Be happy."

His dismissive tone stung, and he went about pouring water from a canteen into the coffeepot and stirring the fire without looking at her even once. The grim expression on his face and the stiff set of his shoulders sounded an alarm in Caitlin's mind.

The coffee was finally ready and Cole filled two cups, handing one to Caitlin. She took the cup, swallowing back the lump rising in her throat, and tried not to read too much into his silence. The coffee was too hot, so she set the cup aside to cool and let her hands rest on her knees.

When he leaned against a tree at the edge of the clearing rather than sit with her to drink his coffee, she knew something was wrong. Something that had nothing to do with Will Thornton.

"We should get going as soon as possible." He spoke without looking at her. "If you plan on feeding the boy breakfast, you'd better wake him up."

"His name is Jamie."

"I know what his name is." Cole sipped his coffee as if they were discussing the weather. "Just do whatever you need to do so we can get going."

"Where are you taking us?"

He turned his head slightly. "I'm taking you back home to your father where you belong."

"We belong with you." She wasn't prepared for this. She couldn't believe he felt nothing for his own child. "You said so last night, when Sally asked—"

"I told you I didn't mean those things I said," he reminded her. "I said what I did to get us out of there alive."

Caitlin's joy over finding Jamie had filled her with all sorts of wonderful plans for the future, and he was tearing them all down around her. "You said we were going to be a family."

"Don't, Caitlin." He pitched what was left of his coffee onto the ground and packed the cup away. "Don't make this more unpleasant than it has to be."

Her heart sank. "You're just going to leave us behind? Abandon your son?"

"He's better off not knowing I'm his father."

"How can he not know?"

"Because you're not going to tell him. As far as he's concerned, I'm just a man who helped you bring him home. A month from now, he won't even remember me."

"Cole, please don't do this to Jamie." She swallowed hard and forced herself to speak calmly. "Just because you don't want me anymore."

His hands stilled. "What are you talking about?"

"I know our situation is unusual, but there's no reason you shouldn't be part of Jamie's life." She struggled to remain practical and think of Jamie's feelings and not her own. "You can visit him from time to time, and when he's older—"

"When he's older, he'll wish you'd left well enough alone." Cole still wouldn't look at her. "I know what I'm talking about, Caitlin. Last night when I made out like I was mad at you and told you to shut up, that's the way my pa was every day of his life." He shook his head. "Of course, he'd probably backhand you across the mouth for good measure."

"You're nothing like your father."

"How do you know?" he demanded. "You saw him only once, for five minutes, and he scared the daylights out of you."

She couldn't deny it, but she wouldn't believe Cole could ever be anything like that. "You make it sound like you have no choice in the matter."

"Maybe I don't." He shrugged and looked away for a minute. "I haven't told you very much about the last three years, but believe me when I tell you I'd be dead if I weren't like my father."

"What do you mean?"

"I mean I've killed men to survive, Caitlin." He paused long enough for her to absorb the statement, but cut off her response. I don't just mean killing men who were trying to kill me. I mean killing men who were out to take what belonged to me. I found out I can be ruthless when it comes to protecting what's mine."

"But you can turn your back on us without hesitation?"

"It's the only way I *can* protect you."

Before she could respond, he turned and stalked out of their little camp, leaving her to stare at his retreating back.

Caitlin reached down for her coffee and took only a sip, disappointed to find it had grown cold and bitter. She tossed the dark brew onto the ground and let the cup fall to her feet.

"Mommy?"

She started at the sound of Jamie's voice, soft and raspy from sleep, and walked over and knelt down on the bedroll. She smiled at him and opened her arms. "Good morning, sweetheart."

He scrambled into her embrace, his tiny arms finding their way around her neck, and she brushed a kiss on his neck. She didn't have to look to know he was rubbing the sleep from his eyes with the back of his fist, and she stroked his back with her fingers. "Did the sandman find you last night?"

He leaned back to look at her and said, "So'd you."

"Yes, I did." Her throat was nearly raw with unshed tears and the words would barely leave her mouth. "I missed you so much."

He raised a tiny finger to her face and traced the line of a tear on her face. "I live with you, don' I? At Papaw's house?"

She kissed the tip of his nose. "Of course, you do."

"Not with Sally and that some-bitch."

"Jamie!" Caitlin gasped and pressed her finger against his lips, choking back startled laughter. "That's not a nice thing for little boys to say."

She couldn't keep from smiling, and his tiny mouth curled into a mischievous grin beneath her fingers. Caitlin hugged him close, hating to think what other choice phrases he'd learned.

Memories.

Cole had envied the memories she carried of Jamie, and she remembered the longing in his eyes when he asked about the child. She knew Cole believed he was doing what was best, but she didn't see why she should make it easy for him. They had a long trip ahead of them, and she intended to give Cole enough memories of Jamie to last a lifetime.

She combed Jamie's hair out of his eyes with her fingers. "Let's get ready so we can go back home."

The water from the stream was cold, and, despite his protests, Caitlin washed Jamie's face and hands as best she could. Cole kept his distance while they ate the biscuits he left waiting by the fire. As soon as they were finished, Cole doused the fire with the last of the coffee and asked if they were ready to leave.

"Yes, we are." Caitlin took Jamie's hand and led him toward the horses. "Honey, I need you to ride with Mr. Thornton on his horse. Can you do that for Mommy?"

Cole was more reluctant than Jamie. "He can ride with you just fine."

"No, he'll be safer riding with you." Caitlin wasn't backing down. "My horse is too small to ride double, and I'm not as good a rider as you are."

She didn't wait for his answer, but swept the child up and placed him astride Cole's horse. "Hold on to the saddle horn as tight as you can."

Cole scowled at her but mounted up behind Jamie without a word, leaving her to manage her climbing into her own saddle alone. She did so with a bit of trouble and smiled sweetly. "Whenever you're ready."

Without a word, he turned his horse and led them out of the ravine, onto the main path.

Fifteen

Cole had never felt as sorry for anyone in his life as he did watching Jamie suffer through what had to be the most thorough washing any kid ever had. Caitlin had scrubbed him over twice, and the skin on his fingers and toes was starting to prune up. Now she had his hair lathered up, and Cole wondered if she meant to scrub him bald.

"I have never seen such a dirty little boy," she said for at least the third time. "Close your eyes, so I can rinse your hair."

At last she hauled him out of the tub and began drying him with a towel. Cole leaned back in the chair and tried to ignore the silly things Caitlin said to the boy and the way he giggled when she tickled his belly.

Once they had checked into the hotel and ordered up hot water, Cole had taken off. He stabled the horses overnight at the livery, purchased the things Caitlin needed from the mercantile, and took his own bath at the bathhouse. Finally, there was nothing else he could do but return to the hotel room, hoping they would both be asleep.

Instead, Caitlin had done everything backward.

Jamie had his nap first and was just now getting a bath, and Caitlin insisted Cole wait so they could decide what to do about dinner.

"I got the stuff you wanted." He motioned toward the bundles he'd placed on the bed.

"Good. I appreciate you doing the shopping for me." She finished drying Jamie and searched through the store-bought clothes. Soon she had him decked out in new underwear, socks, a blue flannel shirt, and brown corduroy overalls. She combed his wet hair with a side part and slicked it back. "Now you look like my sweet little boy."

"He looks miserable."

Caitlin's head popped up at that. "What are you talking about?"

"You've got him buttoned up like an old-maid's corset." Reluctantly, he looked at Jamie. "Come here, boy."

He unbuttoned the top two buttons of Jamie's shirt and loosened the straps on his overalls. "That's better, isn't it?"

Jamie nodded, casting a mutinous look Caitlin's way.

"Well, suit yourself, young man." She folded the wet towel and hung it over the back of a chair. "You two run along while I take my bath."

Cole shot to his feet. She hadn't said anything about him taking the boy anywhere. "What do you mean?"

"The maid is going to empty the tub and bring more hot water. I'd like to have a little privacy.

Surely, you can entertain him for a couple of hours."

"A couple of hours? What all have you got to do?"

"A lady needs more time." She shooed them toward the door. "I saw a restaurant down the street. You can take him for an early supper."

"We can wait for you downstairs."

"Don't be silly. I'll have something later. Right now, all I want is a tub of hot water and privacy. Run along."

Cole stepped out into the hall, and the door shut in his face before he could say anything else. He looked down to see Jamie peering up at him skeptically. Somehow he had to get through the next few hours alone with the boy and not let himself fall into the trap Caitlin was setting for him.

Caitlin brushed and braided her hair, pinning the long braid into a coil at the nape of her neck. She had been dressed for over half an hour, and she wondered where on earth Cole had taken off to with Jamie.

She peered out the window and saw Cole moving down the sidewalk, Jamie trotting alongside holding on to his hand. The child was wearing a new hat, a hat that looked suspiciously like the one Cole wore. Cole's steps halted, and he leaned over to hear what Jamie was saying. Cole hefted the child into his arms and carried him the rest of the way to the hotel.

She hurried across the room and settled into a chair, pretending to read a newspaper. The doorknob rattled, and Jamie burst into the room followed by Cole.

"Mommy, look!" He waved his new hat, holding it out for her to see. "Cole buyed me a hat!"

"He did?" She took the miniature Stetson from him and admired the color and the material. "I've never seen such a fine hat."

Jamie smiled and pointed to the hatband. "See there. Just like Cole's."

Caitlin glanced up in time to catch the smile sneaking up on Cole's face. She understood only too well the warmth and pride he felt for his son, but she also saw the restraint and forced aloofness in his posture. The smile disappeared before he thought she saw it, and the indifference returned.

"What time did you want to leave in the morning?"

Her question caught him off guard, and he hesitated. "We're not leaving tomorrow . . . not together, anyway."

"What on earth are you talking about?"

"I sent a telegram to your father as soon as we got to town. He's already on his way, and he'll be taking you home."

"I can't believe you did that." Caitlin was flabbergasted. He'd wired her father to come take them off his hands like a burden he couldn't wait to be rid of. "I can't believe you did that without asking me first."

"What you want doesn't matter." He pinned her

with a look so cold she shivered. "I know what you're trying to do, and it isn't fair." He glanced at Jamie. "It's not fair to anyone."

Fair! He was telling her about fair! Caitlin was tempted to tell him a few things about fairness, but the confusion in Jamie's eyes silenced her heated reply. Instead, she only nodded. "Life is never fair."

He shrugged. "I won't leave town until your father gets here."

She supposed that was meant to be comforting. "In case I need you?"

His eyes narrowed slightly, but he only said, "Good night, Caitlin."

"Wait, Cole!" Jamie ran toward the door. "Wait for me!"

"You stay here with your ma."

"Where're you goin'?"

Caitlin wanted to know where he was going, too, but knew he wouldn't tell her that. "I thought we could at least have supper together."

"The hotel has a kitchen. I'll have them bring something up for you." He opened the door and stepped out into the hall, but he paused long enough to ruffle Jamie's hair. "You remember what I told you about taking care of your ma."

As an afterthought he glanced back at Caitlin over his shoulder. "Keep this door locked."

The door closed and Jamie's lip began to tremble. Caitlin carefully placed his hat on the dresser and hurried to gather the little boy in her arms. "Don't be sad, sweetie. He'll be back in the morning."

Jamie nodded against her shoulder, but she felt him draw a ragged breath and fight back tears. She'd set out to coerce Cole into caring about his son, but she'd failed to consider how Jamie would feel when he walked away.

The window had no screen or curtain, and Cole had made the mistake of taking a room that faced east. He groaned as the sunlight bolted into the room without warning, and he rolled over to shield his eyes. The thin, lumpy mattress and the boisterous lovers in the next room had kept him awake most of the night, but he didn't regret settling into a hotel other than the one where he'd put Jamie and Caitlin.

It was the only way he could stay away from them. Caitlin was temptation enough, offering him body and soul, but keeping Jamie at a distance was unbearable. Cole had never seen a smarter or more lovable kid, and he had wanted so badly to tell Jamie that he was his father.

Instead, he'd kept his mouth shut and let the little boy think he was just a nice man who was taking him home, and even that had been a pitfall. Cole thought buying the boy a hat would ease his conscience, but that backfired, as well.

"I want one just like yours," Jamie had told him, and his eyes filled with hero-worship. "We'll be just alike."

Anxious to get this day behind him, Cole rolled out of bed and crossed the room to the battered washstand. He hunkered down over the basin and splashed cold water on his face, studying his reflection in the scarred mirror. Without any sleep, he felt like hell and it showed, but he wasn't going to meet Duncan McDonnell looking like a saddletramp. He collected his shaving gear and did the best he could to salvage his appearance.

Just as he was dressed and pulling on his boots, the sound of gunfire erupted in the street below. Without hesitating, he grabbed his gunbelt and ran down the stairs toward the hotel entryway. He'd barely cleared the doorway when several like-minded men stumbled onto the sidewalk along with him, all armed and ready to defend themselves and their town.

It took a few seconds to realize they'd all been fooled, and every man tried to shrug off his chagrin and watch as the Wild West show paraded into town. Kids filed onto the sidewalks to cheer and wave at cowboys, Indians, and assorted characters. The parade stopped in the middle of town, and the leader invited all the children to attend the show that would be starting within the hour and plan to return that evening for the full performance.

The parade resumed, and Cole swore he recognized at least one man sporting a mountain man getup and waving to the crowd. At least a dozen kids trailed after the outfit, and a dozen more squalled because their mothers wouldn't let them go. He glanced across the street and saw Caitlin, holding Jamie, wave at him and smile.

Cursing himself a fool, Cole sprinted across the

street and stepped up onto the sidewalk beside them. Jamie was staring after the parade in wide-eyed amazement and took little notice of Cole, but Caitlin ran her hand along his arm, and said, "Good morning."

"Cole!" Jamie cried, pointing in the direction of the winding parade. "Look at that!"

Without warning, Jamie lunged out of Caitlin's arms and Cole barely caught him. Heedless, the boy locked his arms around Cole's neck. "Take me! Take me!"

"Jamie!" Caitlin scolded. "Settle down."

"Please, Cole, please!"

"There may not be enough time before my father arrives." The halfhearted excuse Caitlin offered didn't dissuade Jamie in the least. "Do you know what time he'll be here?"

"No, I don't."

Cole knew he was being wheedled into something he didn't want to do, but he could only blame himself. If he had gone back inside that hotel instead of crossing the street, he would have escaped the entire conversation. Instead, he found himself looking into Jamie's pleading eyes and was unable to refuse anything the child wanted.

Just a few more hours, he told himself, wouldn't do any more damage than had already been done, and there was no true reason the child shouldn't enjoy something so simple.

Cole lowered Jamie to his feet and straightened the little Stetson atop the boy's head and said, "I think we have plenty of time to see the show."

Jamie squealed with delight and clapped his hands, and Cole felt ten feet tall just from being able to give the boy something that meant so much to him. Regret knifed through Cole's heart just thinking of all the times that lay ahead for someone else to provide for this child who asked so little. He hated to think of Jamie peering up at another man with that same gut-wrenching adoration, but he would hate even more for Jamie to ever look at him and see what Cole had seen in his own father.

Cole glanced over at Caitlin and shrugged. "Let's go."

"You two run along," she insisted, giving Cole a gentle shove. "I haven't packed the first thing, and I know Papa will be anxious to return."

Dismayed, Cole could only look at her in silent reproach. *This won't make any difference.*

She smiled slightly and replied likewise. *It already has.*

Caitlin knew Cole resented her for backing him into a corner where Jamie was concerned, but she was determined not to let him walk away from his son unscathed. All the years before he hadn't known about the boy and sorely blamed her for not telling him. Well, now he knew, and what he did was his choice.

She watched them cross the street and make their way to the grassy field at the end of town where the show was about to start. Cole had slowed his pace, but Jamie still had to hurry to keep up with his long strides. A lump rose in Caitlin's throat as she watched Jamie's tiny hand reach up to grasp Cole's much larger one.

When they reached the edge of the clearing and disappeared down the slope leading to the field, she turned around and ducked inside the general store. She took her time selecting the few items she needed and headed back to the hotel, preparing to face her next battle. Her father.

No doubt, Papa would be furious with her, but she was none too happy with him. Thanks to his interference, Cole almost ended up in jail. She hoped her father would finally trust her judgment when he learned how easily Cole was able to reclaim Jamie for her. Papa would be pleased, at least, to learn that Cole had no intentions of claiming his family or taking them away.

Caitlin made her way inside the hotel room and set about packing their things. She tried to tell herself that she didn't want Cole if he felt only obligation toward her and Jamie, but deep inside she knew she wasn't too proud to accept obligation if he wouldn't offer love.

The room was warm, and she opened the window to allow a little fresh air inside. In the distance, she could hear the Wild West show in full swing, and she smiled, imagining Jamie's awe at the sight of those whooping Indians and lasso-wielding cowboys. She peered out the window to see if she could catch a glimpse of the production, but the view from the hotel was blocked by the other buildings.

She considered walking over to the show once the packing was done, but she wanted to talk with her father before he saw Jamie or Cole. Somehow, she would make him listen to reason.

A knock at the door startled her, and her heart began to race knowing that Papa was here so soon to take them home and away from Cole. Steeling herself for the confrontation, Caitlin crossed the room and opened the door.

And found herself staring into the lecherous gleam in Will Thornton's eyes.

"Well, well, look who we have here," he sneered and blocked Caitlin's hasty attempt to slam the door in his face. "Why, Caitlin, you weren't going to invite me in?"

Caitlin stumbled backward, but he caught her arm and hauled her into his embrace, leering down at her with the devil's own smile.

"We just keep running into each other, don't we?"

She pushed hard against his chest and tried to twist out of his grip, but he held tight. "Please," she gasped. "Please let me go."

"Uh-uh." He shook his head and tightened his hold so that she could barely draw a breath. "Last time I saw you, you wanted to come with me. Change your mind?"

"For your own good, Will, you'd better get out of here." She knew he was looking for Cole, and her mind was groping desperately for the lie that would send him away. "My father will be back any minute, and he'll kill you."

"Your father?" He didn't believe her. "I thought you'd be with Cole."

"He left me," she gasped, her face only inches away from his. "He refused to go after Jamie. We had a fight, and he left."

Will's eyes narrowed. "Did he refuse or weasel out?"

She knew what he wanted to hear. "He was afraid you would kill him."

"He was right," he assured her. "So that leaves you and me to settle this thing."

She nodded, realizing he didn't know that Jamie was no longer with Sally. "Yes, it does. If you return my child unharmed, I'll see that nothing happens to you."

He laughed at her, and the cruel delight in his eyes only made her more determined to keep him away from Jamie.

"Who's gonna see that nothing happens to you?"

"I sent a telegram to my father, and he came to take me home." She meant it as a warning, but Will didn't scare easy. "He should be back any minute. I thought that was him knocking at the door."

"I was hoping to surprise you."

"Please, Will." Caitlin's pride deserted her and she begged. "Please leave me alone."

"I imagine your pa would be real anxious to get you home." Will smiled, combing his fingers through her hair. "I bet he'd pay any amount of money to have you back alive."

"If you leave right now, I'll see that he sends you anything you want."

"Oh, he'll do that all right." Will drew a wicked-looking knife from his belt and twisted his other hand in her hair when she tried to pull away. "Money ain't all I want, Caitlin. You owe me. You owe me a lot more than money."

Before she could even scream, he raised the knife and sliced a thick lock of hair from her head. "Let's leave Daddy a little somethin' to remember you by."

"What do you mean, leave something for him?"

"You and I are going on a little trip." He lowered his head so that his breath fell against her ear. "Just the two of us."

Panic clawed its way into her brain, and she barely choked back a scream. Even if someone could hear her over the shouts of the carnival performers and their clamoring audience, the last thing she wanted was for Cole to rush to her aid, dragging Jamie along with him.

Caitlin knew what would happen when Will and Cole encountered one another. One of them, if not both, would end up dead, and the odds against Jamie escaping the crossfire were too great to risk. Right now, the child was safe with Cole, and that's where he had to stay. She wouldn't risk Jamie, even to save herself.

Without warning, Will drove the knife into the wall, and a guttural scream tore from her throat but died on her lips as she watched him loop the shorn lock of her hair around the blade and fashion it into a knot. It looked to all the world like a scalp hanging on the wall.

"Think Daddy will know what that means?"

She nodded mutely. The feel of his hand on her arm brought her back to reality, and he was dragging her out of the room. Her survival instincts reared inside her, refusing to let her go meekly to her doom, and she dug in her heels and fought him.

"Let go of me."

She twisted against his grip like a wild animal caught in a trap, and too late she saw his fist hurtling toward her face. She saw stars, but only a few, before she sank into his arms and into oblivion.

"Carry me."

"Carry you?" Cole scooped Jamie into his arms, and his little body fell limp against Cole's shoulder. "I thought you were going to hunt buffalo."

Jamie yawned in reply, and Cole had to smile at his sleepy companion. "Your mother is going to skin me alive for being gone so long."

Every time Cole tried to coax Jamie away from the show, another thrilling spectacle would unfold in the ring and Jamie would beg to stay. Secretly, Cole enjoyed the show more than he thought he would, but the best part came at the end.

An Indian claiming to be a Cheyenne shaman, decked out in buckskin, feathers, and war paint, rode into the center of the ring and announced that he was looking for one paleface with enough courage to be a warrior. Cole had never heard any Indian spout off so much nonsense, but Jamie was enthralled.

The shaman caught sight of Jamie perched on Cole's shoulders and called him into the ring. Wide-eyed, Jamie stepped forward when Cole set him down. The Indian lowered himself to Jamie's height, spouted a few mysterious phrases, and drew twin stripes of war paint across Jamie's brow. With the ceremony complete, he turned Jamie toward the crowd and declared him to be Running Fox, who would be a great warrior when he grew to manhood. The crowd cheered, and Jamie scampered back to Cole, breathless with excitement.

Cole wondered what Caitlin would have to say about that war paint. Jamie found a feather on the ground that had dropped from one of the elaborate costumes and had Cole tuck it inside his hatband.

Cole stepped inside the hotel, halfway expecting Caitlin to meet him at the door, but the lobby was quiet and the desk clerk only nodded in their direction.

"Are you Cole Thornton?"

Cole jerked around at the sound of his name, one hand on his pistol. He lowered Jamie to his feet and moved to stand between the child and the stranger.

"Papaw!" Jamie pushed past Cole and ran toward the man, hurling himself into the older man's arms.

"Jamie, thank God."

"Look, Papaw, I'm an Injun." Jamie pointed to the paint streaking across his forehead. "Hey, Uncle Cam!"

Jamie ran toward the second man who scooped him up in a bear hug. "How are you, scamp?"

"I'm Running Fox," Jamie corrected.

Cole knew the first man had to be Duncan McDonnell, and he never looked away from the man's intense, accusing stare. At last, McDonnell spoke. "Where's Caitlin?"

"What do you mean? She's waiting for us in the room."

Cole couldn't have anticipated the violent reaction to such a simple statement, but Duncan McDonnell grabbed him by the collar and shoved him against the wall. "What have you done with her, you bastard?"

"Duncan!" his brother shouted.

Cole's first instinct was to smash his fist into McDonnell's face, but he caught sight of Jamie looking on in fright. The last thing he wanted the boy to remember about him was seeing him strike his grandfather. Instead, Cole looked the man in the eye and spoke calmly, "Get your hands off me, Mr. McDonnell."

"Duncan, let him go. This isn't accomplishing anything."

McDonnell released him, but he was no less angry. "Where is my daughter? We knocked on the door but no one answered. The clerk thought she might be with the two of you at the circus."

A tingle of apprehension ran up Cole's spine,

and he nodded toward the stairs. "Let's go." He glanced over at Jamie and said, "Wait here with your uncle."

Cole knocked on the door, but there was no answer. He knocked again and called her name. He withdrew the key from his pocket and tried to ignore the scowl on McDonnell's face.

They stepped inside the room and found things pretty much in order, save for some clothes lying on the floor and the window left open. Cole crossed the room and closed the window.

"Sweet Jesus."

Cole turned around to see what McDonnell had found and caught sight of a knife driven into the wall with a length of pale blonde hair knotted around the blade.

Cole swore out loud and jerked the knife from the wall. "This is Will's doing. His way of letting me know she's with him and daring me to come after her."

"How can you be sure?"

"This knife belonged to my father."

Sixteen

Duncan McDonnell was beginning to believe this nightmare would never end. No sooner than he saw with his own eyes that his beloved grandson was unharmed, he was facing the possibility of losing his daughter. Again.

Cole Thornton would give him no assurances that his uncle might only want money in exchange for Caitlin's safe return.

"He might tell you he wants a ransom," Cole explained. "But that doesn't mean he intends to release her unharmed once he has the money."

Bile rose in his throat, and Duncan thought he might actually be sick with anger and fear. "I'll have every lawman in the state after him by nightfall, but I'm holding you responsible for whatever happens to Caitlin. None of this would be happening if you had left her alone."

"Do you really think I need you to tell me that?"

Duncan glanced over at the young man his grandson favored so strongly. He was used to men dodging his anger, but Cole looked him right in the eye and spoke without hesitation.

"If you send an army after her, she's as good as dead. Like you said, I'm responsible and I'm going after her . . . alone."

"That's suicide!"

"It would be, if this was about me." Cole wound the length of blonde hair around his fist and shoved it into his pocket. "Caitlin is all that matters . . . I'll get her back or die trying."

Duncan recognized the steely determination in the younger man's voice and posture, but he wasn't ready to relinquish responsibility for his daughter's welfare. "I'm going with you."

"No," he said. "This is between me and Will."

"The hell it is!" Duncan advanced on him. "He'll answer for hurting Caitlin, and he'll answer to me."

"We have to think about Jamie," Cole reminded him. "If neither Caitlin nor I return, I know she would want you to raise the boy."

Duncan ran his hand along his jaw, ashamed to admit he hadn't even considered the consequences Jamie would face. His parental instincts compelled him to save his child, and everything else had been blocked out. Still, he couldn't sit idly by while someone else went after Caitlin.

"My brother will take care of Jamie," he finally said. "While we're gone and if we don't come back. I trust him with my life."

Cole studied him for a moment before nodding in acceptance of the proposition. It was a hesitant agreement at best.

Duncan made his way downstairs to find Cameron seated in the lobby with Jamie sleeping peacefully in his lap. After more than forty years, Cameron had no trouble reading Duncan's troubled expression.

"What's happened?"

"Will Thornton has taken Caitlin."

Cam eased Jamie onto the sofa and rose to his feet. "My God, Duncan, what are we going to do?"

"Cole is going after them, and I'm going with him." Duncan placed his hand on his brother's shoulder. "I need you to stay here with the boy."

Cameron recoiled from his touch and glared at him with a fury Duncan would not have thought him capable of reaching. "Damn you, Duncan. Must you always dismiss even the slightest possibility that I am man enough to do more than wait behind while you conquer the world?"

Stunned, Duncan couldn't believe his ears. "What are you talking about? I've never considered you incapable."

"But it didn't even occur to you that I should go with you to find Caitlin," he countered. "You have more confidence in a man you just met half an hour ago than the brother you've known all your life. All you're willing for me to do is stay behind with the child like a wet nurse."

"Are you really fool enough to believe that?" Duncan's anger matched his brother's. "I'm not just asking you to care for Jamie while I'm gone. There is a strong possibility Caitlin may already be lost, and it's very likely that neither the boy's father nor I will return. I'm leaving the boy's life in your hands because I trust you more than any living soul."

But Cameron wasn't ready to relinquish his fury. He'd been waiting his whole life to stand up to his older brother. "That doesn't explain everything else . . . leaving me behind while you worked and fought. Why didn't you want me beside you?"

Duncan couldn't believe, after all these years, Cameron felt cheated. His brother wanted answers, and, by God, Duncan would see that he had them. "Because you were the son our mother wasn't willing to lose!"

Disbelief masked Cameron's anger. "What are you talking about?"

Duncan had tried to forget the past, but even now it hurt to recall his mother's words. Cameron, she decided, was meant for better things than working in coal mines and sweatshops.

"I didn't leave you behind." His voice was husky when he spoke at last. "I was sent to work so there would be money for you to go to school."

"That's not—"

Duncan held up his hand, refusing to hear any denial of the truth. "You were born with a quick mind and I with a strong back. Mother didn't see any sense in wasting either of us."

"My God." Cameron sank down on the sofa. "She never said anything like that to me."

"It doesn't matter now." Duncan gripped his brother's shoulder. "I just wanted you to know that I never considered myself above you."

Cameron only nodded. "I'll take care of Jamie. You don't have to worry about him."

"I won't. Not as long as he's with you."

Caitlin was dimly aware of cold water trickling over her face and down her neck, but she fought consciousness, knowing the torment facing her.

"Wake up, sweetheart." Will laughed and poured more water in her face. "I know you can hear me."

She blinked, her eyes drifting open to find him hovering above her. She started scrambling to her feet, but he forced her to the ground. Caitlin glanced around, trying to determine their whereabouts. Nothing looked familiar, but she was grateful to have Will out of town and away from Jamie.

"I hope you'll be a little more cooperative." Will ran his fingers along her jaw, and Caitlin winced as he touched the swollen skin around her eye. "There's no reason to make this hard on yourself."

She slapped his hand away. "If you're going to rape me, don't expect to enjoy it."

He drew back, as if burned, and she braced herself for another blow. Instead, he laughed bitterly. "I'll enjoy it, Caitlin. Even if I have to kill you first."

The image his words conjured made her shiver, and he went on to say, "I've waited too long for this, and I know just how it's going to be. Nothing you say will make any difference."

He rose to his feet and claimed the horse he'd left to drink at the stream. Her eyes followed him, and she wondered how far they had traveled. The sun was low in the sky, and she guessed the time to be about four o'clock. By now, her father had surely arrived to claim Jamie, and her heart lurched when she realized the conclusions Papa would jump to when he found her missing. Suddenly, she was more afraid for Cole than she was for herself.

Cole refilled both canteens and handed one to Duncan McDonnell. They had spoken less than ten words to each other since leaving town, but Cole was developing a grudging respect for the man who despised him. They had ridden hard for several hours, but McDonnell showed no signs of fatigue or slowing down.

They had stopped only for the sake of the horses, and Cole tried to imagine how formidable the older man must have been twenty years ago. While the horses drank, McDonnell followed a path leading away from the stream toward a grassy spot under some trees.

When he lingered for several minutes, Cole followed him and asked, "See anything?"

McDonnell nodded. "That's what bothers me. He isn't making any effort to hide his tracks."

Cole scanned the area and saw for himself the trampled grass and blackened matchsticks. At least two people had been here earlier but only one horse. There were no signs of a struggle and no blood, and he tried to take that as proof that Caitlin had not been harmed. Not yet, anyway.

"No, he's not hiding from us," Cole agreed. "He definitely wants me to find him."

McDonnell frowned. "Why is that?"

Cole took a deep breath. He had no idea what Caitlin had told her father about him or his family, but there was no point in trying to save face with the man now. "Three years ago I led Will and a man named Jess Martin into an ambush. Martin and another man were killed, and Will went to prison."

"That was the stage robbery they wrote about in the newspapers?"

Cole nodded. "The U.S. Marshal's office didn't want it to be public knowledge that they cut deals with outlaws. So they made up a story declaring the Thorntons dead and sent me away a free man."

"I never questioned Caitlin's reasons for coming back home. Did this have something to do with it?"

"She found a telegram from my uncle and thought I had left her to rejoin the outlaw gang." Cole realized the bitterness he'd carried all these years was gone, and in its place he felt only regret. "I should have followed her, made her listen to the truth."

"As if I would have let her hear it." The older man removed his hat and ran his fingers through his hair. "I suppose you've already figured out that I've known for sometime now that you were alive. I even knew where you were living, but I kept it from Caitlin. Deliberately."

There was a time when Cole would have been infuriated by the admission, but now he understood too well what motivated a man to shield his child from harm. "You were only trying to protect your daughter."

"Perhaps. I was terrified of Caitlin leaving again—afraid I wouldn't see her again. Afraid she wouldn't need me anymore."

"Caitlin loves you." Cole found himself wanting to comfort this man who had done everything in his power to keep him separated from his family. "Even when she's angry at you, she still defends you to me."

Duncan nodded and smiled slightly. "My wife always said I was the most stubborn man she'd ever known."

An awkward silence followed, and Cole turned away to gather the horses and lead them back where McDonnell was waiting. They mounted up and exchanged a look declaring a silent pact of solidarity. From that moment all that mattered was finding Caitlin.

"What's the matter, darlin'? You waiting for me to carry you across the threshold?"

Caitlin glared at Will over her shoulder, and he gave her a none too gentle shove inside the abandoned dugout. She stumbled into the darkness and batted away the sticky shadows. Waves of sickening revulsion washed over her when she realized she was swathed in spider webs. A sob tore from her throat, and she knew the horror had only just begun.

She couldn't see, but she knew Will was just behind her. She could hear his breathing and smell the scent of whiskey that seemed to be a part of him. Even so, the feel of his hands on her body was still a shock, and she recoiled from his touch.

"You don't know when you're done for, do you, gal?" He slid one hand over her breast and squeezed the tender flesh. "You'd better treat me right if you ever want to see that boy again."

Caitlin's chest tightened at the mention of Jamie. She kept telling herself that he was safe. No matter what happened to her, Jamie was safe with Cole and her father. She still felt a tremendous sense of despair knowing she would never see her child again, and the fight drained out of her.

"You'll never take me to see him," she whispered, determined not to die letting Will Thornton think he'd beaten her. "He's safe. Safe with his father."

Will spun her around. "What the hell are you talking about?"

"Cole and I found him . . . at Sally's house." Enough light spilled through the dugout's narrow entrance for her to see the disbelief in his eyes. "You told Sally that my family wanted to get rid of him, and she thought Cole was there because you sent for him. I think she was really happy to see us all together."

"You're lying."

"No, not now. I did lie to you before. When you

found me in the hotel, Cole and Jamie were just a few hundred yards away . . . at the Wild West show, and my father wasn't anywhere near."

He believed her. She saw the rage in his eyes, but she didn't look away. Even when slapped her across the face, she faced him, bolstered by the knowledge that she had spoiled the sweetness of his revenge. The coppery taste of her own blood filled her mouth, but she knew Will's failure was far more bitter.

He shoved her to the dirt floor, but she didn't resist. He was looking to vent his frustration, and Caitlin was unwilling to give him the satisfaction of a new fight. His mouth swooped down on hers, and she parted her lips so that he would taste the blood in her mouth. He jerked away from her and swore out loud.

"All right, Caitlin. You want to fight dirty? That's fine with me." He seized her hands and began coiling a length of rope around her wrists. "I'll leave you to the snakes and spiders, and what they don't want, the rats will finish up."

Will drew the rope tight, chafing her skin, and secured the other end to an iron stove that had long since been abandoned to rust in the damp, earthy shelter. Without another word, he turned and made his way outside, allowing her just a glimpse of the faint twilight before the makeshift curtain fell back in place.

Caitlin huddled her knees to her chest and began rocking back and forth. She had never felt so alone or abandoned, and she recalled the Bible story about Joseph and the coat of many colors. His brothers had thrown him into a pit and left him for dead, but Caitlin had never imagined the aching hopelessness and terror that now filled her soul.

She cried until she wore herself out, and she fought desperately against sleep. As long as she was awake, she didn't feel as vulnerable as she would be lying unaware of the danger creeping up on her. She drew a deep, shuddering breath, and the musty smell of the earthen walls filled her lungs. Dear God, she thought, this must be what the grave is like.

The image made her shake with fear, but the far-off sound of gunfire startled her out of hysteria. She strained her ears and once again heard the blast of a rifle, this time accompanied by the unmistakable sound of hoofbeats. She filled her lungs with stale air and screamed as loud as she could.

"Help me!" she cried. "Please, someone, help me!"

"Son-of-a-bitch!" Duncan lowered his rifle and peered down the steep hill. "I know I hit him. I know it!"

Cole hoped he had. He, too, had seen the flash of white in the darkness, a man's shirt perhaps, and the sudden eruption of gunfire was all the confirmation they needed. Whoever was boxed in in the narrow canyon didn't want them around, and the

trail had been too clear to believe it was anyone
other than Will. And Caitlin.

"Will Thornton!" Cole called out. "It's me—Cole!
Are you man enough to come out and face me?"

The reply came on the hiss of a bullet that rico-
cheted off a wall of rock not two feet above their
heads.

"There's your answer." Duncan raised his arm to
fend off the shower of shattering stone. "He'll stay
holed up in there 'til doomsday."

"Not if he thinks we left."

"What do you mean?"

Cole raised his rifle and fired in the general direction from which the previous shot had come. He
drew return fire immediately, only this time he cried
out in agony.

"I'm hit!" he shouted, motioning for Duncan to
move back from the cliff. "Ah, God, I'll bleed to
death."

Cole knew Will would relish the thought of
wounding him, and sure enough Will couldn't resist
hollering, "Serves you right, you yellow bastard!"

Duncan hurried around the far slope of the canyon while Cole made his way toward the sound of
Will's voice. He heard the crunch of gravel beneath
a man's boots and bolted toward the shadow rising
from behind a rocky outcropping. The surprise of
the attack gave Cole the advantage, and he leveled
his pistol even with Will's temple while the man was
still too stunned to draw his own weapon.

"Where is she, you son-of-a-bitch?"

Will gasped for air. "Who?"

"Don't try my patience, Will." Cole nudged the pistol barrel more firmly against Will's skull. "Answer me or I'll kill you without thinking twice."

"Cole! Help me!" a voice cried out, so faint Cole thought he had imagined it.

He listened. "Help me, please!"

This time he was certain. It was a woman's voice. It had to be Caitlin's, and he didn't have time to waste prying information out of Will. He cocked the revolver and realized he would committing cold-blooded murder. It shouldn't matter, but it did. Only a coward would kill a man whose weapon lay ten feet away.

"Cole, please!" she cried again.

He swore and struck the butt of the pistol against Will's skull, feeling cheated out of his revenge. Will Thornton would have to answer to the law, though he deserved far worse.

Cole raced across the canyon, listening for any trace of Caitlin's voice. The wind picked up, and Cole feared her cries would be blown over the canyon walls. He caught sight of a length of cloth flapping in the wind and hurried to see for himself, desperately grasping at straws.

The fabric hung across the narrow entrance of a crude shelter fashioned in the side of the hill. The interior was black as pitch, and he started to turn away, but an anguished sob reached his ears.

"Caitlin!" he shouted.

"I'm down here!" she cried. "Hurry, Cole, please. I'm frightened."

He was inside the dugout the moment he heard her voice and scanned the dark walls. "Caitlin!"

"Over here."

Her voice was weak now, and he found her slumped against the dirt wall, tethered to an ancient iron stove. He swore and drew his knife, severing the rope binding her wrists. Cole gathered her close, but she was too weak to do little more than smile up at him.

Her breath caught in her throat and she rasped, "Where's Jamie?"

"Don't worry about him," Cole assured her. "He's with your uncle and he's safe."

She nodded, and he scooped her into his arms and turned to leave the darkened cavern.

"Not so fast." Will stood before them, blocking the only exit. "You didn't think it was going to be that easy, did you?"

"Stand aside, Will." Cole felt Caitlin tremble and tightened his hold on her. "If you're determined for one of us to end up dead, so be it, but leave Caitlin out of it. Let me take her outside."

"So she can watch while we have ourselves an old-fashioned shoot-out?" Will laughed. "You know, Cole, you're just like your pa. He was always looking for some kind of honor, but all he ever found was the bottom of a bottle. I tried to tell him, honor don't figure into things on this side of the law. Stealing is stealing whether you need something or not."

"And killing is killing . . . whether you're facing an armed lawman or a helpless woman."

"Don't preach to me." Will advanced on them, and a thread of moonlight glinted off the barrel of the gun in his hand. "If I don't kill you, you'll try to kill me. So why wait until the fight is fair?"

"That's a damn good question."

Will spun around at the sound of Duncan McDonnell's voice, and Caitlin screamed as the roar of gunfire filled the tiny dugout. Will's pistol fell from his hand, and he staggered backward slightly before crumpling to the ground. Smoke curled from the barrel of Duncan's rifle as he stepped heedlessly over Will's lifeless body, intent on seeing that his daughter was unharmed.

He felt her brow and said, "Let's get her outside."

Once free of the darkness, Cole could see the evidence of Will's cruelty on her face. Duncan swore and knelt down beside her, clasping her outstretched hand.

"Papa," she croaked. "Please don't kill Cole. I love him."

Duncan never looked away from her face. "I know you love him."

Caitlin looked up at Cole for confirmation, but he could only nod and brush a kiss against her forehead, unable to speak for the lump clogging his throat. The feel of Duncan McDonnell's hand on his shoulder spoke volumes, and Cole knew the older man was struggling against his own emotions.

To his shock, Caitlin began to laugh. Cole glanced

up at Duncan and back at Caitlin. She winced and tried not to smile, but she couldn't help herself.

"What is so funny?" Cole finally demanded.

"This is just what I was afraid of." She looked up at them and sighed. "You two are just alike."

Seventeen

"All things considered, you're a very lucky young woman." Dr. Carroll carefully removed the bandage from Caitlin's forehead. "Everything is healing nicely, and I don't see any signs of scarring."

Caitlin nodded and tried to smile. "Thanks to you. I appreciate your concern."

He placed his supplies back in his bag to leave but paused and covered her hand with his. "If you need anything . . ." He paused and covered her hand with his. "Don't hesitate to send for me."

"I will," she promised.

Once he was gone, Lily sank down in the wicker rocker across from Caitlin and smiled. "He's right. I can barely see where the stitches were."

Caitlin raised her fingers to her forehead, relieved by the smooth feel of her skin. She wasn't ready to look in a mirror yet, but she knew Lily would tell her if it looked bad. She should be happy about having no scars, happy to be home again and have her child with her, but Caitlin couldn't shake the sadness she felt knowing Cole would be leaving today.

She had talked until she was blue in the face,

but he wouldn't listen. She and Jamie, he maintained, were better off where they were than they ever would be with him. He dismissed the land and cattle he'd acquired as only a pittance compared to her father's wealth, and her suggestion that he remain in Eden with her family had clearly insulted him.

"Caitlin, have you heard anything I've said?"

Lily was clearly exasperated when Caitlin started at the sound of her voice and glanced up as if she'd forgotten all about her friend's presence. "I'm sorry. I can't seem to think straight today."

"Well, you'd better get your wits together," Lily said in a low voice just before rising to her feet and smiling her most gracious smile. "Good morning, Mr. Thornton."

Caitlin didn't have to turn around to know Cole was crossing the courtyard in her direction. She could hear his boots on the flagstones right behind her. She cast a pleading expression toward Lily and mouthed "Don't leave."

"Good morning, Miss Faulkner." Cole removed his hat and let his eyes settle on Caitlin. "I wanted to talk with you before I leave."

"If you two will excuse me, I need to check on something in the kitchen."

Before Caitlin could object, Lily breezed back inside the house and left Caitlin with no choice but to listen to Cole. "What is there to say except goodbye?"

His expression was grim. "Nothing that you would understand."

She didn't deny that and wished he would just leave. Tears hovered just behind her lowered eyes, and she could feel moisture gathering on her lashes. She wished she could be angry with him and say something hateful that would hurt him as badly as he was hurting her. Instead, she sat silently staring down at her folded hands.

"Caitlin, promise me you won't tell Jamie I'm his father. Ever."

She nodded.

"When you tell him I've left, just explain—"

"You haven't said goodbye to him?" The anger she'd wished for came in a rush. "You're just going to walk away and leave me to break his heart?"

"He'll understand," Cole insisted. "Just tell him I had to leave unexpectedly."

"What do I tell him when he asks if you'll be back?" She glared up at him. "He adores you, Cole. He won't understand why you don't ever want to see him again."

"This isn't about what I want."

"Of course, it is!" She wasn't about to let him feel noble about this. "You don't give a damn how I feel or what Jamie needs. All you want to do is run back to New Mexico and hide behind your land and your horses. Well, I won't try to stop you anymore."

She couldn't look at him anymore, so she let her gaze fall back to her lap.

"Caitlin, you know—"

Whatever he was going to say dissolved into a muttered oath, but she didn't look up, even when she heard the heavy fall of his footsteps marching away from her. She sat there for a long time, telling herself she'd done the right thing. If he didn't want her, they were both better off this way.

When she did finally look up, Caitlin saw her father lingering in the doorway. He looked troubled, and she didn't want him worrying about her any more than he already had. She got to her feet and pulled her dressing gown more closely around her, twisting the ends of the belt around her fingers.

Duncan closed the distance between them and put his arms around her. His voice was hesitant. "Caitlin, I know I was wrong about Cole. He's a fine young man, and I swear I didn't send him away."

"I know that, Papa," she whispered against his shoulder. "He didn't need anyone to send him way, because he never really came back to me."

Caitlin felt somewhat better after getting dressed and having lunch in the dining room rather than in her room. The mood at the table had been somber, at best. Papa and Uncle Cam said very little, and Lily tried her best to make conversation but her heart wasn't in it. Caitlin focused all her attention on Jamie, who was in a delightful mood.

Caitlin just couldn't bring herself to tell him that Cole was gone and wasn't coming back. She'd made the excuse of wanting him to eat lunch first, then he needed a nap, but there would never be a good time to tell him such heartbreaking news. She would at least wait until she was certain she wouldn't fall apart herself and make matters worse.

While Jamie was asleep, she started a letter to her aunt but put it aside. She couldn't concentrate on needlework, either, and her head began to ache when she tried to read. Finally, she went back out onto the patio to nurse her misery. She huddled into one of the roomy wicker chairs and drew her knees to her chest. The anger she'd wanted to feel had deserted her, and the thought of Cole living alone and never knowing his son was a steady ache in her chest.

"Caitlin?" Lily's voice barely registered. "Caitlin!"

She looked up. "What is it?"

"There's someone here to see you."

"Lily, please tell them to go away," she begged. "I'm just not up to visitors right now."

"I told him that." Lily's voice was hushed and worried. "He won't take no for an answer."

"Who won't?"

"I never take no for an answer."

Caitlin nearly tumbled out of her chair at the sight of Shane Weldon strolling out onto the patio, but she managed to get to her feet. She didn't know what to say, and stammered, "Sergeant Weldon, w-what a surprise."

"I'm sure it is." He turned toward Lily. "Miss McDonnell and I have personal business to discuss. Would you please excuse us?"

"You have no right to barge in here uninvited."

Lily was never one to leave a friend in a lurch. "I told you she doesn't feel like company."

"I'm not company."

"It's all right," Caitlin intervened. "He won't leave until he's had his say."

"If you think it's all right, Caitlin." Lily raked him with a disapproving glare. "I won't be far if you need me."

Caitlin didn't know what to say to Sergeant Weldon, and she was suddenly glad Cole had left when he did. At last, she asked, "What brings you to Eden, Sergeant Weldon?"

"I heard you found your son," he told her.

"Yes, I did. He's doing very well."

Another long silent pause stretched between them, and good manners forced her to invite him to be seated. When he sat facing her, she caught the unmistakable look in his eye of someone who was waiting for her to admit to something.

"I know how worried you were." When she said nothing, he added, "I suppose I can understand you going along with Thornton for the sake of your child."

Caitlin felt everything inside her freeze, and she knew he was watching for even the slightest reaction on her part. She didn't trust her voice not to tremble or her eyes not to widen in alarm. However, no reaction was no less condemning.

She swallowed and managed to sound calm. "The sake of my child was all that mattered."

"That's what Thornton said."

She forgot all about guarding her reactions. "What do you mean?"

"I don't take kindly to being made to look like a fool, Miss McDonnell." He nailed her with a look of pure contempt. "You stood right there in that sheriff's office and let Thornton leave me behind bars like a common criminal."

"No . . . Cole didn't . . . You don't understand."

"Why don't you explain it to me then?"

"Sergeant, I pleaded with you, but you wouldn't listen." Caitlin shivered at the cold fury she sensed in him, and she couldn't let him blame Cole for what she had done. "I'm the one who drugged you, and it was my idea to leave you in that jail."

"You're still determined to protect Thornton, aren't you?" He shook his head as if he would never understand women. "Even after he left you and the kid behind."

Caitlin recognized that was no idle comment. "What do you know about what Cole did?"

"I know he was heading back to New Mexico . . . alone."

"Why don't you tell me why you're really here?"

"Just to wish you well, Miss McDonnell." He rose to his feet. "Now, if you'll excuse me, I need to get back to town, claim my prisoner, and be on my way."

"What prisoner?"

"Miss McDonnell, you underestimate me. I knew just where to find Thornton, and all I had to do was wait for him to ride right to me." He paused thoughtfully. "Don't get any ideas about helping him escape. I might just forget you're a lady, next time."

Cole winced from the effort to breathe, and he didn't dare try to adjust his position on the jail cell cot. He figured he had some broken ribs, and his shoulder throbbed as if it were out of joint. He knew he deserved worse, but he hated the thought of being locked up in Eden, even overnight.

Weldon may have been the one who turned the key, but it was his own foolishness that landed him right back where he started. He never should have come back to Eden. Never. Caitlin didn't need him to see that she arrived home safely, and Jamie had his grandfather and his uncle to look after him.

Cole was only fooling himself—making excuses to stay around them just a little while longer. A little while had turned out to be too long. He loved Caitlin more than he ever had, and Jamie had worked his way so deep inside Cole's heart he'd been afraid not to leave. A few more days and he would have convinced himself that they would be just as happy with him as he would be with them.

He hated leaving with Caitlin so angry with him, and he knew Jamie would hate him for leaving, but it was better to hurt them once than destroy them little by little over years of disappointment.

The door to the cell block opened, and Cole groaned inwardly at the sight of Troxler's deputies. He would be glad when Weldon hauled him out of here, just to be away from that pair of heathens.

"What's the matter, Thornton?" Nichols leered through the bars. "Tired?"

Powell grinned. "Naptime is over. You got company."

Caitlin rushed inside the cell block with Jamie in tow. "Cole, are you all right?"

"Miss McDonnell, civilians ain't allowed back here!"

Cole wished Weldon had just shot him and been done with it. The wide-eyed look on Jamie's face was all too familiar. How many times had Cole gawked through bars and seen his father sprawled on a dingy mattress? He knew how that made a kid feel, and he would have died rather than have Jamie feel that way for one second.

"Unlock that door!" Caitlin demanded. "This minute!"

Cole had never seen Caitlin so angry, and he figured she wouldn't be satisfied until Jamie was so ashamed of him he wouldn't *want* Cole to be his father. Holding his side, Cole managed to sit up on the side of the cot. At least, Jamie wouldn't think he was passed out drunk.

"My God, you're hurt!"

He looked up to see Caitlin's eyes filled with tears, not anger.

"Caitlin, don't do this," he pleaded. "Just because I hurt you, don't make the boy suffer."

She blinked, as if she hadn't heard him right, but before she could answer the door burst open again, and Duncan McDonnell stormed into the cell block followed by his brother. Everyone held their breath, but Duncan stood back and let Cameron speak.

"Deputy, if you don't release my client this minute, I'll telegraph a federal judge in Austin, and this place will be a feed store before sundown."

Both deputies swallowed hard, knowing that Cameron wasn't making an idle threat. Nichols managed to find his voice. "The marshal is the only one who can release him."

"No one is releasing my prisoner!" Weldon made his way inside the cell block followed by Marshal Troxler. "Are you people crazy?"

Everyone started talking at once, shouting to be heard over the others, and Jamie started crying. Cole got to his feet and glared at Caitlin. "Get him out of here. Now!"

The men fell silent, ashamed for scaring an innocent child, and the marshal moved to unlock the cell. "Let's all go out front and discuss this like sane people."

When everyone was assembled in the marshal's office, Troxler tried to make sense of things. "Weldon, you told me you had cause to hold this man and take him back to San Antonio."

"By God, I do!" Weldon was furious.

"On what grounds?" Cameron demanded.

"He kidnapped her." He pointed to Caitlin. "And then he tried to poison me!"

"I'm the one who poisoned you," Caitlin snapped. "And who said I was kidnapped?"

"I did." Duncan looked chagrined. "This is all my fault."

Cameron spoke up. "So you want to drop the charges?"

Duncan nodded, and Weldon exploded. "You can't do that! This man is wanted by the law, and now you just want to turn him loose?"

"He has every reason to withdraw the charges," Cameron put in.

"But why?"

Jamie wiggled out of Caitlin's lap and ran to stand in front of Cole. "Because he's my daddy! You leave him alone!"

Everyone fell silent, and Cole turned to Caitlin. "You promised you wouldn't—"

"I didn't," she insisted, moving to gather Jamie in her arms. "Sweetie, how did you know that?"

The boy would have none of her coddling, stretching his arms out toward Cole. "He took me away from the bad man and watched over me and Mommy."

Cole lifted the boy in arms, ignoring the pain in his side. He didn't know what to say, and Jamie put his little arms around Cole's neck.

"You love me and Mommy, don'cha?"

The question sounded so simple, and Cole realized the answer was indeed that simple. Yes, he loved them, and they loved him. All the grown-up excuses he'd made to Caitlin sounded foolish compared to the wisdom of a child.

"Yes, I do." He stroked Jamie's dark hair. "I love you and your mother very much."

Jamie twisted in Cole's arms and held his hand out to Caitlin. "We love him, don't we, Mommy?"

"Yes, we do." Her voice was little more than a whisper. She caught Jamie's outstretched hand and stepped into Cole's embrace. "We always have."

They were blessed with a beautiful day for a wedding. There wasn't a cloud in the sky, and a soft breeze swept through the courtyard. Cole took her hand as the priest instructed, and Caitlin smiled, coaxing a hesitant smile from her groom. She knew he would have preferred a private ceremony, and she had kept her word to invite only her family and closest friends.

The courtyard was full, but Cole's expression reflected only pride and contentment. Their wedding served more than the purpose of joining them in matrimony. Jamie finally had the family he deserved and his father's name. Duncan was content in the knowledge that he would always be part of Caitlin's life, even if that life took her away from him.

Even Shane Weldon was able to recoup his pride when Cole asked him to stand up for him as best man. Despite the risk to his career, Weldon had defended Cole to the Rangers and had all charges dropped against him. Weldon intended to bring charges against the local deputies for their ill treatment of Cole, but Cameron beat him to it.

Father Dante cleared his throat and began reciting the rites of marriage, and Caitlin couldn't help blushing when he instructed Cole to kiss the bride. The guests broke into applause and surged around them, offering heartfelt congratulations to both her and Cole, and Jamie clamored for Cole to pick him up.

Lily embraced her and said, "Caitlin, I'm so happy for you."

"Maybe you'll be the one to catch the bouquet, Miss Faulkner." Shane Weldon's smile was absolutely wicked. "If you're lucky."

She dismissed his brash remark with a toss of her head, but Caitlin didn't miss the blush that brightened Lily's face. Uncle Cam embraced her and shook hands with Cole, and Caitlin caught sight of her father wavering just beyond the well-wishers.

"Papa," she whispered, slipping through the crowd, into his arms. "You are happy for me, aren't you?"

"Of course, I am." He kissed her forehead. "All I want is for you to be happy."

"I am happy," she assured him. "I only wish we weren't going to be so far apart."

He gently gripped her shoulders and pinned her with an admonishing look. "You'll never be far away from me. Now, go and find happiness with Cole. He's waited long enough."

Caitlin turned and rushed toward her husband and her son, laughing even as tears slipped down her face. Happiness, she knew, would always be hers as long as they were together.

<u>BOOK YOUR PLACE ON OUR WEBSITE</u> <u>AND MAKE THE</u> <u>READING CONNECTION!</u>

We've created a customized website just for our very special readers, where you can get the inside scoop on everything that's going on with Zebra, Pinnacle and Kensington books.

When you come online, you'll have the exciting opportunity to:

- View covers of upcoming books
- Read sample chapters
- Learn about our future publishing schedule (listed by publication month *and author*)
- Find out when your favorite authors will be visiting a city near you
- Search for and order backlist books from our online catalog
- Check out author bios and background information
- Send e-mail to your favorite authors
- Meet the Kensington staff online
- Join us in weekly chats with authors, readers and other guests
- Get writing guidelines
- AND MUCH MORE!

Visit our website at
http://www.zebrabooks.com

ROMANCE FROM FERN MICHAELS

DEAR EMILY   (0-8217-4952-8, $5.99)

WISH LIST   (0-8217-5228-6, $6.99)

AND IN HARDCOVER:

VEGAS RICH   (1-57566-057-1, $25.00)